WHAT REVIEWERS SAY ABOUT
THIS AUTHOR'S WRITING

"Buckle your seat belts and hang on!...Fine and funny! ...a unique and utterly loveable voice...a fabulously authentic voice!"
—Lucie-Jane Bledsoe, *Lambda Book Report*

"Jack Fritscher writes wonderful books full of compassion, humor, lyricism, and insight."   —Geoff Mains, *The Advocate*

"Literary and cinematic...heart-warming and heart-breaking... outspoken and overwhelming...an *evocation poetique* of an era..."
—Michael Griffiths, *Time Out*, London

"Fritscher's book of fiction is lean writing laced with witty observations and a couple of tear drops of genuine human compassion. The author deserves credit for diversifying his 'voice' throughout his long career." —Terry Solomon, *The Petaluma Post*

"Gore Vidal...James Baldwin...Andrew Holleran...Jack Fritscher... Classic!"   —David Van Leer, *The New Republic*

"Jack Fritscher's gift for language makes me think of the poet Dennis Cooper."   —Ian Young, *The Body Politic*, Toronto

"Mythic...Comic...Graphically elegant style!"
—David Perry, *The Advocate*

"There's more variety in a dozen stories by this one author than in most anthologies with a dozen different authors."
—Richard Labonté, A Different Light Books,
    In Touch, Los Angeles

"Fritscher has carved out a niche in the world of short-story fiction that is hard to match...unique and memorable. What an unsettling, and surprising, writer." —John F. Karr, *Manifest Reader*

"Literary…with enough wit to keep readers on their toes."
      —*Gay Times, London*

"A fun read…"   —*Playguy*

"The cascade of words that fills Fritscher's style is perhaps its greatest asset."—Jack Garman, *Lambda Rising*

"Fritscher is concerned with the psychology of…life and love, the intricate interplay of self-expression and self-destruction, the erotics of autonomy and dependency…characters are heroic but not invincible, brave but not always successful…unflinching honesty."
      —Michael Bronski, *First Hand*

"Real characters…well portrayed…fascinating…important… deserves to be read."
      —Michael Yates, *The James White Review*

"Fritscher's 'The Story Knife' is a beautiful tale of a priest's journey through desire to peace." —Jim Nawrocki, *Bay Area Reporter*

Also by
Jack Fritscher

The Geography of Women
Some Dance to Remember
Mapplethorpe: Assault with a Deadly Camera
Love and Death in Tennessee Williams

Sweet
Embraceable You

Coffee-House Stories

Jack Fritscher

PALM DRIVE PUBLISHING
SAN FRANCISCO CALIFORNIA

For author history and literary research:
www. JackFritscher.com

Cover photograph, shot by and ©2000 Jack Fritscher
Cover design realized by Mark Hemry, Sebastopol, California
Cover ©2000 Jack Fritscher and Mark Hemry
Coming Attractions photographs ©1976 Jim Stewart
Generation photographs 1968 courtesy Kalamazoo Civic Theatre

Published by Palm Drive Publishing, Sebastopol CA 95472
EMail: Publisher@PalmDrivePublishing.com
Library of Congress Catalog Card Number: 99-067124
Fritscher, Jack 1939-
    Sweet Embraceable You: Coffee-House Stories / Jack Fritscher
    p. cm.
    ISBN 978-1-890834-35-7 (print)
    ISBN 978-1-890834-19-7 (eBook)
1. Fiction. 2. LGBT Fiction. 3. Short-Stories. 4. Women's Studies. 5. Lesbian & Gay Studies 6. Plays & Screenplays. I. Title.

Printed in the United States of America
First Printing, June 2000
Second Printing, June 2018
9 8 7 6 5 4 3 2 1

www.PalmDrivePublishing.com

For my sweet, embraceable
Mark Hemry

Contents

Sweet Embraceable You

Murder me," Ada said.

"The reception began at eight." Cameron set his second bourbon glass down on his newspaper blotting Herb Caen's Tuesday, August 15, 1972, column. "It's now eleven-thirty, precisely. Time is not your forté, my darling. Must you always run on your own clock?"

"Don't tick me off," Ada said. She was chilled from the San Francisco night. Her coat hung from her shoulders. "I hate when you play daddy. Next you'll be into spanking."

"We've never tried that."

"Keep it that way." She stood her ground across the tiny cocktail table.

He smiled under his thick black moustache. "Let me help with your coat."

Cameron Vicary rose to his full height. Ada watched him grow taller than she, and she was tall enough to be striking. Her coat rode like a cape across her shoulders. He lifted it and dropped its smartly tailored lines across the chair he intended for her.

She sat.

A waiter stepped from the piano bar. He looked up at Cameron who said something Ada could not hear. Cameron sat down.

"I asked you to murder me," she said.

"Don't change the subject." Cameron lit a cigarette. "I never do anything uncivilized." He handed it to her.

"I've stopped again."

"Start again," he said. "You prefer yourself with vices."

She took the fresh cigarette and held it. "God, I hate this place.

All of San Francisco and here we sit." She tugged at the light fold of dark tricot falling down from her throat. "We come here so often. I'm suffocating." She ground out the cigarette. "Must we always come here?"

"Where were you?" Cameron asked.

She looked at him.

He looked at her.

"I had a reception of my own to attend," she said. "Stop trying to make me obedient."

"Simple, isn't it?" He knocked down neat the last of his scotch.

"Simple? What is? For godsake, do you need such a big bush to beat around?"

The waiter hovered for a moment. He served Ada. He served Cameron. He disappeared.

"Cheers," Cameron said.

"To what." Ada said it flat. "Our one-thousandth visit to this bar?"

"Bistro. This bistro," Cameron said. "Remember? You picked me up here."

"Correction," Ada said, lifting her glass. "I met you here. I picked you up later."

"You love this place. We're old faces here."

"Being an old face anywhere is something I don't love."

Cameron lifted the single candle. His hands cupped the warm glassful of wax through the white plastic mesh. He lifted the wavering light to Ada's face. "An old face, Ada, you'll never be."

She began to melt in tenderness to him, but caught herself. Was he joking? "You could be fatal to me," she said. "So lay off the mood swings."

Cameron lowered the candle to the table. "Well?" he said.

"That's a deep subject."

"You're so sophisticated for a professor's wife."

She glared at him. She had her own degree, her own teaching certificate, her own car, what had been—before he moved in—her own Victorian flat. She bit her lower lip. From tables nearer the bar came brief applause as the pianist finished her set. Ada's ears rang in the sudden silence. Cameron stroked his chin, waiting. She knew the feel of his sharp clean face when his midnight stubble raised just enough to rasp her body raw. There was no part of her he had not scraped. Night by passing night the tiny bristles of his strong face were sanding her smooth. She felt she was losing herself to him.

"Don't be abrasive," she countermanded. Her word choice pleased her.

"Where-have-you-been is hardly an abrasive question. Not when a husband asks a wife who has stood him up publicly in front of his colleagues for two hours."

"You mean those goddam geologists actually noticed?"

"Yes."

"All eight of them?"

"And their eight wives. And the chairman. And the woman who was the guest of honor."

"You've never cared what they thought."

"So where were you, Ada?"

"I was having an affair with a rich man from China. A kinky little fellow. You know: whips and chains. *Spanking.* And a special little gadget that..."

"I don't care where you were." Cameron gulped down his drink.

"Then I'll tell you. We had a department reception of our own at the St. Francis."

"Why didn't you call?"

"Why didn't you?" She smiled at him. Things were always shifting tectonically between them. "Can this marriage be saved?" she asked.

"Why not?" Cameron reached for her hand.

"That'll cost you two-bits, buster." She stood up.

"What for?" He dug into his pocket for change.

Ada held out her hand and took his quarter. Leaving the table, she signaled the waiter for another round. "If my students could see me now," she called in the silence left by the stilled piano. "Hi, honey," she said, passing a young, balding ex-jock. He was all teeth and curly blond hair. She patted his butt the way she had seen players pat rump on the Bowl games Cameron insisted she watch with him. She made sure that Cameron saw her action. "What this joint needs," she said to Mr. Touchdown, "is some sounds." She headed to the jukebox.

Ada hated herself, taking a too-cute finger-in-the-mouth eternity deciding on her selections. She felt the ex-ballplayer heating up behind her.

Cameron watched her through his lifted glass. She rippled in the soft psychedelia of the jukebox. He knew her every trick and he liked watching her.

She fed the coin into the machine and danced onto the floor by herself. Her arms were slender and bare, silky against her rich mauve dress. The barkeep to amuse himself more than the patrons turned a flashing strobe on the lone and lovely woman. Her body flowed, flicked out in instants by the light. For half a lyric she was lost in her exhibition. Then with a fast move the blond jock joined her on the floor. Cameron watched her pull away with short, jerky motions. She left him, standing bewildered, alone in the middle of the floor. She made her way back to the table and stood: "He says he played a little ball in college."

Cameron smiled. "I bet he wanted to play ball with you." He leaned into the table, pulling her soft hand to his chin. The strobe caused Ada's eyes to divide his tender movements into rhythmic spasms, but the feel of him pulling her hand to him felt smooth. Between the appearance and the reality, she often lectured her classes, is the difference of what isn't and what is.

"Come on," he said. "Let's get out of here."

"I drove my car," she said.

"My bike's outside."

"On your motorcycle in this dress? I'll die."

"You wanted me to murder you." He took her by the arm.

"Come on. We'll get the car in the morning." They both of them knew they were odd. Not so anyone else took notice. Just late-at-night odd: confessing, prevaricating, revealing to each other their apt match.

*

"I should have written a different thesis," Ada said. She turned on her side in the bed toward Cameron and ran her hand down his back.

"Lower," he said. He liked the feel of her hands. Her light touch floated across the dark hair downing his cheeks.

"My master's thesis," Ada said. "I should have written on Emily Dickinson."

"Lightly," Cameron said.

"An American woman poet." Ada sat up in bed.

"Don't stop," Cameron said into the pillow.

"Not a poetess," Ada said. "A poet." She hiked her nightgown above her knees. "A bit of tippler, Emily was." She straddled Cameron's thighs from behind. "A spinster like me." She massaged from the small of his back up the twin muscled ridges leading to his strong neck. She touched lightly the scar on his left shoulder. It was a bullet wound from the war that he had hated.

Cameron moaned in pleasure, his face buried in the pillow.

"What?" Ada said. She pushed hard on the base of his spine.

"You're no spinster. You're a married woman."

"Then I haven't been a spinster twice."

Cameron rolled over beneath her light straddle. "You're my first marriage," he said.

Ada laughed. "But hardly your first fuck!"

"I'm cold," he said. "Come here." He pulled Ada down, her face to his face. "You're beautiful," he said.

She kissed his ear. "Then there's a pair of us....Don't tell."

He began the familiar rocking motion, holding her. She was a little girl and a grown woman, in a boat, holding the sides, laughing and screaming, holding Cameron now, because years before Curtis had rocked her so wildly in the rowboat on Stow Lake lagoon that the Golden Gate Park attendant had called to them through a megaphone.

Cameron slipped her cotton nightshirt over her head and inside it she smiled remembering how she had been so embarrassed by Curtis, mortified, when at the end of their row, the attendant with the megaphone had helped her from the boat. She and Curtis had been married a week then. The attendant had reached for her hand. The marriage lasted into that winter. The attendant, throwing a quick look at Curtis, had apologized to her, as if he, and not Curtis, had frightened her nearly out of her wits in the middle of the wide lagoon. The week after Christmas she had, with justifiable anger, left her groom of five months.

The last of the nightshirt trailed off her arms. Cameron tossed it to the floor and Ada descended at her own speed full on to him. He was perfect. She knew he was perfect. But nothing, not even this, she had felt—long before she had nearly drowned in public embarrassment—was ever going to be enough. She could never forgive Curtis.

"Be here now," Cameron said. "Ada, be here now."

With his call, her mind came back into her head. "I love you," she managed and floated away again. This time to the porch glider. Cameron had spent the warm afternoon watering the lawn. He had worn white flannel trousers rescued from a resale shop. She had drowsed idly lying in the porch glider. Its gentle squeak had lulled her half to sleep, dreaming she lay aboard a gentle sloop rocking lazy at anchor. Through the white porch railing, she watched Cameron, all in white, wrap the dark green garden hose around his forearm, his thumb pressed hard into the water to fan the pressure into a wide spray.

He'll have arthritis when he is old, she mused. His thumb will grow stiff and gnarled because this one August afternoon he has meticulously watered every inch of grass.

She closed her eyes.

He was too bright. He was far brighter than Curtis. He was perhaps always too bright for her. Out there, white on the lawn, against the wet green, he soaked up the very heat of the sun. She was cool and he was too warm. At night he glowed, as if the sun had gifted him with dazzle. Sometimes she lay awake next to him and watched him sleep. Once she had awakened, cold as death. The old dream of Curtis clutched her throat. Her breath had been pressed out. She had wanted to wake him, to say, "Hold me." But then, as now, finished, he lay asleep, dark moustached and naked. She knew he would gladly hold her, but she said nothing. He was a good man and she rolled off him, reaching out her hands, chafing them together, holding them over his sleeping body, warming herself in his sweet animal heat. She watched him glow in the moonlight streaming down past Sutro Tower and in through the old Victorian windows.

He turned toward her on his side. She turned away and snuggled her back into his belly. It was their favorite way of sleeping.

The moon hung low and full outside the windows. The tower blinked a hundred tiny red lights on and off. Ada, her face in full moonlight, smiled.

*

In the morning, Ada smelled the coffee. In the kitchen, Cameron stirred his cup with a silver spoon. She pulled the blankets tighter around her. An ocean chill had crept over the City and into the room. Unusual even for August. A lock of her long black hair caught on her lip. Her tongue pulled in one of the hairs. Her teeth bit it lightly, nervously, careful not to cut it through. The hair had thickness and resiliency. It had sides, definable, as she turned it between her teeth. She had slept soundly, but she had not slept well. The blankets had weighed her down. She threw them back and shuddered as the cold air of the room sank into the warm sheets. She lay studying the ceiling. "Might as well," she said outloud, and she meant get up, which she did, pulling her terrycloth robe around her.

From the bathroom, she shouted to Cameron, "Good morning!"

"Coffee!" he shouted back.

She splashed water in her face and pulled a brush through the pleasant tangle of her hair.

She headed down the hall, past two photographs Cameron had taken of the City. Both showed the Golden Gate Bridge shrouded in fog. In the background of the second, the tip of the new Trans-America Pyramid pierced the fog bank with the rising sun haloed directly behind it. "You ought to sell postcards," she shouted into the kitchen.

He looked at her framed in the doorway. "Lay off," he said quietly.

"That's not what you said last night." She swept into the kitchen and went straight for the coffee. "What are you reading?" she asked, stirring three teaspoons of sugar into the small cup.

"Nothing," he said. His forearm, peeled out of his rolled up flannel shirt, shielded the book.

"Come on!" She pulled at his big soft fist.

He relaxed.

"*Dickinson*," she said. "the *Collected Poems of*. Really, Cameron, I'm touched."

He took a long slow pull on his coffee. He said nothing. He was expressionless.

"Here's one for you," Ada said, turning the pages. "Pain has an element of blank."

"I'm cycling out to the park," Cameron said. He stood up.

"Someday you'll be killed on that motorcycle. Someday you'll leave me all alone."

"Maybe today," he said.

"And that will be my proof."

Cameron pulled on a light leather jacket. "What proof?"

"That we're alone."

"That you're off-balance, sweetheart." He kissed her. "And out-of-whack, out-of-synch." He touched her breasts lightly.

"And out-of-bounds," she said, pushing his hands away.

In his big silence he moved away from her. Something they both needed more than they recognized, something that had not quite melded together from their separate spiritual lives, sometimes hung unspoken between them. He turned at the door, and said, "Whatever," as if she, not he, held the mystery.

The ancient front door closed. Beneath her, the garage door of the old Victorian ratched open. Cameron kicked his bike into muffled life, paused on the lip of the drive, returned, pulled closed the garage door, and roared away into the sounds of the City.

Ada put both elbows on the table and interlaced her fingers across her forehead. She stared down into the steam rising from her coffee. She had papers to grade. Errands to run. And the telephone was ringing.

It was Cassiopeia.

*

Unhelmeted, Cameron cruised west out Fell Street, along the green boulevard of the Panhandle. The morning cool felt wet and good on his face. He angled his Harley Sportster smoothly into Golden Gate Park and roared loud down Kennedy Drive. The park lay emerald in the morning light: meadows, rose gardens, eucalyptus groves. Every stick and bush and tree transplanted into perfect place. He passed behind the DeYoung Museum and prowled the tarmac circle wrapped around the Stow Lake lagoon.

He laughed thinking of Curtis years before rocking Ada insanely in the rented rowboat. He gunned his bike. Hard. Fast. Breaking down curds of inertia inside his own flesh as the bike ate up the parkway. He turned right, in full shot of the ocean, roared past Point Lobos, Land's End, and out El Camino del Mar toward the Golden Gate Bridge.

*

Once he had taken Ada for the thrill of her life, speeding in an earlier dawn, in and out of the fogclouds, across the Golden Gate. She had held him tight as the lover she was then, tighter than when she made love to him now. Her raven hair had whipped around his face as she buried her head into his shoulders. He caught a mouthful and pulled on it. She clung tighter. He thought he heard her scream, "Balance!" as she dug her nails into the insides of his jeaned thighs.

They had ridden that Sunday to Tiburon. She was furious. "You're worse than Curtis," she said. "What is it with men? Don't ever scare me like that again."

"How should I scare you?"

"The usual way will be just fine," she said cupping his crotch.

"That's never scared you," he said. "Come on."

"Where?"

"Brunch, kiddo." He stooped down to chain up the big bike. The sunlight caught in his hair. It reddened his moustache. He hadn't shaved. He clamped the padlock shut and smiled up at her. He grinned around the butt of a small burnt-out cigar in his perfect white teeth. "You're some looker," he said.

"You're no Bogart."

"Thank God," he said.

Ada followed him into the dark interior of the restaurant-bar. At the end of the hall, sunlight burnt bright enough to hurt her eyes. Cameron headed straight for it. She squinted as he pulled her out onto a floating deck with a hundred or so summer people brunching over eggs and gin fizzes. Three waiters and a busboy seemed to manage the whole affair for an invisible chef.

"There's no place to sit," Ada said. "It's too bright. I can't see a thing."

"I can." He took her gently by the hand.

"Must you always lead?" she said.

He pulled her through the maze of close tables. She bumped a chair, pushing a matron's leather-tanned face into the foam of her gin fizz. "Sorry," Ada said. The woman tried a smile, then napkined it away along with the ridiculous moustache of fizz beneath her nose.

"Sunday's House Specialty," Cameron said over his shoulder.

"What is?" Ada giggled.

"Gin fizzes. They're terrible, but they're In." He pulled her down to one of the two vacant tables. They leaned back against the railing. A yacht rose and fell at anchor twenty feet down a short gangway.

"This whole place is floating," Ada said. She panned the entire Sunday morning scene. "If I don't go blind, I'll get seasick. This better be good."

"Watch this," Cameron said. He pointed to a couple newly arrived into the glare. No one seemed to notice them. The woman's hair was lazily knotted on top her head. She wore big-rimmed shades. Her blouse and jeans looked comfortable enough to scrub floors in. She was warm. She walked a short-leashed mongrel dog. Ada liked her. But the man with her projected something: breeding, aristocracy, cool.

"That's California for you," Ada said. "That's pure San Francisco."

The couple headed straight for the empty table next to them.

"What do you mean?" Cameron said.

"The men are more chic than the women."

"Chic? No," Cameron said. "That's the wrong word."

The couple sat down. The woman excused herself as she bumped into Cameron's chair.

"That face!" Ada whispered. "Cameron, do you know who she is?

Cameron put the mock of his fist to his mouth. "And who do you think the guy with her is?"

"Don't let them know," Ada said.

"Don't let them know what?" Cameron whispered back. "You're acting like a groupie."

"Don't let them know we know who they are."

"Nobody seems to care," Cameron said.

"Nobody else recognizes them."

"They're off-camera," Cameron said. "Movie stars aren't what they used to pretend to be."

"Quiet," Ada said. She had this fan-madness about her. Cameron had witnessed it before. She had a passion for the fabulous, for fabled people. She collected fame the way a philatelist collects stamps. Once in Union Square, Clint Eastwood had smiled at her between takes in one of his films.

"Do you think he recognizes me?" Ada said.

"You're kidding."

Six months before, Ada had been in the right place at the right time, the corner of Broadway and Columbus, when the cast and crew of *The Streets of San Francisco* carried Edmund O'Brien costumed like a cop out of a little jeweler's shop on a stretcher. Ada had worked her way to the front of the crowd and planted herself smack between Karl Malden and Michael Douglas. Malden's line had been to the crowd: "Move back, everybody. Move back." And she had, frowning, but not too much, under-acting for the Panavision camera, determined not to end up on the cutting room floor. When the take was over, Michael Douglas, like Clint Eastwood, had smiled at her. She had been wearing a tight T-shirt of alternating blue and yellow stripes that she had then folded into her cedar chest as a souvenier.

"Ada," Cameron whispered. "I think he recognizes you."

"No, he doesn't. He couldn't." Ada looked for a menu. "Why do you think so?"

"By the way he keeps his back to you." He nudged her ribs.

A gull reconnoitered greedily overhead.

"Call a waiter, will you, Cameron? For godsake, I'm starving. I need a menu."

The woman with Michael Douglas turned around. "Here you go," she said. Her voice was husky. "We seem to have three." She handed the menu to Cameron.

"Thanks," he said.

Ada smiled. The woman turned back to her section of *The New York Times*. "Don't let her know," Ada said. Her eyes narrowed from more than the glare.

"Know what?"

"She's Brenda Vacarro."

"She probably knows that," Cameron said. "What are you doing with the menu?"

"I'm folding it up for my collection. It's not everyday a movie star hands you a menu."

"Ada, you're putting me on."

Ada's eyes narrowed even more in the Tiburon sunglare.

"Omigod," Cameron said. "You're not putting me on."

"Right," Ada said. "Indulge my little fantasy."

"You'll laugh about this when you have a saner moment," Cameron said. "Don't you dare ask for an autograph or I'll tell our future children."

"You hate children."

"I forgot."

A waiter took an order from Michael Douglas, who did not smoke, while Brenda Vacarro lit up a filter king, and tossed a bread-crust to a cruising gull. The waiter, oblivious to Ada and Cameron, spun his exit still scratching on his pad. Douglas returned to the "Arts" section of the *Times*, looking up only when Vacarro interrupted to show him a recipe which his father's wife, Mrs. Kirk Douglas, had been asked to supply to the "Gourmet Supplement" she was reading.

"What about our order?" Cameron said. "We were here first."

"We're not famous," Ada said.

The waiter returned with two gin fizzes and a Sanka for Brenda Vacarro. So close were the two tables, he kept his position and turned on point to Cameron and Ada. "Have you decided?" he asked politely.

"We'll have..." Cameron began.

"Whatever they're having," Ada interrupted, triumphant.

*

Cameron grinned as he sped north off the Bridge. Sausalito lay below him to the right, and that crazy Sunday in Tiburon lay even farther off in time and space. Ada should have written her thesis on Millay, he thought. With her little petulant hand an annotation of her greatly petulant life. He took the off-ramp from 101 and headed up the canyon roads, past the Muir Woods turnoff, shifting gears and climbing the snaking asphalt up the mountain, above the Pantoll Ranger Station, roaring beyond the natural Mountain Home Theater, to the top of Mount Tamalpais, the highest point in the Bay area, a forest and crest sacred to the old Miwok Indian gods.

Cameron loved the mountain.

It was worn and smoothed, twisted with trails as ancient as the fog that rolled through its pines. Hikers puffed up and down its paths, rediscovering traces of the old gravity-pulled Mt. Tamalpais Railway that before the San Francisco quake had pulled fashionable ladies and gentlemen up the steep grade for picnics of chicken and lemonade in the sun.

Cameron kicked up his bike in the asphalt parking lot below the peak. The ladies with the lemonade had vanished. A tie-dyed hippie replaced them, lounging in the mountain heat against the stainless-steel sides of a pickup truck fitted out to serve cellophaned sandwiches and coffee.

"Black or white?" the hippie asked.

"Black." Cameron took the styrofoam cup of coffee in his hand and flipped the kid a half-dollar.

"It's sixty cents, man." The boy hooked his long hair back behind his ears and dropped his hands to his hips. "Overhead," he said, looking up at the clear blue sky. "The cost of doing business, man."

"Yeah." Cameron flipped him the dime.

The kid caught it. "Have a nice day," he said.

Cameron headed back to his bike. "Whatever," he said over his shoulder. He set the coffee on the asphalt, zipped off his leather jacket, pulled off his flannel shirt, picked up the coffee, and lay back on his bike, head and shoulders padded with his rolled jacket against the handle bars, feet stretched back over the hot leather seat and rear fender, his torso exposed to the sun.

He sipped the coffee and watched the valley below the mountain. Brown grasses, dry with August, waved in heat shimmers between him and the water of the Bay. A road below, white and winding, wended its way up and down ridges and rises, leading toward, and then disappearing, before it reached the Golden Gate Bridge and the white City of Oz itself shimmering across the Bay in the translucent August sun.

He closed his eyes.

Be here now. He relaxed into his mantra. *Be here now. Three. Here.* Counting backwards. *Two. More here. One. Really here.* He breathed deep from within his center and through his eyelids saw not the Fire Watch Station at Tam's peak but the clear unspoiled way the mountain had been when holy men roamed its trails fasting and praying, dreaming visions for their hunting shields.

Cameron had dreamed once of a bull's head, horned and cocked left, nostrils flaring. A tattoo artist in Oakland had needled it deftly on the outside of his shoulder above his left bicep. He had never regretted the rite. He had opened his flesh to the ink and the needle like a burning razor blade. It had been his first willful and completely irretrievable freewill act.

"How terribly," Ada had drawled, mocking his machismo, "existential."

Behind his eyes, he smiled and opened his pores to the sun. Energy flowed into him. Sweat beaded on his chest, grew to a rivulet, and inched down his side. A fly buzzed, circled, landed, sampled. Cameron felt its feet gigantic on him, treading up and down in place, the way Ada's cat at night often stood atop the blankets padding its paws up and down on his chest as if he were so much dough to be kneaded. He relaxed into the fly, tried to become the fly, but finally the itch was too much. Eyes still closed he swatted, missed, and had only his own sweat to lick from his hand. The fly landed again. This time it marched strangely across his chest. A bead of sweat headed fast down his belly toward the pool in his navel. He opened his eyes.

"About time," said the figure silhouetted against the sun.

Cameron was momentarily blinded. Startled. The man had been tickling his belly with a stalk of mountain grass.

"Curtis!" Cameron said. "You're late."

Curtis brought the stem of grass to his mouth. He bit off the end and smiled. "I like to talk to people when they least expect it." He spit out the butt end of grass. "Guess you'd say I'm strange."

"Curtis," Cameron said putting his feet on the ground, "you're more than strange."

"Come with me," Curtis pointed partway down the slope. "We can talk better down at the old Tam Railway Station. My car is parked over by the lovely hippie." He climbed uninvited on the motorcycle. "You can drive us down," he said. The straw twitched between his teeth.

"So get off so I can start it," Cameron said pulling on his shirt.

Curtis obeyed.

Cameron kick-started the bike into roaring life. "Okay," he said. "Get on."

Curtis swung his leg across the machine. "Where do I hang on?" he asked.

"Sit on your hands," Cameron said. "Don't play so dumb."

"It's time we talked," Curtis said. "Really time."

"About what?"

"About Ada."

"What about Ada?"

"I married her before she married you."

"That makes you some kind of expert?"

"Exactly."

Cameron shifted the bike, angry, and peeled out of the parking lot with Curtis hanging on for dear life.

*

Ada sat naked on the marble floor of her shower watching the water sputter down the brass mouth of the drain. Once she had read of an elderly woman who had slipped in the tub and laid in five inches of water for six days before anyone found her. She was alive but wrinkled as a prune; she had kept warm by adding hot water every hour or so. Ada had filed that information away for her old age. "If there's going to be an old age," she said outloud. "I wonder if other grown-ups ever sit on the shower floor and play?" She laughed thinking of Cassiopeia sitting on the shower floor, if Cassiopeia ever showered, with the water pelting down, filtering through her hip Brillo-frizzy locks.

Cassiopeia had been Cameron's prior old lady. He had met her in the Haight, five years before, during the Summer of Love. Ada had visions of Cassiopeia leaning provocatively against the Haight-Ashbury street sign with her madras skirt up over her head and her mattress on her back. Or at least her sleeping bag.

The little lady's birth name, before she had rechristened herself Cassiopeia by taking an extra large hit of magic mushrooms and shouting "Here I go," had been simply Margaret Mary O'Hara. After her christening, she had felt the need for a lysergic communion service; she had renounced her Catholicism, but adored its sacramental choreography: her confirmation ceremony had been a strung-out drug-bang of chemical mysticism.

Cameron, at that time a mescaline novice overdosed on Alan Watts' books, had been certain that against the Hashbury street sign leaned his spiritual guide. Margaret Mary O'Hara was buying none of it. "St. Theresa of Avila, honey, I'm not." She raised her hands. "With these," she said, cupping her 36-D breasts like a treasure, "I am Cassiopeia Star Child."

Ada knew Cameron had said something ridiculously trendy like: "Far out!" She shook her head violently under the shower spray, shimmying like a retriever run in from the rain. Her hair whipped water around her face. As far as Ada was concerned Cassiopeia was a burnt-out chick. Talking to her was harder than running on foot across a twelve-lane freeway.

She turned off the shower, splashed herself with baby oil, wiped down with a soft sponge, then wrapped her waist with one towel and turbaned her head with another. She stepped carefully from the shower and met her bare breasts in the medicine cabinet mirror. "Thank God," she said, "I'll never be as mystical as Cassiopeia."

She toweled herself dry in the bedroom. A few beads of water flipped onto the ungraded student papers stacked on her vanity. Her students hated papers. She hated papers. Still they wrote and she corrected. She tried to towel dry the top paper. A blot appeared across the title. It made no difference. The paper, twice as long as assigned, was from an ardent little feminist who always wrung political relevance into everything. Ada checked the blotted title, something about "'Women in Literature: Enter as Juliet; Exit as Ophelia' by Ms. Pat Leavitt for Ms. Ada Vicary, MA."

Ada grabbed a red felt-tip. "All these abbreviations," she wrote petulantly on the title page, "remind me of writer S. J. Perlman who wished he had become a Jesuit so he could have signed himself S. J. Perlman, S. J." Ada appreciated Perlman's chiastic sense of humor, knew that it would be lost on the intense Ms. Leavitt, and added, "Sorry about the blot." She threw the marking pen on top the stack; that was at least a start on the thirty-four research papers for English 252: Shakespeare.

Ada felt mean pulling on her jeans and knotting her blouse above her midriff. She had neglected to tell Cassiopeia that Cameron had roared off for the day. She blow-dried her hair and was almost finished when the doorbell rang. She grabbed her lipstick, drew a bit of color across her mouth, blotted her lips together, tossed the tube on top the "Juliet-Ophelia" paper, said, "Whoops! Sorry, Ms. Leavitt," and headed down the stairs to the door. Through the stained glass, she could see the dark silhouette of the one, the only, the original.

"Cassiopeia!" Ada said, opening the door. "How are you?"

"My nose hurts," Cassie said.

"I can see why," Ada said. "Come in."

Cassiopeia's nose had been pierced with a gold ring, or, more accurately, her left nostril had been.

Cassiopeia also had a Janis Joplin tattoo on her wrist and Bette Midler tweezed eyebrows. Her body was a map of fads in and out.

"Why have you done that?" Ada asked.

"Makes me think twice about Kung Fu fighting," Cassiopeia said.

"It would be hell to have someone grab your nose in a catfight," Ada said.

"Worse than pierced ears, but I'm a nuclear pacifist now. No fighting." Cassiopeia swooped into the Victorian parlor. "Far out!" she said.

"What a lovely saffron robe you're wearing," Ada said. "Sit down, please. Have you joined that dervish group? What are they called? The ones who shave their heads except for the ponytail and play drums for the tourists down at the Powell and Market Street cable-car turnaround?"

"Still the same old Ada," Cassiopeia said. She pulled a joint from her totebag.

"Still the same old Cassie." Ada threw her a box of footlong wooden fireplace matches.

Cassie toked up. "Where's Cam?" she asked, her voice whistling and high as she spoke on the inflowing blue air.

Ada settled back into a large wicker chair, one leg under the other. "Cameron's out," she said.

"Just us girls then, huh?" Cassie said, hitting her joint again. "Say," she said, "does Cam still leave the toilet seat up?"

Ada knew they were off and running.

"Cam always used to leave the toilet seat up," Cassie said. "More than once with that man I crawled out of bed at night and plopped my buns right down into the water."

"How refreshing," Ada said. "Did you have to change your jammies?"

Cassie was deep into her joint. "Do you have any peroxide?" she asked. "For my nose."

Ada shifted a cushion behind her back. "In the bathroom. Left side, second shelf."

"Thanks," Cassiopeia said. She billowed up from the couch like a saffron cloud.

Ada checked out her spreading size. "You want to go to aerobics class with me?"

"You've got to be joking," Cassie said. "Hold this, will you?" She handed the jay to Ada who sat holding the burning joint. Across the front bay of windows hung Ada's precious Boston ferns, four huge bushes with fronds bursting up and then down through the macrame hangers. She laid the joint in an ashtray, crossed to the windows, picked up her misting can and sprayed the jungle-sized plants.

"I can't find the peroxide." Cassiopeia's far-away voice whined a child's ploy.

Ada set down the misting can and headed down the long hall. "I'm coming," she said. She turned into the bathroom. "It would help," she said to the stoned Cassie, "if you opened the cabinet." Ada pointed. "What's this mess on the mirror?"

Cassiopeia grinned at Ada. She held up a bar of soap. "I was feeling inspired."

In the mirror both women were reflected. Over their reflections handwriting was scrawled with soap.

Ada attempted a smile. "When did you become a graffiti artist, dear."

"My latest poem," Cassie said. She began to read: "Chameleons are not furious. They color themselves to fit their world. Suddenly this long here...." She studied Ada's face. "What do you think so far?"

"Terrific," Ada said.

"Suddenly this long here," Cassie continued, "I no longer speed on the urgency of there. Chameleons are." She stopped. "That's all the farther I wrote when you came in."

"Too bad," Ada said. "You and Coleridge."

"Huh?" Cassie said. "I don't get it."

"He was a poet. Here let me squeeze this cotton over your nose. Someone interrupted him in the middle of a poem and he never could finish it. Hold still."

Cassiopeia gasped like a fish as the peroxide foamed in her nostril. "But I finished mine," she blubbered.

Ada capped the peroxide. "That figures." She tossed the soaked cotton into the wastebasket.

Cassiopeia stood between her and the door. "Chameleons are adaptable."

"Move aside," Ada said.

Cassie moved, still reciting: "Chameleons will be here long after the rest of life, extinct, has died of a mushroom ulcer." She smiled at Ada.

"That's it?" Ada asked.

"Far out, isn't it?" Cassie said.

"No wonder Cameron thought you were a muse lately sprung up in America."

"What's that supposed to mean?"

She led Cassie into the hall. "Care for some tea?" she asked.

"I have some ginseng in my tote," Cassie offered.

"Thanks, dear," Ada said, "I'd as soon not swallow anything in your bag."

"Don't be smart," Cassiopeia said. "Just because your toilet seat is down."

"You noticed."

"You've broken him, paper-trained him like a lap dog." Cassiopeia looked genuinely sorrowful.

"Don't be ridiculous," Ada said.

"No. Really," Cassiopeia said. "Signs and omens are everywhere."

"You've confused peace, love, and granola with life," Ada said.

"In the universe. In the cosmos. In the constellations of stars. It's all magical."

Ada busied herself with a pot of Mu tea.

Cassie rattled her costume bracelets across the old white-oak table. Silence stretched between them. Once, when she was eleven years old, Ada had connected a wire between two soup cans and had given one to her best girlfriend. They had been barely able to hear each other.

Cassiopeia stared vacantly at her fingers full of rings.

Ada switched on the 1932 Philco that Cameron had restored. KFOG crept around the aspidistra and wandering jew plants, filling the kitchen with guileless music. At least once an hour they played an instrumental version of "I Left My Heart in San Francisco."

"That station makes me feel like I'm in a dentist office," Cassiopeia said.

"It calms me," Ada said. "In the room," she clung for balance to her favorite line of poetry, "the women come and go, speaking... speaking..."

Cassiopeia was not listening. She nervously twisted her rings. "I think I'm leaving Frisco," she said.

It grated on Ada. "Never call San Francisco 'Frisco,'" she said. "What's the matter with you?"

"Nothing," she said. "It's all over here, unless you're gay. I just want to go away."

"Then go." Ada said it flat.

"You've never liked me." Cassiopeia looked about to cry.

"I could cheerfully murder you," Ada said. "Hand me your cup. The tea's ready."

"I tried to leave before."

"That was a happy day till you called us late that night." Ada poured the tea.

"Long distance."

"Collect," Ada said. "I accepted your call when Cameron

refused." She poured her own tea. "Why should I like you? My husband's old...." Ada stopped pouring in mid-cup.

She felt reversed, turned around. It was the New World the liberated Ms. Leavitt loved: Ada, the princess, out defending, rescuing again, perhaps, her prince.

She set the tea-cosy down on a mirrored tray in which she saw the upside-down face of Cassiopeia. "Okay," Ada said, "take a sip of your tea."

"Thank you, Nurse Rat Shit," Cassiopeia said.

"Furious this may make you, my tired little hipster, but you're going to hear me out for once. Stoned or not. Try to focus your fried-out brain."

Cassiopeia rose up in her seat. "Nobody talks to me like that."

"Except me," Ada said. "And you look straight at me, Margaret Mary O'Hara. "Watch my face. Read my lips."

Cassiopeia bolted. Lectures frightened her. She stood straight up, knocking over her chair. "Dear, dear Abby," Cassie said, "I'm not one of your sophomores. Who needs this? I'm leaving."

"Good-bye, good luck, and good riddance."

Cassie grabbed her tote and ran down the hall, heading toward the front door. She stopped. She turned. "I'm pregnant," she screamed. "Tell Cam that!" She slung her tote over her shoulder. "From what I figure about you, Ada Tomato, that's more than you'll ever be able to tell him!"

Ada started for her, walking fast, then faster down the hall. "I'm going to tear your nose off your face," she screamed.

Cassie yanked open the front door. The afternoon sun hit her directly, exploding her into a ball of saffron light.

Ada was momentarily blinded. She stopped in her tracks. The door slammed. The hallway grew quiet, except for the tiny sniffle Ada stifled with the back of her hand. This wasn't what she had meant to happen. Not at all. "Oh damn," she said.

*

Curtis directed Cameron down the dirt fire-road to the old Mount Tamalpais train station. The sign on the stone-and-timber building read West Point Club. Cameron pulled the bike up under three shady pines. The dust ball that had followed the bike down the trail caught them and sifted into their clothes. Curtis hopped off, preening himself like a swan. Cameron wondered if Curtis, neat old Curtis, sportscar nut and terror of women, wasn't just a bit of a fag, even if he had married Ada who refused to rate Curtis' performance on a scale of one-to-ten. He kicked the stand under his bike. Why give fags a bad name, he thought. Curtis is Curtis.

"Hey, Mala!" A raspy voice called down from the porch. At first Cameron couldn't see to whom the man at the railing was shouting. Then a streak of gray flashed out of the bushes. Curtis moved quickly behind the bike as the gray Malamute loped her panting way up to the newcomers.

"Hey there, girl," Cameron said. The dog looked up at him and rolled over on her back. Cameron stooped down.

"That's it," the man on the porch said, "scratch her."

Cameron pulled the white hair on the dog's belly back and forth. Her back wriggled through the dusty gravel. Her eyes rolled ecstatic back into her head.

"Be careful," Curtis said. "She might bite."

"Come on, Mala," the man said coming down from the porch. "Don't be a pest." His chin was grizzled with whiskers. He was shirtless and wearing brown leather hiking shorts he had crafted himself. "She found a rattler this morning," he said, "curled up on the porch steps." He held out a hand to Cameron stooped over the dog. The tips of two fingers were missing. "Name's Jerry," he said. His grip was strong and he was so veined with muscle he easily pulled Cameron to his feet. "I killed it with a stick." He pointed to a nail on the porch railing. "Come on up. You can see the rattles."

The dog followed the three men up to the porch where she lay down possessively guarding the steps. Four hikers, two couples, in their late fifties, early sixties, sat at one of the many tables on the porch, one sipping hot tea, and three lemonade.

"What a view," Cameron said. "From down in these trees I didn't think you could see anything."

"Everything from out in the Pacific, in past the Golden Gate, all of San Francisco, Oakland, on around to Berserkley and the Richmond Bridge," Jerry said. "On a clear night, the ocean and Bay are black as the sky. You can hardly tell the constellations of stars from the constellations of city lights."

"A poet," Curtis said, "and you know it."

"Nope, the caretaker." Jerry spit over the railing. He liked most people, but already he disliked Curtis. "Lemonade?" he asked.

"Fresh squeezed?" Curtis sat in one of the heavy wooden porch chairs.

"Wyler's Brand," Jerry said. He toyed with a chain hanging heavy with keys at his left hip.

"Make it two, okay?" Cameron said. He shot a .22-caliber look at Curtis.

"Come on, Mala," Jerry said.

The dog rose, looked with dumb affection at Cameron, and passed on into the club rooms. Cameron looked in. The floors were rough and unfinished. The walls and ceiling were an ancient enamel yellow. Some of the leaded glass had fallen out of a built-in cupboard, and the fireplace had been converted to a gas burner. Even the globes hanging from the ceiling burnt gas. Directly opposite the door hung a portrait of John Muir.

"How long has this place been here?" Cameron asked.

"Forever," Curtis said. "Sit down. I want to talk to you."

"Yessir!" Cameron said and saluted smartly.

The woman with the tea took a quick look at Curtis and then whispered something to her husband with the lemonade. They both laughed.

Cameron sat down, back to the view. Curtis began talking.

Cameron studied the map of trails that hung framed under glass over Curtis' head.

"Here's your lemonade," Jerry said. He set the tray down between the two men.

"Pay the man," Cameron said to Curtis. "It'll be good for your soul."

Curtis looked hurt. Ada always said money was Curtis' only friend. "How much?" he said.

"Fifty cents," Jerry said.

Curtis laid five dimes on the table. Jerry's stubbed fingers deftly flicked the change into the palm of his hand. "For the West Point kitty," he said.

The other hikers called him to sit with them.

Curtis drank the lemonade in one gulp. "Everything tastes like chemicals," he said. "Even if you could afford it, where could you find any quality to buy these days?"

"What makes you think you could ever buy it?" Cameron sipped his lemonade.

"As I was saying," Curtis said.

"What were you saying?"

"I was saying the trouble with Ada is..."

"There's no trouble with Ada," Cameron said.

"...is the same as the trouble with me." Curtis was relentless. "When we were married, such a short time, we both were very young. She was in school. We were both in school. We were peace activists in the streets, but we fought each other. All the time. About everything. We needed, well, a referee."

"Someone to count you out? 8-9-10?"

"I loved...no, love, Ada." Curtis looked about to whimper.

"That makes two of us," Cameron said. "But I have my doubts about you."

"No doubts," Curtis said.

Mala crept over next to Cameron's chair. Jerry was playing the harmonica, one of three he kept on a shelf inside the door, and the four hikers were singing a German song.

"So what do you want me to do?" Cameron asked. He scratched the dog behind the ears.

"I want...." Curtis hesitated.

"Go on," Cameron said. "Good girl, Mala. That's a good girl, Mala."

"I want," Curtis said, "to live with Ada."

"You're crazy," Cameron said. "She thinks you're a joke."

"No." Curtis leaned into the table. "I want...and this is really hard to verbalize."

"Try," Cameron said.

"I want to move in with Ada. And with you."

*

Ada lay prostrate on the couch with laughter. "Poor Curtis!" she said. "What did you say to him?"

Cameron fell across her, stretching down the length of her body. Her laughter was infectious. He laughed too. "What do you think I said?"

She roared. "Yes!" she screamed. "You said *yes*! We're no longer a marriage. We're a *menage*!"

"He wants us to be his mommy and daddy."

Ada's hilarity ignited her immense energy and she pushed Cameron off her to the floor. "You idiot," she said, gaining control of herself. "Of course, you didn't really!"

"You hurt my back," Cameron said. "Of course, I did. I couldn't help myself."

"You didn't!" She began to strike his shoulders with her small fists. "I'll hurt more than your back. I'm not ready to adopt. Any-one." She meant Cassiopeia especially.

"Watch your knee," he said. He rolled into a fetal position.

"Say you didn't," she said. "I'll positively murder you!"

Cameron was laughing, tickling her, teasing her, driving her crazy. She pounced across his butt, snatched a pillow from the couch, and pummeled his head.

"I didn't." He confessed, but he never surrendered. "I didn't. I really didn't."

"That's more like it." Ada stood up triumphant. "Curtis and Cassie are both children, and we agreed not to have children."

Cameron rolled over and unhitched the belt on his jeans. He held out his arms to her. "We can change our minds," he said.

"Is that all you care about?" Ada reached for the misting can and walked indignant toward the windows.

"Go drown your ferns," Cameron said.

She sprayed the ferns so heavily they began to drip on the hardwood floor. "That's all you care about," she said. "That tramp Cassie might have been your trampoline, but not me!"

He locked his hands together under his head. "I used to care about a lot of things."

"Here it comes," she said. "Whatever it is we never talk about." She pulled a red bandana from her back pocket and tried to wipe the wet floor.

"Yeah. Here it comes," he said. He leaned up on an elbow and stuck a cigarette between his teeth.

"You ought to trim that moustache before you burn yourself up."

"Here it comes," he said. He lit the cigarette and pulled the smoke down deep.

Ada took advantage of the pause. "First there were the Kennedys," she recited. She repeated his litany by heart. "Assassinations. Executions, you say. And second there was…"

"Nam," he said.

"Sometimes I think the only heart you have is purple."

"Smart-assing doesn't become you, Ada."

"Don't forget drugs," she said. "You and your sacred mushrooms."

"And drugs."

"And Cassiopeia, the human air-mattress."

"Lay off," Cameron said.

Ada rose from her knees waving the wet red kerchief. "Would the bull like a surprise?"

"What surprise?"

"She was here today."

"Cassie?"

"Yeah."

"What'd she want?" Cameron let the cigarette hang forgotten in his mouth.

"Same as Curtis I imagine." Ada folded the wet kerchief deliberately into squares. "But you know Cassie. She always says the opposite of what she means. You have to read her in a mirror." Ada never believed in telling anyone everything. She decided not to lighten up with a joke about Cassie's chameleons.

"What'd she say?" Cameron rose and crossed to the bottle tucked away in the bookcase.

"She said she's leaving San Francisco. She said she stopped over to say good-bye. She said she'd never call us again. Not even collect. She said she was a chameleon. Her hints were as broad as her hips. I think she wants to live with us too. Fuck her!"

"Cut it, Ada," Cameron said. He was flashing on the night Cassie had called them long distance, desperate and sick on junk. "That poor kid," he had said. He had spent the night in the Greyhound Bus Depot waiting for her to get back from Santa Cruz.

Ada had been furious. "You can't really expect me to go down to that filthy bus station practically on our honeymoon to meet your whore," Ada had said. "What kind of woman do you think I am?"

"I don't know," he had said. "I suspect I'll find out. Sooner or later."

*

Even through that long night waiting for Cassiopeia, Cameron hadn't blamed Ada. Strangers in the station had surrounded him, deathly alive at 3:30 AM. They had breathed on him. Everyone smoked. Their blue exhalations had yellowed the air, thickening the pallid fluorescent light.

He hadn't blamed Ada and he hadn't blamed Cassie.

The longer he had waited that night the more he had needed the men's room. He had stalled leaving his seat in the crowded terminal, mainly because an old woman, a white choir robe folded over her arm, had stood sentinel, waiting, like God's Righteousness at the end of the full row of seats. She had tried to stare Cameron into relinquishing his chair. But he had sat, steadfast, bladder hurting, because her face, over the folded choir robe, because her face, over the righteous folds of her melting flesh, was so mean.

From the moment of Cassie's emergency call, Ada had given him no peace; and Cassie wasn't due till 6:47. Cameron had reached for a cigarette. Out. He had frisked his pockets for a stray pack.

Another predator had eyed his nervous movements. Seated in the row opposite, a young hooker, in shorts and leg-warmers, had been clipping her nails, licking each finger after each snip, rubbing each cuticle meticulously dry on her denim blouse. That night among desperate travelers going nowhere had been terrible.

Cameron took his drink and turned to Ada. "If nothing else," he mumbled, "here and now...."

"What?" she said.

"Nothing." He took a good slug of the whiskey. "There's too many people in the world to care anymore," he said.

That night in the bus station, too far away to hear, Cameron had watched a security cop hassle two men lounging without luggage. One, a young black, had produced a ticket. The cop had reached for his eyeglasses. He took the ticket, examined it, and handed it back. The other man, a wafer-thin Appalachian with red hair, had fumbled through his pockets, offering at last to the cop a shred of paper. Even at a distance, Cameron had felt the failure. Outside, a bus roared. The cop had jerked his fist, thumb extended, back over his shoulder. Obediently, the red-haired man had risen, defeated, cast out, and shuffled out towards Seventh Street and Market Street.

"How can anyone care anymore?" Cameron lay back on the couch. "There's just too many."

The depot had been a mess with people. Too many people always meant a mess. They had drained him of sympathy. All their patience. All their hurry. Their smell. Their sound. He knew he was the same to them. Just another body taking up the last available seat. If the security officer had shot the red-haired man in the face, Cameron would have felt no pity. No more sorry than watching an actor like Edmund O'Brien get shot in a TV series. Maybe the cleaning woman might have minded the red-haired Appalachian brains blown under the bus station seats about as much as she minded the hooker's snipped crescents of dead-white fingernail.

*

"Hello in there!" Ada rubbed Cameron's forehead with the cool wet bandana.

"Cassie's really gone then," he said.

"As much as Cassie ever goes," Ada said. "I wouldn't worry. She has her own ways of coping, weak as they are."

"She'll keel over out there, Ada." The hand with his drink sank to the floor beside the couch.

Ada lifted the glass to her lips and finished the burning whiskey. "Cassiopeia will be alright. So will Curtis," she soothed, climbing on top of Cameron's outstretched body. She kissed him. She loved him. "Everything's alright," she said. "Everybody drops people now and then." She kissed him again. "We're alright, Cameron. We're here now."

She cupped his head in her hands, nuzzling his lips, nose, eyes. "They're both gone," she said.

"They'll come back."

"And we'll send them away."

"We have no choice."

She kissed him. "We're all alone."

"We need to be alone together," he said. He brought his arms up around her, pulling her down on to him. "We two." He needed to hold her, just hold her.

She let him embrace her sweetly.

She relaxed across the full length of his body. She rose and fell with his breathing as he drifted off to sleep. She felt his unshaven face chafe against her cheek. Some things she sometimes accepted. She was not sleepy in her vigil, holding him, protecting him, but she could not afford to look too long at his face. Maybe he wasn't the best man in the world, but he was the best who had yet come along.

Everyone thought they were a great couple. They were charmed, emerging from the burden of their pasts. He was as handsome as she was attractive, and, lord knows, something in the very look of him warmed the cold Curtis had left deep inside her when his dose had killed her fertility. Someday when Cameron was ready, when she was ready, when she could afford the astonished look in his face, when she could chance his disappointment might not drive him away, she promised herself to tell him why, really why, she didn't want, couldn't have, children.

God! His radiant heat made her eyes burn. She closed them, in self-defense, closed them tight against his seductive, engaging brightness that was like the beautiful blinding brightness of San Francisco itself when tour boats pull away from the Embarcadero at noon into the windswept cross-currents of the Bay.

Coming Attractions
Kweenasheba

A Snappy San Francisco Comedy
1 Act in 2 Scenes

"Kweenasheba" was first produced by the Yonkers Production Company, San Francisco, premiering March 13, 1976, at the Society for Individual Rights SIR Center Theatre on a double bill with "The Madness of Lady Bright" by Lanford Wilson. The author adapted his 1975 play from his 1972 short story, "Sweet Embraceable You."

Time: Christmas, 1972
Setting: San Francisco, Castro Street, Soap-and-Floral Shop
Four Characters: two women, two men

Ada Vicary: 30, with an MA, teaching in a junior college; her own woman; sveltly attractive; first married to CURTIS, she is now divorced and living with JOHN; independent; clever; as a girl she bound her own books, hunted bugs, and invented animal nicknames for her relatives. In many ways, ADA is a compensatory swinger; owner of a restored Victorian on San Francisco's Castro Street.

John Stack: Early 30's; a craftsman-motorcyclist; dark and handsome and into an ironic trip as owner of a Soap-and-Floral Shop located in Ada's Victorian. JOHN, formerly the lover of KWEENASHEBA, is now ADA's lover. JOHN is the straight foil to both KWEENASHEBA and CURTIS.

Kweenasheba: 29, formerly named Mary Margaret Chase until her lysergic rechristening in the Haight-Ashbury. She is amply endowed as any Rubens nude; she fancies herself "the one and only reincarnation of the Queen of Sheba": Kweenasheba. Her body is a tracery of fads: a Janis Joplin tattoo, tote bags, saffron robes, and a pierced nose. Basically she's been around and she's winded. She is a photographer snapping her borrowed camera.

Curtis Boughner: 34, pansexual; even more masculine of body and voice than John; sometimes lilting in manner of delivery when he chooses; as handsome in his fair way as John is in his darkness; Curtis, formerly Ada's husband, is now KWEENASHEBA's lover.

This comedy should be played light, lively, and fast—midway between the madcap comic style of vintage Hollywood and fast-paced TV sitcoms.

TWO SCENES. ONE SET.
Playing time: 40 minutes

SCENE ONE

A morning before Christmas in the storefront Soap-and-Floral Shop of a restored Victorian on San Francisco's Castro Street. The calendar says December 1972. Two couples share this house: Ada Vicary and John Stack, upstairs; Kweenasheba and Curtis, downstairs behind the shop.

The single set is decorated for Christmas and divided by the service counter to the left of which stand the soap baskets, the green plants in white wicker, and the inevitable macrame-bilia. To the right of the counter is strewn a combination work and living area. To the left is the street entrance. Coming down at rear center stage is the last curve and landing of a stairs from the second floor.

To the right, behind the clippers and styrofoam frogs and 1940's couch is a door curtained with nostalgic floral draperies. An old coffee dripolator sits steaming on a hotplate. A vintage 'Forties radio, receiving a contemporary station, plays Christmas carols.

John: (Off-stage, singing with the radio)
"Tis the season to be jolly;
Fa La La La La La La La La!
Time to sell the goddam holly!"

JOHN ENTERS

The shop is his and he readies it for the day. His voice is big enough to sing his own lyrics over the radio.

John: "Don we now our gay apparel..."
Ada: (Entering, switches off radio) Not you!
John: (Rising from plants) What?
Ada: I smelled the coffee.
John: (Closing in to embrace ADA) Then good morning. (He kisses her lightly)
Ada: Thanks for the stroking. I'm beat.
John: Tired?
Ada: All last night I could hear them.
John: Curtis and Kweenasheba? They'll be here forever.
Ada: They giggle. Too much. What could they have in common?
John: Your Curtis? My Kweenie? Once upon a time, each one of them had each one of us.
Ada: Comparing notes, I suppose. Curtis always was one to kiss and tell. God! I loathe the smell of fried bologna. What are they cooking back there?
John: Roses.
Ada: Roses?
John: In these boxes are 20 dozen roses.
Ada: You're the only florist in San Francisco who smells like fried bologna.
John: You think I like it? Your Ex and my Ex living in a room behind my shop.
Ada: (Pouring coffee) Darling....I own the building. The smell permeates. And I hate the way it curls up...

John: (Tossing yesterday's wilted flowers aside)... Everything curls
    up...
Ada: ...Bologna when it fries, curls up. I hate it.
John: My customers buy with their noses.
Ada: Business is off? It's Christmas!
John: They buy roses. They buy bayberry soap. They smell bolo-
    gna.
Ada: I know what Curtis is telling Kweenie.
John: Flowers are one thing. Meat is another.
Ada: Those two have to move.
John: Said Mohammed to the mountain.
Ada: They've crashed here long enough.
John: Once you loved Curtis.
Ada: Once you loved Kweenie.
John: A good case of changing partners.
Ada: Two bad cases of unrequited love. They've got to move.
John: A crime of passion might make us colorful in the neigh-
    borhood.
Ada: The unveiling of the mysteries inside all these marvelously
    restored old Victorians!
John: Curtis and Kweenie cling to each other...
Ada: ...because I love you and Kweenie loves you and you love
    me and Curtis loves me.
John: May I have the envelope please?
Ada: I never told you why I divorced Curtis.
John: Because Curtis likes...
Ada: ...what Curtis likes. No. Particularly why I divorced Curtis.
John: You promised to spare me the gory details.
Ada: You pumped Curtis about me.
John: You pumped Kweenasheba about me.
Ada: So what?
John: Fair is fair.
Ada: A dump is a dump.
John: What are you teaching this morning?
Ada: Children's literature.
John: Nice...
Ada: Kiddy litter.

John: Don't be cute.

Ada: To a bunch of reluctant adolescents who think they want to teach when they grow up. Hell. I don't even know what I want to be when I grow up.

John: You are a real junior-college thrill.

Ada: Listen. Curtis and I were on our first vacation. Driving down Route 1. Eating Four-Bean Salad from a Safeway can. I was feeding Curtis...

John: Now *that's* cute!

Ada: ...because he was driving. I'd eat a bite, then lean over and feed him a bite. He'd open his mouth and I'd fork in the beans.

John: That's why you were never invited to the French Embassy!

Ada: A whole year we'd been married and it hit me. Who is this person? How'd we get to be driving in the same car? Me feeding him.

John: Things happen.

Ada: How do things happen? I hardly remember meeting Curtis. I sort of always knew him. One day he said it seemed like a good idea to get married.

John: So you tied the bean cans to the car and took off to the No-Tell Motel.

Ada: Curtis made me promise to tell him all my fantasies.

John: Did you?

Ada: At night. In bed.

John: Sort of a game?

Ada: Sort of therapy. It got to be fun.

John: You were made for each other.

Ada: He seemed to love me better if we played games.

John: He performed better?

Ada: He seemed to love me more.

John: What kind of games?

Ada: Children's games, really. He called me "The Doll Lady" and once every week or so he became one of my baby dolls.

John: Freud lives...and he's dating Tennessee Williams.

Ada: Don't try and stop me now.

John: Not for the world.

Ada: He had two favorite dolls he liked to be. One was Baby
   Bunting.

John: You'd be his mother.

Ada: I'd bathe him and talcum him with baby powder. It was as
   exciting as...

John: ...*Oedipus Rex.*

Ada: I'd diaper him and we'd cuddle on the bed while I sang to
   him and he kissed me here. (ADA touches her breast) He
   made me feel like a Madonna. Then we'd make love.

John: Baby Bunting stuck it to Mommy?

Ada: No! When the loving started the gaming stopped.

John: It was always foreplay?

Ada: For me. But Curtis let the fantasy part stretch on longer
   and longer. He invented a new doll called Gladys Mae. I had
   to dress him up in little girl clothes from Macy's.

John: Curtis as Shirley Temple?

Ada: He kept the motions of loving me.

John: Sweet Jesus and Dear Abby!

Ada: He needed mothering.

John: He should marry Kweenie.

Ada: No more than I should marry you.

John: You played along?

Ada: Till I went mad.

John: Sure.

Ada: One of my liberated lady students wrote in her term paper,
   "With a man, a woman enters as Juliet and exits as Ophelia."

John: Virgin to virago.

Ada: I complained to him.

John: What did he say?

Ada: That I wanted to tie him down. That I was tying him down.

John: What did you say?

Ada: I was furious. I'd been a good sport all along.

John: I'd say so.

Ada: He made me so mad standing there looking so goddam cute, so ridiculous in the cotton pinafore and white
   kneesocks. He stuck his tongue out at me. So I hit him.

John: Punched him?

Ada: Slapped him. Knocked him stunned into my vanity chair.
    He just sat there.
John: Really turned you off?
Ada: Then I tied him into the chair.
John: Tied him?
Ada: With cord from the electric blanket. Kind of poetic revenge.
    "Tied down?" I said. "I'll show you tied down."
John: He whimpered?
Ada: He cried.
John: You liked it.
Ada: I loved it. I faced him into the mirror and brushed lipstick
    and rouge all over his face. The powder caked in the tears on
    his cheeks.
John: You hurt him.
Ada: He was happy. I let him alone. I made him stare at himself
    in the mirror. I went into the kitchen and scoured the sink till
    the pad disintegrated.
John: How long?
Ada: I don't know. Twenty minutes. Then I started to worry
    about the circulation in his hands.
John: So you went back to the bedroom.
Ada: He was grinning.
John: From earring to earring.
Ada: I said: "What are you smiling at?" He wouldn't answer me.
    So I hit him again. You know what he said?
John: What?
Ada: This grown-man's voice. It came out of his powdered, dim-
    pled dollface and all he said, so matter-of-factly, was: "Curtis
    just came in Gladys Mae's panties.
John: That's the Big Secret? Pantyhose.
Ada: I never let him touch me again.
John: Because of the games?
Ada: Because at that point I was included out.
John: Joe Namath wears pantyhose.
Ada: Curtis' only love object was Curtis.
John: You gave up too easy.
Ada: Easy!?

John: You could have dressed up like Gladys Mae yourself.

Curtis: (Enters through floraled drapery door) And to think students think their teachers hang in suspended animation between classes.

Ada: Curtis, I want you to move.

Curtis: Who kisses and tells? Walls have ears, doll. Good morning, John.

John: Hello, Curtis.

Ada: You and Kweenie both. Out!

Curtis: If they fired the weirdos, they'd have to close down every school in California.

Ada: Don't threaten me.

Curtis: Do you feel threatened?

Ada: I feel crowded.

Curtis: Crowded? By a cast of thousands.

John: It's San Francisco kharma. If you've got an extra bed in your apartment, somebody from the Midwest will crash in it.

Curtis: The Midwest is the pits. Whatever happened to the Midwest?

John: I'm still figuring what happened to you.

Curtis: Someday I'll tell you the whole truth. If awful "Ophelia" doesn't tell you first.

Ada: Someday I'm going to cut you up in itsy bitchy pieces. Very little pieces.

Curtis: Your favorite size.

Ada: As John Wayne said in *Red River*....

Curtis: I live and breathe movies.

John: Movies are such garbage.

Ada: As John Wayne said, Curtis, in *Red River* to all the fat cows: "Move out"

Curtis: Ada Tomata!

Ada: Curtis Schmurtis!

John: Kiddies!

Ada: How can an adult respond to THAT?

Curtis: You're just jealous because my parents live on the planet Krypton.

Ada: As I recall your parents....

Curtis: My mother said you'd do for a first wife.

Ada: She did?

Curtis: You didn't.

John: Before dawn I was at the Flower Mart on Harrison Street. I watched the sunrise over the East Bay.

Curtis: You're so pure.

John: I saw wet dew in Dolores Park.

Curtis: You felt "peace."

John: I hosed down the sidewalk out front.

Curtis: May the Castro Street merchants pin a rose on you.

John: But my head cannot get behind the trip you two lay on each other.

Curtis: Still crazy after all these years.

Ada: I'm sorry.

John: This is a big house and we're adults.

Ada: Adults!

Curtis: Keep saying it, Ada. Adults! Clap your hands and believe with all your heart and Tinker Bell will menstruate.

Ada: (Pulls on her sweater with a vengeance. She moves in on CURTIS, thumb-tip to thumb-tip, forefingers up at right angles to her thumbs framing CURTIS' face for a mocking movie close-up) How's that, Mr. DeMille? Is it a take? Or is it a fake?

Curtis: (Blows the sounds of "raspberries" all over ADA's palms)

Ada: (Retreating) Some adult!

Curtis: My diary entry about you today won't be nice.

Ada: It never is.

Curtis: You've read it.

Ada: You leave it lay out on purpose. (She tosses the diary to him)

Curtis: It was a test.

Ada: Then I failed.

Curtis: God will get you.

Ada: Curtis?

Curtis: Yes, darling?

Ada: Move out. You and Kweenie. Together. Separately. Bag, baggage: out! I want you and Kweenie gone. I want to smell

John's roses. I loathe your fried bologna. I want my privacy
back. (ADA picks up books and satchel, slams door, and exits)
Curtis: She once was so sweet.
John: What happened?
Curtis: She became a teacher. Why Ada teaches is beyond me.
Sensitive people used to go into teaching. Kindly gentlemen
like Robert Donat in *Good-bye, Mr. Chips* and nice ladies like
Jennifer Jones in *Good Morning, Miss Dove.*
John: Sensitive people still teach.
Curtis: For sure. If they can balance a textbook with a whip, a
chair, and a pistol. I personally am thinking of turning to a
life of crime.
John: You could use a career.
Curtis: A career I got. A job I need. All these film schools turning
out hundreds of little Francis Ford Corpulents.
John: Class tells.
Curtis: What's that mean?
John: Get a job. Get an apartment.
Curtis: There's not much call for film editors right now.
John: Use your connections.
Curtis: What connections?
John: Your famous gay underground.
Curtis: *My* famous? *My* gay? My *underwear!*
John: Come on, Gladys Mae; admit it. *Newsweek* says the gay
mafia controls the media.
Curtis: I'm not gay.
John: Neither is your closet full of underwear. Pour me some
more coffee.
Curtis: You ought to have your consciousness raised.
John: Women raise my...consciousness.
Curtis: (Pouring coffee) We also shovel who only stand and
pour....Your consciousness about men.
John: I never think about men.
Curtis: About alternative ways of being a man.
John: I'm sick of your gay *schmerz.*
Curtis: I'm sick of your macho paranoia.

John: Okay, Curtis. The Bottom Line: as a person, I like you. As
    a fag, you're a drag.
Curtis: ...said the Flower Queen. (JOHN threatens) Excuse me.
    King. Flower King.
John: Men used to box.
Curtis: I didn't mean because you were interested in flowers that
    you were a "flower." I swear by St. Genet, NO!
John: You implied.
Curtis: You inferred what I did not imply.
John: I love women. Like I love Ada.
Curtis: I can love anyone.
John: How catholic.
Curtis: You really get your rocks off dumping on me.
John: You make good coffee.
Curtis: Someday you'll have the empathy to understand.
John: Coffee-making?
Curtis: When a man and a woman make love....
John: "Strangers in the night, beedoobeedoobee."
Curtis: ...among other things they do is celebrate their co-sexual-
    ity. When two women make love...
John: Interesting!
Curtis: ...they celebrate, yes, celebrate their femininity.
John: Why don't you wake up Kweenasheba?
Curtis: She's tired. We were...celebrating.
John: Kweenie's tired all right.
Curtis: Kweenie's a hot woman.
John: And I thought it was burning bologna!
Curtis: What you won't let me say, John, is that I'm freer than
    you.
John: Freer and queerer.
Curtis: Hold on to this wire.
John: Why?
Curtis: So your death will look accidental.
John: Go arouse Lady Astor.
Curtis: When I want to celebrate manhood, I bed down with a
    man.
John: I admit: you're honest.

Curtis: I'm natural.

John: You're not normal.

Curtis: I'd rather be natural than normal.

John: I think you're unemployed.

Curtis: Film companies are hiring only women editors.

John: Go roll out Kweenasheba.

Curtis: Women are chic. From the silent movies on, they've always been the best editors. Dede Allen cuts all of Arthur Penn's films: *Bonnie and Clyde*.

John: I need her to dust up the shop.

Curtis: Kweenasheba?

John: The one, the only, the original.

Curtis: Get off Kweenie's case.

John: "A case of do or die..."

Curtis: Shut-up.

John: I run this shop.

Curtis: Ada owns this house.

John: So I should shut-up?

Curtis: I'm going to marry Kweenie.

John: You and the Marines.

Curtis: I'm going to marry her and move her out of this house.

John: In a world of terrorists and pay toilets, you want to marry Kweenasheba?

Curtis: We'd be a team. A couple. Judy and Mickey. Tracy and Hepburn. Sonny and Cher.

John: A fag and his hag.

Curtis: Those words today are not acceptable.

John: May you have twins. You can name them Butch and Nellie.

Curtis: (Amused) Why do I like you?

John: You think marrying Kweenasheba will make you straight?

Curtis: But I *do* like you.

John: Your brain's in neutral. Your mouth idles on.

Curtis: You are a Straight Chauvinist. (Expansively dramatic) "The Adventures of Macho Man"!

John: Sue me. I'm a white Anglo-Saxon male.

Curtis: Macho do about nothing!

John: We males are an endangered species.

Curtis: I can see why.

John: Just man-to-man trying to protect you, boy. Kweenie's been around and she's winded.

Curtis: You whirled her around in the Haight-Ashbury when she was still Mary Margaret Chase.

John: And I fed her valiums for a month after a freaked-out methadone Marxist baptized her in acid. He told her she was the reincarnation of the one, the only, the original Queen of Sheba.

Curtis: And she's loved you ever since.

John: You drill that old rig, Curtis, you better dynamite through a million layers of old deposits.

Curtis: *Oklahoma Crude*!

John: You'll really get off thinking of all the dudes who beat you to first base. Hell. To Home Plate.

Curtis: All four of us have been around.

John: One rock musician after another.

Curtis: Is that all? Kweenie's dated the United Nations. With your bad-boy vocabulary, I expect you can peel off some really cute names for Blacks, Latins, and Asians.

John: Besides a Turk or twelve. And now a reformed faggot. That figures.

Curtis: So she has a talent for loving a lot of men.

John: Armies have marched over that chick.

Curtis: You stood in line.

John: Poor old cow.

Curtis: Stop, pig!

John: I guess I loved her once.

Curtis: I guess you maybe still do.

John: In a way....You freak me out, Curtis.

Curtis: Why?

John: I guess I'm a little jealous. Kweenie will marry you. Ada won't marry me.

Curtis: Sure.

John: I guess I'm a little shocked.

Curtis: I'm a little shocked myself.

John: Ada will freak out when I tell her.
Curtis: I know. So will Kweenie.
John: You haven't asked her?
Curtis: Marriage just seems like a good idea at this time.
John: You better go wake her up.
Curtis: Sleeping Beauty.
John: What will she say?
Curtis: She'll say, "Wow!" She'll say, "Far out!" She'll say, "YES!"
Kweenie: (Appearing grandly through the floral draperies and
    holding a big bologna sandwich) I'll say, "NO!"

**Lights hold three solid beats
freezing the action to
END SCENE ONE**

**Lights fade down for five beats
and then come up on
SCENE TWO**

Evening of the same day. The shop is closed. Incense is burning.
Christmas lights are a glow. Alone, KWEENIE whistles boisterously
a couple lines of "Silent Night." She has obviously been photograph-
ing, without much satisfaction, a still-life of soap and flowers. She
seems ponderous and pondering. She addresses her soliloquy to the
absent ADA and JOHN and CURTIS.

Kweenie: May I speak? May I speak without being spoken to?
    May I make a personal remark?...A personal remark? Oh
    my....Oh yes. A personal remark? Please do. (Then flatly) I
    think I'll go kill a rock star....Nothin', huh? How do you get
    somebody's attention? "You can tell us anything." (She snaps a
    flash picture) My parents always said that. I'll bet every parent
    on the block, every parent in the nation, in the western hemi-
    sphere, in the world, in the mind of God has said, "You can
    tell us anything. We'll understand." Call *The National Enquir-
    er*! EXTRA! EXTRA! Read All About It! BLIND PARENTS
    RAISE INVISIBLE CHILD!" I'll bet even killer sharks pump

their kids for information. (She lines up another picture and snaps it) Personally, I prefer still-life. (She whistles one more line of "Silent Night") I must not whistle. What was it the nuns at good old Misericordia taught us? "When a girl whistles, the Blessed Virgin cries." (She whistles a fast "wolf" whistle) Who runs the Kleenex concession in heaven? "Bless me, Father, for I have whistled." I am the by-product of a long procession of parents and priests and nuns. They told me to be good. I'm good okay. Very good. But, mommy, what's "good"? Be good. You and daddy never finished that sentence. Be a good what? A good lawyer. A good doctor. Anything but a good virgin-martyr-saint. Right now I'm good...and pregnant. (Sings) "Round yon Virgin, Mother and Child." Tch! They'd never believe that!

Ada: (Entering) Is this the mad scene from *Hamlet*?

Kweenie: Just helping an old lady across the street...of her life.

Ada: Found an apartment?

Kweenie: You missed supper.

Ada: A-part-ment. As in a-part.

Kweenie: Maybe I should marry Curtis and be a housewife in Daly City.

Ada: Somehow that must be against zoning laws.

Kweenie: My nose hurts.

Ada: That's more barbaric than pierced ears.

Kweenie: It's PRIMAL!

Ada: Primal? It's positively Neanderthal.

Kweenie: It's only my left nostril.

Ada: ...and what a lovely saffron robe.

Kweenie: I may join that Dervish group.

Ada: And shake your tambourine for the tourists down at Powell and Market.

Kweenie: The same old Ada. (KWEENIE pulls out a joint)

Ada: The same old Kweenie. (ADA tosses KWEENIE a box of footlong fireplace matches) Where's John?

Kweenie: Out. (KWEENIE has struck the match and lets it burn close to her face)

Ada: Just us girls then.

Kweenie: Am I just another candlelight beauty? (KWEENIE waves the match before her face. She is baiting ADA as the "older" woman) What does youth do to a face?

Ada: Usually it leaves.

Kweenie: (Blows out match) Say, does Johnny still leave the toilet seat up?

Ada: We're off and running.

Kweenie: Johnny always used to leave the toilet seat up. More than once with that man I crawled out of bed in the dark of night and plopped my fanny down into the cold water.

Ada: How refreshing. Did you have to change your jammies?

Kweenie: Peroxide. I need peroxide. For my nose.

Ada: John stores a first-aid kit under the counter. (ADA busily waters plants)

Kweenie: Let me recite my latest poem.

Ada: You're so creative. Photography. Poetry. Hooking.

Kweenie:

> "Chameleons are not furious.
> They color themselves to fit their world.
> Suddenly, this long here...."
> What do you think so far?

Ada: Terrific. I hate it.

Kweenie:

> "Suddenly, this long *here*,
> I no longer speed on the urgency of *there*.
> Chameleons are..."

Ada: Stop!

Kweenie: You'll make me forget.

Ada: You and Coleridge.

Kweenie: He was into opium.

Ada: He was also a poet. Let me squeeze this cotton over your nose. Someone interrupted his composition of a poem. Hold still. He never could finish it.

Kweenie: But I finished mine.

Ada: Like I said: he was a poet.
Kweenie: "Chameleons are adaptable."
Ada: Move aside.
Kweenie:

"Chameleons will be here long after
the rest of life,
extinct,
has died of a bleeding ulcer."

Ada: That's it?
Kweenie: Far out, isn't it?
Ada: Care for some tea?
Kweenie: I have some ginseng in my tote.
Ada: Thanks, dear, I'd as soon not swallow anything in your bag.
Kweenie: Don't act superior. Just because your toilet seat is down.
Ada: (Very angry) You were forbidden ever to go upstairs!
Kweenie: You've broken Johnny, paper-trained him like a little
    dog.
Ada: Ridiculous.
Kweenie: Signs and omens are everywhere.
Ada: When I was eleven, I connected a wire between two soup
    cans. I could barely hear my best girl friend.
Kweenie: In the universe. In the cosmos. It's all allegorical.... My
    horoscope says I should leave San Francisco.
Ada: Good-bye. Good luck.
Kweenie: Good riddance, you mean. You've never liked me.
Ada: I could cheerfully murder you. Hand me your cup.
Kweenie: I tried to leave once before.
Ada: Try again. Try moving tomorrow.
Kweenie: I tried to leave when I thought that Johnny had mar-
    ried you.
Ada: Hurry. I have a short attention span.
Kweenie: I called you from the bus station in L. A.
Ada: Collect.
Kweenie: You've never liked me.
Ada: I accepted the collect call John had refused....Why should I
    like you? John's old....

JOHN AND CURTIS ENTER TOGETHER

John: (Pushing CURTIS aside) May I cut in?

Ada: Kweenie-says-she's-leaving-San-Francisco-She-promises-
     never-to-call-again-Not-even-collect-and-she-said-she-is-a-
     chameleon.

Kweenie: Ada, you're a stitch.

Ada: In time, I'll save nine. What's wrong with Curtis?

Kweenie: Curtis wants me to marry him.

Ada: Wonderful. You can move out bride and baggage.

Kweenie: I won't marry him.

Ada: That's wonderful too. You can move out separately.

Kweenie: Never will I marry him.

Ada: You're nobody's fool.

Curtis: (To ADA) You married me.

Ada: Curtis, you and I weren't married long enough to fight for
     custody of the cake.

Curtis: Kick me when I'm down.

John: (To CURTIS) Were you beaten as a child?

Ada: For the extra point, I could dropkick you into the street.

Curtis: I'd feel right marrying Kweenasheba.

Ada: Sometimes "no" is a positive answer.

Curtis: (Pulls KWEENASHEBA into a clinch almost like tight
     dancing) Marry me, Kweenasheba.

Kweenie: Let go of me, you big ape.

Curtis: Marry me.

Kweenie: You're suffocating me.

Curtis: Marry me.

Kweenie: I'm getting claustrophobic.

Curtis: I can't let go of you.

Kweenie: Let go of me.

John: (To ADA) Let's go watch Channel 12's Big Time Wres-
     tling.

Curtis: I need you.

Kweenie: I don't need you. Let loose!

Curtis: You can change your mind.

Ada: Five'll get me ten, she won't.

Kweenie: Wicker bedpans in hell!
Curtis: We're never too far into anything that we can't turn back.
Kweenie: I got along without you before I met you.
Curtis: I can't get along without you now.
Kweenie: Let loose.
Curtis: I can't let go of you.
John: May I have this dance? (JOHN softly hums "Silent Night")

JOHN AND ADA DANCE SLOW, CLOSE

Kweenie: Can't you tell where you're not wanted?
Ada: Neither one of them can tell where they're not wanted.
Kweenie: You have to let go of me.
Curtis: No!
Kweenie: I'm leaving you.
Curtis: No!
Kweenie: I'm leaving San Francisco.
Curtis: I can't deal with this.
John: (Sings *sotto voce*) "Sleep in heavenly peace."
Kweenie: Let go of me.
Curtis: I'll go with you.
Ada: Go get their suitcases.
Kweenie: No.
Curtis: Why can't I go with you?
Kweenie: I won't let you. You *must* let go of me.
Curtis: I'll never let you go.

John and Ada, dancing, are just going into a dip. The next line freezes them at the bottom of the dip where they do a "take" until John's line.

Kweenie: Speaking of 'round yon Virgin and Child...I'm going to have a baby. (Curtis releases Kweenie)
John: That's good. We were about to go to sleep.
Curtis: I don't believe it.
John: Cute. A baby brother for Gladys Mae.

Ada: Look at her face, Curtis. You can tell a pregnancy in a
     woman's face.
Curtis: You have a ring through your nose.
Kweenie: I had it pierced this morning coming from the clinic.
Curtis: I don't believe it.
Kweenie: Curtis! The rabbit died!
Curtis: Honey-babe, we're never into anything so far we can't
     change our minds.
Kweenie: My mind's made up.
Ada: Like a hide-a-bed.
Curtis: Now you have to marry me.
Kweenie: No.
Curtis: Then you have to chuck the brat.
Kweenie: Says who?
Ada: That-a-girl.
Curtis: I say.
Ada: "The little Bummer Boy."
Kweenie: You constantly antagonize me.
Ada: Curtis calls it foreplay.
John: I think, Ada, we'll take a walk.
Ada: Says who?
Kweenie: You don't want to see a man nag a pregnant woman?
Curtis: I once let go of a balloon in St. Louis in 1957. Where did
     it go?
John: The same place electricity goes when the lights go out.
Kweenie: Don't try to worm out with your philosophy, Curtis.
Ada: We're all on to your rhetorical tricks, Curtis.
Curtis: I ought to belt you.
John: If you want to box....
Curtis: I mean her.
Ada: Curtis wants to hit Kweenie. That's one of the ways Curtis
     turns on. It makes a big man of him.
John: I don't want to hear this.
Ada: You wanted to know why I divorced Curtis.
John: Because of Gladys Mae's pantyhose.
Curtis: You have to repeat everything!
Kweenie: Shut up, Curtis.

Ada: Shut up, Curtis.
Curtis: What is this, the OK Corral?
John: Shut up, Curtis.
Ada: Do what you want, Kweenie.
Kweenie: I'm beginning to.
Ada: But don't listen to him.
Kweenie: I can't even hear him.
Ada: He beat me up and then he knocked me up.
John: You were pregnant?
Ada: Give me a cigarette. (JOHN starts to light it for her) For
    godsake, I can light it for myself.
John: You were pregnant?
Ada: Yes.
John: Curtis made you pregnant?
Ada: In a motel on Highway 1. Right after the Four-Bean Salad.
John: But I thought Curtis was...
Curtis: You are what you plug.
John: I ought to belt you.
Curtis: For making my own wife pregnant?
John: Really belt you.
Curtis: For making both these ladies pregnant?
John: Really hit you.
Curtis: I could punch you out with one hand.
John: Says you.
Kweenie: (Disgusted) Omigod!
Ada: You're worse than little BOYS!
John: So where's "Little Curtis"?
Ada: Curetted down some drain. God. I hate smoking. (ADA be-
    gins to cry) What do you mean "Little Curtis"? It might have
    been "Little Ada."
Kweenie: This night is going to run up a lot of karmic debts.
 Ada: You're the same as Curtis.
John: Don't get down on me.
Curtis: There isn't enough soap in this shop.
Ada: I'm not any man's incubator.
Kweenie: Who says I am?

Ada: I know, John, what you borrowed from Curtis. Those magazines of Asian women bound in tied-up situations.

Kweenie: Curtis keeps that disgusting junk under the bed.

Curtis: A man needs fantasies.

Ada: Signs and omens are everywhere.

Kweenie: For sure.

Ada: Move out! This is my house. You, Kweenie, out. You, Curtis, double out ...and now that I think about it, you, John, you...out too!

John: Why me?

Ada: Why not you?

John: I'm supposed to be your lover.

Ada: You're a tenant with a lease on a shop.

Curtis: Primitive people always eat the god they worship.

Ada: I'm going to my room.

John: It's *our* room.

Ada: Tonight it's my room again. I'm going up there and have a good cry for Little Ada.

John: This is all a guilt syndrome.

Ada: Out! All of you!

John: No woman should feel guilty about an abortion.

Ada: You utter idiot! I'm not whining for that little Ada. I'm letting it out tonight for *this* Little Ada. The one who counts. Me. The one who lives and breathes and teaches and tries to give up smoking while her lover wants to box, for godsake, with her ex-husband.

John: Don't dare go up those stairs alone.

Ada: Try and stop me. You or the Queen of Sheep Dip.

Curtis: I rather enjoy this.

John: We promised never to end an argument with separate beds.

Ada: This isn't an argument. This is a decision.

Curtis: Ada means not tonight, John. She has a headache.

Ada: Ada means sometimes people just need "alone-time."

ADA EXITS

Curtis: Good-night, Greta Garbo.

Kweenie: So here I stand with the two men in my life. One the soul of the middle class. The other, the heel.

Curtis: What's next?

John: (Pointing upstairs to ADA) First: getting out of Ada's life. (Pointing to Kweenie) Second: getting out of Flower Girl's life.

Kweenie: Not on my account, Johnny.

John: I'm taking my motorcycle out. I'm going across the Golden Gate. I want to feel fog in my face.

Kweenie: Why don't you just go upstairs to Ada.

Curtis: That wouldn't be fog in his face.

John: I'm not in the mood to rape.

Curtis: What about these wilting roses? What about this awful herbal soap?

John: (Tosses Kweenie some keys) Kweenie, open up tomorrow?

Kweenie: Sure, Johnny.

Curtis: I mean what about the shop?

John: My lease has three more months. Curtis, why don't you buy me out? Lock, stock, and barrel.

Kweenie: Maybe Ada will change her mind.

Curtis: Ada Vicary started life as a parson's daughter. Once she starts moralizing on that....

Kweenie: Ada is an Aries with Scorpio rising. She'll change.

John: Ada can sit upstairs in her restored Victorian rocker till she's 90...

Kweenie: Ada will always be full of surprises.

John: ...till she's 95 and drooling in her needlepoint.

Curtis: Remember when making love was fun?

Kweenie: Fun gets complicated.

Curtis: In every grade-B mummy movie, the diamond in the tomb always has curse on it.

John: ...or a Curtis.

Kweenie: Where will you go? It's late.

John: It's early. To the Russian River. A friend has a cabin. The key's under a rock by the porch.

Kweenie: You'll come back?

John: Probably. For awhile. Then I may cycle up the coast to
    Vancouver.
Curtis: Ada likes plays the way I live movies.
Kweenie: She thinks everything is *Romeo and Juliet*.
Curtis: A good thing those two kids aren't alive today.
John: You guys better pack up your bologna and move.
Curtis: "Years from now when you speak of this, and you will
    speak of this, be kind."
John: Curtis, if you couldn't quote movies, you'd be silent.
Curtis: What silent movie would I be?
John: Whatever, you wouldn't be original. (To Kweenie) So long,
    kid. Do it. (John pecks her on the cheek)
Kweenie: I can live on *that* for a month. (John smiles, shrugs)

JOHN EXITS

Curtis: (Musing) What silent movie would I be?
Kweenie: *Intolerance*.
Curtis: And you're beginning to look like *Birth of a Nation*.
Kweenie: Why have you always wanted to change me?
Curtis: To perfect you. Why, Eliza, don't you recognize Henry
    Higgins?
Kweenie: You're hateful.
Curtis: I'm Pygmalion.
Kweenie: You're a pig.
Curtis: You're never happy unless you're miserable.
Kweenie: You're never happy unless you make me miserable.
Curtis: Made for each other. What's the matter?
Kweenie: My film seems stuck in your camera.
Curtis: Have you rewound it?
Kweenie: Of course.
Curtis: You probably pulled the last picture too far and yanked it
    from the cannister.
Kweenie: I wound it right.
Curtis: Let me see. Was the little light on? Could you hear it
    click when you rewound it? I hope you didn't wreck the
    strobe. (The flash camera goes off.) You have to pay attention.
Kweenie: I'm blinded!

Curtis: You're also irreversibly deaf and dumb.

Kweenie: Everytime I get near something electronic, you conde-
scend.

Curtis: Dearly beloved, we are gathered here tonight because
Kweenasheba's film is caught in my camera.

Kweenie: I surrender, Curtis.

Curtis: Surrender?

Kweenie: I never thought I'd come to this.

Curtis: You can't surrender.

Kweenie: I can. I do. I'm beat.

Curtis: You're backing away.

Kweenie: I accept you, have accepted you...the way you are.

Curtis: Time with you is better than time without you.

Kweenie: I'm tired....

Curtis: ...You're chicken...

Kweenie: ...of trying to change you.

Curtis: SQUAWK!

Kweenie: You'll always be lower class.

Curtis: We have that in common.

Kweenie: The only thing we have in common is neither of us has
ever been married to Elizabeth Taylor.

Curtis: Touch your tummy and say that.

Kweenie: The little bugger's mine.

Curtis: How about marrying me?

Kweenie: I think I'll strangle you.

Curtis: I knew you couldn't surrender.

Kweenie: Go to bed.

Curtis: Tuck me in, mommy?

Kweenie: Go to bed.

Curtis: You used to say, "Come to bed." ...I love you, Kweenasheba.

Kweenie: You mean you want me to love you.

Curtis: I do no kidding love you.

Kweenie: Am I supposed to bat that ball back over the net for a
love, game, set?

Curtis: When a person says "I love you," it's civilized to say you
love that person back.

Kweenie: I don't.
Curtis: Kick me some more.
Kweenie: I won't.
Curtis: Kick me.
Kweenie: I can't.
Curtis: Why not?
Kweenie: I surrendered.
Curtis: Then for sure kick me.
Kweenie: Why should I?
Curtis: To the victor go the spoils.
Kweenie: I didn't win, Curtis. I surrendered.
Curtis: If you won't make love to me anymore, then you have to
    kick me.
Kweenie: No!
Curtis: Hit me!
Kweenie: I said no!
Curtis: For godsake, Kweenie, hurt me.
Kweenie: When something's over, whatever happened to shaking
    hands and saying good-bye?
Curtis: Please.
Kweenie: (Amazed) I'm finishing an affair with a punching bag!
Curtis: Time, space, flesh have passed between us.
Kweenie: What's that mean?
Curtis: I can't deal with you leaving San Francisco.
Kweenie: Well good-bye, dear, and amen.
Curtis: Come to bed.
Kweenie: I haven't given up my free-will.
Curtis: I'll be under the covers when you're ready.
Kweenie: You're not hard to get.
Curtis: (Exiting) It's dark back here.
Kweenie: Get a nightlight.
Curtis: Where will you sleep?
Kweenie: Here on the couch.
Curtis: *Voulez vous couchez....*
Kweenie: Pack your pickup truck tomorrow morning.
Curtis: Orders straight from Wonder Woman.
Kweenie: You heard Ada.

Curtis: I hear you, Kweenie.
Kweenie: Sleep tight.
Curtis: I'm glad we don't have to bother to get a divorce.

CURTIS EXITS

Kweenie: (Making up the couch, sings) "...God rest ye merry gentlemen. Let nothing you dismay..." Everyone has gone off to sleep. Alone. (She toys with the blankets, then stands stock still as the realization fills her. She folds her hands across her stomach) I will see...I promise I will see my invisible child....I love you...I love you...I love you, baby. I am. I am the one. I am the only. I am the original Queen of Sheba.

LIGHTS SLOW FADE

CURTAIN

**One San Francisco Play's Gender Journey
From the "Neli-Deli" Sandwich Shop
at Dave's Baths to the Queer Stage...**

Lost Photographs, Found Genders

Pioneering Gay Theater in San Francisco in the 1970s

Coming Attractions: Kweenasheba (1975)
**was adapted by the author from his story
"Sweet Embraceable You" (1972).**

The beloved San Francisco character actor Michael Lewis introduced me to producer and actor Joe Campanella of the all-male Yonkers Production Company that produced my play *Coming Attractions* (aka *Kweenasheba*) in 1976, the year after Campanella himself co-starred in *My Fair Laddie* with head-liner Empress-ario Jose Sarria at the Royal Palace, 335 Jones Street. That Tenderloin venue was not far from the South of Market "Society for Individual Rights' SIR Center Theater," 83 Sixth Street, known, because of its spill of derelict winos propping up the sidewalk, by its camp name, "Wine Country," because that block of Sixth was then a filthy Skid Row providing perfect sanctuary for gay theater coming out of the closet.

The SIR organization produced theatrical events from 1964-1976, and published *Vector* magazine from 1965-1977. In a line of theatrical descent, the year after the free-styling SIR organization closed camp with its double-bill of Lanford Wilson's *The Madness of Lady Bright* and my play, the newly founded Theater Rhinoceros opened its doors with its own remounting of Wilson's riff on Tennessee Williams' Blanche DuBois in *Lady Bright*.

The five-foot-six elfin Michael Lewis was a great performer of any gender. He was legendary as the Lion in the San Francisco camp staging of *The Wizard of Oz*. We met one rainy December afternoon in 1975 at Dave's Baths across from the foot of the new TransAmerica Pyramid in the 500 block of Washington Street, a couple doors west of Sansome Street. Michael ran a little shop inside Dave's Baths where he whipped up desserts and coffee. He called it with a wink: the Neli-Deli. I ordered a sandwich, soup, and decaf. It was a slow day at the tubs, and, between gentlemen callers, I had been editing my script in my tiny dark cubicle which was no beach *cabine*, and brought it with me to sit on a well-lighted barstool at the deli service-counter window. I was barefoot with a white towel wrapped round my waist. We struck up a conversation.

As in all good show business stories, within an hour, we had met cute and were bonded and discussing pairing my one-act with a second one-act, *Lady Bright*, in which Michael was already cast to play the title role.

Pirandello would have approved: Michael was one character in search of an author.

He needed a companion play that would not charge royalties. Seeing that he was the force rather much in charge of creating a double bill for a proper evening's entertainment for Yonkers, I suggested he do a kind of dual-role double feature, and play the lead part of the flamboyant Curtis in my play because he was perfect, to the point of type-casting, for the part.

He and Campanella and I discussed, with Jose Sarria (SIR founder, 1963), the fact that my play featured two evolving men, and two straight women, living together behind a flower shop on Castro Street in 1972. I based that shop on my pal Tommy Zalewski's pioneering urban nursery and gardening shop "Tommy's

Plants" at 566 Castro Street where the hale, hearty, and handsome big blond Tommy—come to Castro from Wisconsin—entertained hot locals and tourist tricks with fat joints and quickie fun in his upstairs office.

Yonkers wanted to cast four men from their talent pool which would have essentially changed the psycho-sexual narrative of my play while adding little but camp to it—which all these diverse years later might be great fun to try. In those olden days, I had been warned against such stunt casting by the example of Edward Albee who, while he approved interracial casting, insisted on cisgender casting for *Who's Afraid of Virginia Woolf.* I had composed for two male actors, and two female actors, because I envisioned a "coming out" comedy whose crusading political point was to *include* and *dramatize* the women—Ada, straight middle-class, and Kweenie, fluid counter-cultural—who in the emerging antics of gay culture in the 1970s were too often forgotten as collateral damage when men, like Robert Mapplethorpe, went gay leaving them, like Patti Smith, all too often behind. Hence, the cautionary title: *Coming Attractions.*

I wanted to examine that particular situation comedy of errors. So when Yonkers understood why I requested gender similitude dramatically and politically, these liberationist theater folk who were anxious to evolve on the subject of gender, made note that although they identified as an all-male company, they were happy to assist such diversified casting. Producer Joe Campanella wrote in the program: "You may ask why Yonkers is involved in serious theatre at this time. The answer is that we, as a production company, feel it is time to express ourselves in a different light. Why should we limit our goals to all-male drag and camp when there are other areas of entertainment to explore. We have a responsibility and commitment to the audience to provide worthwhile theatre, and we feel that tonight's presentation is worthy of your time. As Chairman of Yonkers, one of my first accomplishments was to revise our by-laws so that any person, male or female, would be able to audition and take part in any future production. My basic theory is that the best person for the role—male or female, if that person is the best, then he or she deserves the part. We need to branch out in our casting."

Even so, I was pretty much on my own to find such women.

I had to get creative. I asked my hip and hippie sister and house mate, Mary Claire Fritscher, who at age eighteen was eighteen years younger than I, and a star newly graduated from her high-school and community theater experience of performing the femme fatale "Appassionata von Climax" in *Li'l Abner* and choreographing *Oklahoma!* to stop by the open casting call, and walk right in and audition anonymously on her own merit, identifying herself simply as "Mary Claire," for the role of Kweenie, which was rather much based on her alternative feminist personality in the first place. Her example helped me create two strong roles for women. Without any input from me, Michael Lewis, Joe Campanella, and director Jack Green made all casting decisions. Two weeks into rehearsals after Mary Claire had proven her acting chops and her geniality to all concerned, we siblings announced our backstage ploy to much approving laughter and applause.

Secondly, when Jack Green's choice for Ada, Jeanne Nathans, suddenly got a part in a film, I asked my pal, the elegant Catherine White, to audition for Ada because of her own personal sophistication and because we had the time of our young lives playing the pregnant hippie bride and beaded hippie husband leads in Broadway playwright and screenwriter William Goodhart's 1965 "Generation Gap" comedy, *Generation*, at the Kalamazoo Civic Theater in May 1968. The production, directed by the British theatrical legend Bertram Tanswell, was well received and its run was extended. Catherine was also a dancer who had choreographed *A Funny Thing Happened on the Way to the Forum* for the Civic Theater. She and her husband, with their new baby, had just moved to San Francisco, and she agreed to "come out of retirement" as a favor since we had gotten along so well on and off stage during *Generation*.

Then there was the role of the straight John Vicary. For a year,

I had been friends with the actor Bob Paulson who leased an old-fashioned open-air sidewalk florist kiosk across the street from the Castro Theater. We first met, also cute, standing under his colorful canvas awning in a soft winter rain while I bought one of his delicate rose bouquets. He and I also bonded taking an exam together when the San Francisco Sheriff was recruiting gay men. We both scored. I came in as Deputy Candidate number eleven, but I turned down the job which he took. So he was an authentic new deputy sheriff who was a veteran actor in dozens of San Francisco plays including *Fiddler on the Roof, Pal Joey,* and *Little Mary Sunshine.* (His co-star Mary Claire had also starred the year before in another production of *Little Mary Sunshine.*) His manly presence, brooding matinee-idol looks, and gregarious personality were ideal for the role of John Vicary who also owned a flower shop.

When my longtime sporting buddy, Jack Green, a credentialed and experienced theater director, agreed to direct *Coming Attractions,* I was delighted because in our group of new immigrants reconstituting ourselves *en masse* in San Francisco, we were all inventing new lives, new roles, and new ways of befriending each other while transferring our talent, hearts, and humanity from homophobic towns and cities from which we had fled as sex refugees trying to carry on the natural narratives of our lives.

Late nights, after rehearsals and after performances, our cast and crew retired for food and drink at Pam Pam's coffee shop, open 24/7, one block west of Union Square, 398 Geary Street at Mason, mixing sometimes with professional actors from proper playhouses just across the street, like the American Conservatory Theater's Geary Theater, and the Curran Theater where film director Joseph Mankiewicz shot the "Broadway theater" exteriors and interiors for *All About Eve.*

Lucky for us happy friends rehearsing at SIR, Eve never showed.

In 2017, my dear friend, the photographer and author Jim Stewart was searching his files of negatives and found rehearsal photographs both of us had forgotten existed. We had met in 1973, and when he moved to San Francisco in 1975, he lived with me and my sister at our home for six months before moving to the artsy bohemian Clementina Street where he began shooting for *Drummer* magazine, which I had the good fortune of editing for three years (1977-1980).

Drummer often published plays like *Pogey Bait* and *Isomer* and *Corporal in Charge of Taking Care of Captain O'Malley. Pogey Bait* was written by 1960s Off-Off-Broadway playwright and Gay Games bodybuilder George Birimisa of Caffe Cino and Theater Rhinoceros who produced *Pogey Bait. Isomer* was by Richard A. Steel, a pioneer of New York's Circle Repertory Company, who was also an associate of Sam Shepard and a good friend of Lanford Wilson. My closet drama *Corporal in Charge* was the only play the revered publisher Winston Leyland included in his canonical anthology and Lammy Award Winner, *Gay Roots: Twenty Years of Gay Sunshine - An Anthology of Gay History, Sex, Politics, and Culture* (1991).

Stewart's lost negatives of *Coming Attractions*, shot on the SIR Center's stage, with available light, were dusty and damaged, and have been restored as much as possible for archival purposes by Mark Hemry. The perversatile Stewart, to whom I am so grateful, soon after, only a few blocks from the SIR Center, was the designer and carpenter who built the interior of Oscar Streaker Robert Opel's Fey-Way Studio, 1287 Howard Street, the first gay art gallery in San Francisco, where Opel was murdered in 1979. Author Stewart's 2011 hello-and-goodbye to all that was his best-selling memoir, *Folsom Street Blues.*

Back in that primitive first decade after Stonewall, *Coming Attractions* may have been the first play written on Castro Street (1975) about life on Castro Street. It played weekends to full houses for a month and was noticed on the cover of *The Bay Area Reporter* and in the arts "Pink Section" of the *San Francisco Chronicle.**

**The Bay Area Reporter*, Volume 6 #5, March 4, 1976, and "Date Book Arts and Entertainment" Pink Section of the *San Francisco Chronicle*, Sunday, March 21, 1976

Notes for *Coming Attractions* from the
Yonkers Production Company Program
by Perry George

Coming Attractions [aka *Kweenasheba*] was first produced by the Yonkers Production Company, San Francisco, premiering March 13, 1976, at the Society for Individual Rights SIR Center Theatre, 83 Sixth Street, San Francisco. Joe Campanella, Producer. Directed by Jack Green. Photography by Eye-Onic. *Coming Attractions* was double-billed in a program of two one-act plays with *The Madness of Lady Bright* by Lanford Wilson, and was noticed as the cover of the weekly newspaper, the *B.A.R., The Bay Area Reporter*, Volume 6 #5, March 4, 1976, and in the "Date Book—Arts and Entertainment" Pink Section of the *San Francisco Chronicle*, Sunday, March 21, 1976. [*Coming Attractions* may be the first gay play written and produced in San Francisco reflecting the actuality of the gender mix in early 1970s emerging gay culture on Castro Street.

CAST
In order of appearance:
John Stack: Bob Paulson
Ada: Catherine White
Curtis: Mike Lewis
Kweenasheba: Mary Claire Fritscher

JACK FRITSCHER
Playwright

Jack is an Illinois Gemini who played in Peoria (and Chicago and New York) before arriving, five years ago, in the Gemini City of Oz. His first produced play, for which he wrote the book and lyrics with Lawrence Brandt, was the musical-comedy, *Continental Caper* (1959). He has acted in *Oliver!* and T. S. Eliot's *Murder in the Cathedral*. He played the lead in the hippie comedy, *Generation*, and the five male leads in the musical-comedy, *Canterbury Tales*, also appearing fleetingly in *The Streets of San Francisco*. He has published two books, *Television Today* and *Popular Witchcraft: Straight from the Witch's Mouth* (Citadel Press). Currently he is working on a collection of San Francisco short stories while writing a TV movie, *Duchess: Berlin 1928*. He lives it up to write it down. *Kweenasheba* is dedicated to his lover of seven years, the photographer, David Sparrow.

JACK GREEN
Director

Born the day before Thanksgiving to a theatrical family in Duluth—that's right, a theatrical family in Duluth, Minnesota, Jack fled from the frozen northland at an early age. At a more mature age, he received a B.A. in Theatre Arts at UCLA, after which he became Founder/Director of the "Fifth Corner" company in Los Angeles, an ensemble presenting Off-Off-Broadway plays. *Coming Attractions* makes both his Yonkers and San Francisco theatrical debut.

JOE CAMPANELLA
Producer and Chairman
Yonkers Production Co., Inc.

Yonkers is fortunate to have as its producer, the capable and talented, Joe Campanella, who has been active in all-male theatre in San Francisco for over ten years. Most recently, he played the male lead in *Blithe Spirit* for which he received a Cable Car Award nomination. His background in Gay Theatre includes two Yonkers productions, *That's Show Biz*, and *Michelle Plays the Palace*. Professionally, Joe works as a radio announcer at KEST Radio in San Francisco, and teaches a course in Radio and TV broadcasting. Since coming to San Francisco eleven years ago, Joe has appeared in productions with the Opera Ring, Interplayers, Playhouse, and at the Village in *Ready or Not It's Me* and *It's Me Again*. He also played opposite the famous Jose Sarria in many spoof operas.

Joe is current chairman of Yonkers, a titled member of the Royal Household of Grand Duchess Charlie, and the newly appointed Production Chairman of SIR Center. Joe writes: "You may ask why

Yonkers is involved in serious theatre at this time. The answer is that we, as a production company, feel it is time to express ourselves in a different light. Why should we limit our goals to all-male drag and camp when there are other areas of entertainment to explore. We have a responsibility and commitment to the audience to provide worthwhile theatre, and we feel that tonight's presentation is worthy of your time. As Chairman of Yonkers, one of my first accomplishments was to revise our by-laws so that any person, male or female, would be able to audition and take part in any future production. My basic theory is 'the best person for the role—male or female'; if that person is the best, then he or she deserves the part. My hope with *The Madness of Lady Bright* by Lanford Wilson, and *Coming Attractions* by Jack Fritscher is to establish Yonkers as an open-minded theatrical company."

MICHAEL LEWIS
Curtis, *Coming Attractions*, and Leslie, *Lady Bright*
Producer, *Coming Attractions*

Mike has been a familiar face to San Francisco audiences since 1970, making his "Golden Award" winning performance in the Yonkers Production of *Hello Dolly*, only to be followed by a long line of memorable roles in *The Boyfriend, Dames at Sea, Feather and Leather Follies, CMC Carnival*, and *Little Me*. More recently, Mike claims a Cable Car Award for his unforgettable role of the Lion in *Wizard of Oz*. Active in charities, his characterization as the Lion has been delighting audiences from the Shriners' Hospital to the *Jerry Lewis Telethon*. Mike is re-creating the role of Leslie in *The Madness of Lady Bright* from a previous production staged last year at San Francisco State University. You can find him performing to SRO crowds at his own business, the Neli-Deli, at Dave's Baths.

MARY CLAIRE FRITSCHER
Kweenasheba

From Appassionata Von Climax in the Peoria (Illinois) High School production of *Li'l Abner* to the focal leading lady (and

Yonker's first actual female leading lady) in Yonker's San Francisco production of *Coming Attractions*—that's how far the eighteen-year-old ingenue, Mary Claire has come. Her varied experience has touched on every aspect of theatre: dancing, singing, acting, even set construction and decoration, make-up, children's theatre, and directing. Now she adds gay theatre to her credits. Her credits specifically include the lead in *Little Mary Sunshine, Archie and Mehitabel,* as well as dance director for the choreography for a community production of *Oklahoma!* As a "backstage musical" note, for Yonkers, she auditioned anonymously, as "Mary Claire," winning the role of Kweenasheba, written specifically for her by the author, her brother. They revealed their relationship at a party during the third week of rehearsal. She is a psychology major at City College of San Francisco, studying advanced acting, directing, and philosophy.

CATHERINE WHITE
Ada Vicary

Catherine moved to San Francisco with her husband three months ago from Michigan where she was active in the Kalamazoo Community Theatre. Her credits there include an extended run in the hippie comedy, *Generation,* playing the female lead opposite Jack Fritscher who invited her to step into the role of Ada when actress Jeanne Nathans landed a part in an upcoming film. Six months ago, Catherine gave birth to her newest production, a son, who can sometimes be heard backstage, rehearsing.

BOB PAULSON
John Stack

Handsome Bob Paulson, is a newly sworn and openly gay San Francisco deputy sheriff, whose acting credits include fifteen musicals for Woodminster Summer Musicals in Oakland, notably, George Musgrove in *Little Me,* Hysterium in *A Funny Thing Happened on the Way to the Forum,* Mottel the Tailor in *Fiddler on the Roof,* and James Wilson in *1776.* He also appeared as Arthur Swan in *No Man's Land* and the Gardner in *The Vigil* for Producers

Associates in Oakland. For SIR he has appeared as Ludlow Lowell in *Pal Joey*, Capt. Jim in *Little Mary Sunshine*, and Marcus Lycus in *Forum*. He also directed *Anything Goes* with Michelle, and has appeared in numerous SIR-lebri-te Capades and Revues for SIR. His set design credits include, for SIR, *Anything Goes, Madness '71*, and *Hello Dolly* for SIR and Yonkers. He also designed *Dames at Sea* for Kimo Productions. Coincidentally "type-cast" as John, the owner of a flower shop, Bob, until he was recently picked for the first group of openly gay deputy sheriffs, was the manager of a flower shop on Castro Street.

"YONKERS DOES GAY THEATRE
WITH TWO DRAMATIC ONE-ACT PLAYS"
by Perry George
Reprinted from *Yonkers Free Press*

Yonkers is proud and happy to offer to our theatre-going public a whole new facet, for us, of theatrical endeavor in two one-act plays, *The Madness of Lady Bright* by Lanford Wilson, and *Coming Attractions* by Jack Fritscher. The pairing of these two plays, Yonkers Productions Company's Sixth major endeavor, is not an all-male musical comedy or revue. There is no expensive union orchestra, lavish sequined and feathered costumes, stunningly choreographed production numbers or singing, that have given us the spectacular reputation we have.

It is not Yonkers' intention to abandon this type of theatre, which we have pleased audiences with again and again from *Hello Dolly, The Boy Friend, Little Me, Michelle Plays the Palace*, to *That's Show Biz*, but to enhance this achievement with a branching out, a theatrical coming-of-age and an emergence to the dynamic times this theatre group, our City, state, and nation are arriving at in encouraging and recognizing the blossoming of relevant Gay Theatre where a positive and honest mirror image of ourselves and our friends, as members of the gay and general community, can have both entertainment and insight.

The first play, *Coming Attractions*, an original play by the local playwright, Jack Fritscher, will receive its world premiere and is a vignette of a life-style very likely to be familiar from the neighborhoods of San Francisco to anyone who sees this play. *Coming Attractions* deals with homosexuality in a matter-of-fact positive way, with the homosexual living "happily-ever-after"—no suicides, no murders, none of all the strangely unnecessary retribution that seems inevitable in most gay-themed drama we are exposed to in the "straight world" theatrical productions. It is our belief that the turn of this tide of negativity must start from the Gay Community as it does not seem likely it will from the Straight Community.

Also aware of the fact that all within gay life and the Gay Community is not like a "Gidget Goes Gay" kind of movie, and remembering our often traumatic and painful past, we offer Lanford Wilson's compelling drama, *The Madness of Lady Bright*, a study in the complete schizophrenic breakdown of an ageing fading failure of an effeminate homosexual on a very hot, hot night in New York City. Everyone in the audience cannot avoid seeing a little, a lot, and perhaps too much of Leslie Bright in themselves or someone dear to them.

It is unwise to single out one performer from the many who work so hard to entertain the audiences who see our shows, but I cannot conclude without saying the compelling, powerful, and sensitive performances I have seen blossoming in Mike Lewis as Leslie (Lady) Bright, and as Curtis, "the real Kweeasheba," throughout rehearsals of these two shows will be worth the price of admission for all who see his double tour-de-force. *Lady Bright,* which also stars Shel Kovalski, is directed by Andrew Barron; assistant director, William Howard.

Tickets for this double-bill of one-act shows are available at Macy's Box Office, The Record House, and the Kokpit Bar. They are for unreserved seating and are $4 each, March 13, 14, 20, 21, 27, and 28. After the closing night performance, there will be a cast and audience party at the Kokpit Bar, 301 Turk Street.

CREDITS: *The Madness of Lady Bright*, written by Lanford Wilson, courtesy of Dramatists Play Service; directed by Andrew Barron. *Coming Attractions*, written by Jack Fritscher, courtesy of Spitting Image/Palm Drive; directed by Jack Green. Both plays produced for Yonkers Production Company by Joe Campanella; sets by Bob Paulsen; lighting and sound, Bill Hirsing; program notes and design, Perry George and Bob Cramer; stage manager, Rod Schaefer; crew, Randy Totten; photography, EYE-ONIC; special thanks to Jim Briggs, Mark Barrett, Record House, Kokpit, Dennis Coonan, Bert Arthur, Tadd Waggoner, SIR Board of Directors, and Exactly That Productions.

Top: (L) A pensive Bob Paulson (R) Michael Lewis and Bob Paulson
Bottom: Mary Claire Fritscher and Catherine White. Photos: Jim Stewart

Top: Catherine White and Mary Claire Fritscher rehearse on set
Bottom: Ada (Catherine White) challenges the ironic hipster Kweenasheba
(Mary Claire Fritscher). Photos: Jim Stewart

Top: (L) Mary Claire Fritscher and Catherine White (R) Catherine White
Bottom: Director Jack Green and Mary Claire Fritscher. Photos: Jim Stewart

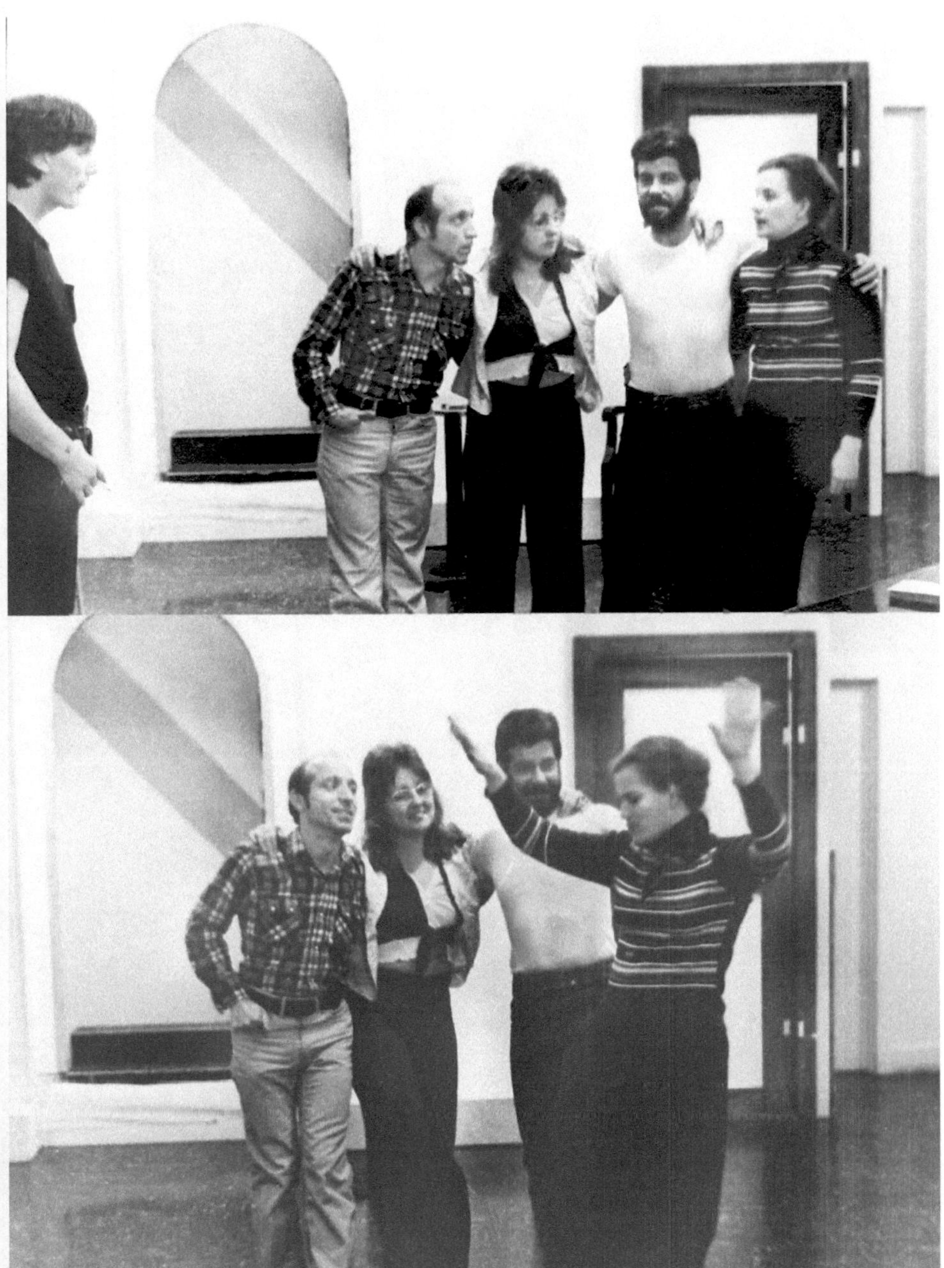

Top: Michael Lewis (Curtis), Mary Claire Fritscher (Kweenasheba), Bob Paulson (John Vicary), and Catherine White (Ada Vicary)
Bottom: Michael Lewis, Mary Claire Fritscher, Bob Paulson, listen attentively to Catherine White. Photos: Jim Stewart

Top: The always buoyant Michael Lewis with Mary Claire Fritscher, Bob Paulson, and Catherine White
Bottom: Rob Schaefer, Stage Manager; Bill Hirsing, Lighting and Sound; Randy Totten, Crew. Photos: Jim Stewart

With director Jack Green, tall and center, Michael Lewis, Mary Claire
Fritscher, Bob Paulson, and Catherine White. Photo: Jim Stewart

Jack Fritscher, Catherine White, and Franklin Smith, *Generation*, May 1968, Kalamazoo Civic Theater

Franklin Smith, Jack Fritscher, and Catherine White, *Generation*, May 1968, Kalamazoo Civic Theater

Top: Michael Lewis and Jack Fritscher, West Hollywood, 1989. Photo: Mark Hemry
Bottom: Jack Green, 1977. Photo: Jack Fritscher

YONKERS PRODUCTIONS
presents
an evening of one acts

Tickets Available at the Record House-Polk & Post, MACY'S Tickets or
FOR MAIL ORDER, ENCLOSE CHECK & SEND TO YONKERS PRODUCTION CO.,
c/o 785 McAllister St. "I", S.F. 94102.

Enclosed please find $__________ for_____ ($4 each) for the
evening/s of MARCH 13 14 20 21 27 28 (circle)

PLEASE MAIL TICKETS TO:

NAME____

ADDRESS_______________________________   TELEPHONE___________

Phone reservations, please call 673-4258 or 474-6919

B.A.R.
free
IN THE BAY AREA
.25 ELSEWHERE
VOLUME 6   NUMBER 5   March 4th   NEXT ISSUE OUT MARCH 18   NEXT DEADLINE: MARCH 12
THE LARGEST CIRCULATION AND READERSHIP IN THE BAY AREA
GAY HATE CAMPAIGN GROWS
... SEE PAGE 4

"Lanford Wilson
writes with
understanding
and
sensitivity"
THE NEW YORK TIMES
Yonkers Presents
"COMING ATTRACTIONS"
by Jack Fritscher
"THE MADNESS
        OF LADY BRIGHT"
by Lanford Wilson
March 13, 14 - 20, 21 - 27, 28   8:30pm   SIR Theatre
TICKETS: 673-4258

The Barber of 18th and Castro

On the last day of spring, June 20, 1973, at high noon, at the corner of 18th and Castro in San Francisco, Robert Place found the Face of God in a pornographic photograph. Not that he was given to dirty pictures. Rather, he had been drawn, by some—what?—thing to this neighborhood, by some thing he had vaguely heard or read or sensed, that had nothing to do with the corner barber shop where he had sought refuge, but had everything to do with whatever was intersecting the intersection which was inventing its flamboyant self even as he watched.

He had parked his 1957 Chevy BelAire with the candy-apple red body, tuck-and-roll upholstery, and the white "Says-who? Says-me!" top, and then he had walked all four of the single-block arms reaching out like a cross from the main intersection which was more like ground zero than anything he'd expected even in California. Everything rushed oingo-boingo right up at him: the omelet-brunch cafes with cake made out of, go figure, carrots; the dandy little flower shop near the corner kiosk where a one-legged ancient eye, maybe the world's oldest newsboy, hawked the call, "*Chronicle!*" like the last screech of a dying species, selling headlines, "Nixon bombs Saigon"; the loud beer bars with slender young men in white tanktops and baseball caps posing and partying in windows open to the street; the chic boutiques selling nothing anybody would ever need after a nuclear attack.

All of it was alien to him. Or he was alien to it. He had entered foreign territory. Fear—not so much the fear of the unknown, but more like the human animal's fear of his own kind—bristled the shorthairs on the nape of his neck. The unexpected thrill of temptation put him on edge. Seeking sanctuary, he spied a revolving red-and-white barber pole. He bolted past the blue arrow pointing up the stairs. On the landing outside the barber's door, he stopped, catching his breath. He was a young man in need of something familiar, and what was more solid than a good old-fashioned barber shop?

Until that bone-bright noon hour when Robert Place actually witnessed what looked like the campus of the world's most flamboyant boys' college, he had little more than a tourist's curious Kodak hope that there, at that world-famous intersection, he'd see people unlike any of the people back home in southern Illinois, people stranger and more festive even than the hippies he'd seen on TV in the Haight, people, who, rumors persisted, had always existed, the way bohemians and gypsies and magicians, all of them outlaws, had always existed, even before the Druids, but had never been seen before, at least not in broad daylight, in such visible numbers. So he had come to see for himself.

Because of his uneasy feeling that he already recognized these new people even if he did not know them, Robert Place immediately affected toward them a distanced attitude which he knew camouflaged his ground-glass fear he might, in fact, be one of them, whatever they really were. After a grueling four-day cross-country marathon in his car, he had come to California for what? A trim? Yeah. Sure. That was it. A little trim and some talk. A simple visit to a quiet barbershop. The best place for some local gossip. Some shaving cream hot around his ears. The scrape of the straight-edge razor across the thin skin over the hard bone of his skull. That was all.

Only a few days and many miles before, he had been driving aimlessly through his small town where he knew every street and every house and everyone who lived, or who had ever lived, in those houses, when one of those almost religious, certainly reckless, transfiguring impulses no one can ever deny had possessed him. He had thrown one suitcase into his Chevy, left a rose on his mother's fresh grave, and headed west. He had driven from Canterberry, in Green County, in southern Illinois to the San Francisco crosshairs of 18th and Castro where, in the heart of lightness, of the California sun at high noon in June, almost the solstice, the day of the year's longest light, the most familiar thing to him, the only thing he understood, man-to-man, as his father always said, was the gold leaf spelling out FLOYD'S BARBER SHOP. His hair was not long and he had not even felt in need of a haircut; yet why else had he pulled his Chevy to the curb in front of the shop, traipsed back and forth three or four dizzying blocks, and then run from his car up the flight of stairs leading to the door of Floyd's Barber Shop that looked down directly on the corner of 18th and Castro?

Floyd sat customerless in his single green barber chair. He wore a white puckered nylon barber's smock. Across his lap were spread the guts of a player piano he was working over with a screwdriver. He looked up at Robert Place. "Come on in," he said. "I have to do it, otherwise I spend all day looking out the window. Take a look. You'll see. What a parade. It looks like half of Noah's ark. The stag half if you catch my drift. The neighborhood's changed."

Robert wanted to ask, from exactly what to exactly what, and was it good, or bad, or neither; but he kept silent, not wanting to tip his hand, because he figured it didn't matter where he'd played before: California was a brand new game.

"I'll be with you in a minute," Floyd said. "Hope you're in no hurry."

Robert checked his watch against the clock on the wall. One of them was ten minutes fast. Inside himself, the clock of his body, the only clock that really mattered, began to slow. He felt the speed built up on the I-80 freeway descent from Reno and Truckee down to San Francisco slowly recede from himself. Time zones like tide in the Bay ebbed from him. He jingled loose change in his pocket. Nickels and dimes from back home mixed through his nervous fingers with quarters and Kennedy half-dollars he won in less than an hour playing the slots at a filling station somewhere in Nevada.

"I hope you're not in a hurry," Floyd repeated.

Robert remembered his appointment book on the front seat of his unlocked car. Never had he ever left his car unlocked. He peered through Floyd's gilt-lettered window. At the parking meter he had forgotten to feed, a white-helmeted metermaid ticketed his windshield. She turned slowly from the Chevy toward Robert as if she could feel him watching her every move. The noon sun glinted from her helmet. Robert could not see her face. He did not want to. He did not need to. Back home he could drop a deer at a hundred yards. She was a dead bitch in his book.

"No," he said, "I'm in no hurry. I was late for the last appointments I made four days ago. I sell, I mean, I used to sell Fuller Brushes door to door." He was warming up, trying to feel like himself again. "I can tell you more than you'd ever want to know about natural bristle brushes for your hair and your bottles and your carpets and your drapes and your dog and your cat."

"That a fact?" Floyd said. More than once he'd been told his droll roll of a phrase reminded the teller of W. C. Fields, which only encouraged him, despite his efforts to speak naturally.

"And the women!" Robert presumed that Floyd, same as all barbers, liked to talk about women, when he should have known only most of them like to talk about women, but they all love to talk about sex, except the Seventh Day Adventist ones who were always closed on a Saturday when a man was most likely to get his hair barbered. "Let me tell you," Robert said, "about those little housewives. Those lonely ladies sure do want to talk, talk, talk. Always saying, 'Well, Robert, enough me talking about me. What do you think about me?' Do you believe the utter conceit of women?"

"Much, much less than I believe," Floyd said, "in the unutterable conceits of men."

"Those girls were always giving me coffee till I thought I was going to drown. Always asking me if the coffee was sweet enough and how they could make it sweeter, shaking their hair down, trying out the sample brushes, teasing me, asking me how I thought they looked. I tell you. More than once before I left, I had to comb my teeth. It was murder. Door-to-door can kill you."

"That so?" Floyd fielded like W. C. "I'm what you might say interested in hair brushes too. Being a barber and all, it's natural."

"I bet you've heard everything too," Robert, doing his best Holden Caulfield, said. "At least twice."

"Frankly, I never hear the half of it. In one ear. Out the other. I'd go crazy if I really listened. We're all maniacs except when we're not. I must confess music's my mania."

"Is that right?"

"Right as rain."

"What kind of music? Grateful Dead? Judy Collins? Lawrence Welk? What?"

"Piano. I play the piano. But not with these hands. These are the hands of a barber. I always play piano with my feet." He surveyed Robert's puzzled face and grinned. "I catch me a rube everytime with that," he said. "Player piano, of course."

"I knew that," Robert said.

Floyd gestured to the plaster-of-paris busts sitting awry on a shelf over Robert's head. He had saved and bought each one of them from Silvestri's statuary company in South San Francisco. "There you see them." He pointed with his screwdriver. "Bach. Mozart. Schubert. Beethoven. Liszt."

"A whole shooting gallery." Robert stared straight at the barber. Floyd was a man dragging age forty-five like it was sixty. He combed his graying hair into the stiff part and pomp he had learned as a boy thirty years before. His glasses were as thick as binoculars. Robert liked that. He liked the way some older men and older women kept on with the styles they got locked into when they were young, like they were fixed in some time warp, instead of changing with the fashions and looking ridiculous in clothes that were too young for them, or too modern, or too ugly, like the new uniform for the old, polyester leisure suits for the men and polyester pant suits for the ladies, topped off with a frizzy reddish short perm, or worse, one of those Dynel wigs that catch the sun like orange copper wire. If he got old, which he doubted, that's what he planned to do. Sort of stay just like he was. Not change a thing.

"Turn around and look," Floyd said. "Bach and Liszt. I like them best."

Robert panned his head to the figurines. They were each ten inches of white plaster with the names chiseled into the bases. "Nice," he said. "Really nice." He surveyed the rest of the room.

This was not the first barber shop, waiting room, or bookstore that Robert Place had cased. In fact, it was a matter of police record that Robert Steven Vincent Place had been found guilty of at least one misdemeanor: slicing articles and smuggling magazines from the Green County Public Library. His mother had paid his hundred-dollar fine, but his year's probation was not half up, and he was on the run.

He had confessed to the judge that he had started with laundromats, that one day he had ripped one article from one magazine in one laundromat. The judge didn't bother to ask his motive, and Robert could hardly have volunteered one. He didn't know exactly why he coveted certain pictures like the first ones he had ever stolen, photographs of blond bodybuilders on Venice Beach hoisting even blonder starlets high as the American Dream onto their broad shoulders in the brilliant California sunshine.

From stray magazines in laundromats and doctors' offices, he had moved on to stealing the neighbors' mailed magazine subscriptions, and from there on to harder stuff, to the *pieces de resistance*, the photo-books on reserve at the public library. He had moved from a noisy tearing the pages to a quieter slicing them with a single-edge razor blade, and he had cut out for himself quite a collection of classical Greek athletes. His most prized theft was from a portfolio of reproductions of Lumiere's 1903 photos of the legendary strongman Eugene Sandow in an appealing variety of masculine, but modest, figleaf poses.

His satisfaction with his secret addiction had given him a false confidence that he figured out later had made him greedy and all too careless. He constantly needed more pictures to satisfy himself. Sometimes the actual tearing felt better, bolder than slicing.

Pleasant little dangers thrilled him.

It was his own fault when Miss Ollie Thomas, the head librarian, and his mother's cousin, had herself pinched him red-handed and called the sheriff. She had caught on to him, because he never coughed except when he was in the library, which, as his second cousin once-removed in a family inclined to TB, she thought was worrisome, but then she divined that he only coughed when he was, of all things, tearing out pages, and the louder he coughed the more pages he was tearing out at a pull. She was, of course, incensed, even when she apologized to his mother for calling the law.

The week after his sentencing Robert had returned to one of the two laundromats he frequented with a half-filled basket of clothes. He disliked washing his laundry in machines which he suspected harbored the curlicue hairs of strangers. He added his soap and extra bleach, dropped in his quarter, and settled back to pass the time reading.

Unexpectedly, as he leafed through an old 1964 issue of *Life* magazine, he came across the ragged seams of the pages he had ripped out the week before. The photospread had featured what they termed a man's-man kind of motorcycle bar called The Tool Box in San Francisco. Oh, he'd ripped that one out right away! Yessir! He liked cars and motorcycles both! And now he had the same gutted issue in his hands again. He looked neither to the right or left in the laundromat. He grinned at touching the ragged tear, the evidence that he had once before been in this place. Getting caught once was thrill enough, but better was the thrill of returning to the scene of an undetected crime.

In his switch of his clothes from washer to dryer, he stuffed the evidence, the rest of *Life*, unnoticed by the hawk-eyed manager, into the bottom of the basket on whose canvas he had carefully marked with a red felt-tip pen: "If found, return to R. S. V. Place." He didn't need to put his street address, not in Canterberry where everybody knew him.

"I don't really play piano," Floyd said. "I'm not a pianist. I'm a mechanic of the piano."

"I don't really sell Fuller Brushes," Robert said. "But I did. People like to meet me. I like to meet people." He reached for a small stack of magazines that lay next to him on the burgundy leatherette seat.

"Why don't you flip through a few of those," Floyd said. "Being from back East, you might never have seen those kind of pictures."

"I'm not from back East. I'm from the Midwest. The southern part of the Midwest. New York and New England's back East."

"It's all back East here in San Francisco which has nothing to do with California which has nothing to do with the rest of the country, if you catch my drift." Floyd adjusted a wire and a screw in the board across his lap. "Nossir," Floyd added, as if he were changing the subject to answer a question Robert had never asked. "I never get lonesome up here looking down on the boys and girls in Rainbow County."

"Is that a bar?" Robert asked.

"Nope," Floyd said. "It's the other foot of the rainbow arch from Oz. It's just a T-shirt I made up. It's a state of mind. What size do you wear? Maybe I should give you one."

"Hey, don't injure yourself doing me any favors," Robert said. "I can pay."

"I got a hundred of them," Floyd said. "A man has to be enterprising."

By the late Sixties, Floyd had nearly gone under. He had standards. He had tradition. He figured men and boys should be groomed a certain way. He hadn't been able to see himself as one of those fancy-nancy men's salons that other barbers changed to when nobody wanted Princetons or flat-tops or, his favorite, crewcuts anymore. He figured to ride out the long-hair fad. But here he was forty-five, with a one-chair shop and a steady but small clientele of older balding gentlemen of the sort people once kindly called "born bachelors" as opposed to "eligible bachelors." His trade kept him comfortable. The brisk pace that had once been Friday's and Saturday's had fallen off taking with it the strain from his eyes and the pressure from his varicose veins.

"I been closed for four months, yeah." Floyd said. "Just a second and I'll have all these wires tied up. Out for four months. Back for three."

"Vacation?" Robert asked. He was vaguely bored. The magazines were nothing to write home about.

"Operation," Floyd said. "Eyes. Yeah. Wouldn't be able to see today but for those two operations."

He smiled with such a general gratitude for his health that Robert, who in his own life was grateful for nothing, felt uncomfortable. Robert wished for another customer, preferably a mother with a small boy who would have to be hoisted to a kid's chair inside the big one. With commotion like that he could easily slip one or two of the crummy nudist magazines into the sleeve of his jacket.

"I always figured," Robert said, "that little boys always understand the world earlier and better than little girls."

"Why's that?"

"Because little boys get taken younger to barber shops. You sit them up on that little chair. You wrap that big cloth around them. All of a sudden they see what it's like to be a disembodied head caught between two mirrors. That's why little boys cry at the barber shop, because, all of a sudden, they're scared. They're face to face with the secret how we're all just curving off into infinity."

"I like that myself," Floyd said.

"Maybe that's why you barber."

"Could be." Floyd looked up at a hundred mirrored images of himself.

"To tell the truth," Robert said, "I think everybody ought to have two full-length mirrors facing each other in their house."

"Why's that?"

"So in case you ever need to escape for any reason, like, you know, to get away from whoever's after you, you can just stand yourself between the two mirrors and walk right out of space and time into some infinite dimension."

"That sure is another reason to be able to see," Floyd said. "If I was blind, I'd never know if you were telling me the truth about mirrors or not."

"You are so right," Robert said.

"Of course," Floyd continued, "more practically speaking, if I was blind, I couldn't barber. Whoever heard of a blind barber?" He thought a moment. "Guess it's possible to have, you know, the touch without the eye for it." He paused lost in the thought. "Me? I got the eye and the touch. Mmmm. Must be a blind barber somewhere."

"I figure," Robert said, "if the human mind can think of it, somebody somewhere is doing it. You should hear some of the things my human mind thinks about."

"Damn!" Floyd shifted his piano tools hand to hand. "That sure would take a trusting customer."

"What would?"

"A blind barber."

Robert began a careful roll of the magazine next to him.

"I can see now," Floyd said. "Good as you."

Floyd kept his eyes on the piano board, but Robert felt accused. He flipped the magazine away casually. The guilty flee, he thought, and he meant not from the barber but from back home. For crissakes, what am I doing here?

"It's funny," Robert said.

Floyd looked up with a vaguely cross expression.

"That I came up here, I mean. I came into your barber shop not wanting or really needing a haircut and I'm not getting one. I came into your shop and I'm not getting what I didn't want."

"Oh," Floyd said. He folded his tools into a felt bag. "I thought you meant that I could see was funny."

"Oh no," Robert said. "I guess I came up here looking for something else. Barbers always know what's going on around town."

"I mean," Floyd said, "it would be funny if I couldn't see and I was a barber. But it wouldn't be funny if I couldn't see and I was a pianist. You see them on the TV all the time. Pianists who can't see. They say it helps them play better. They feel it more. But you never see a barber who can't see cutting hair on TV."

"I guess not," Robert said. "Too bad for you that good old Ed Sullivan isn't on anymore. He eyed the morning's *Chronicle*. A sensational murder, one of a series of murders by the Zodiac Killer, spread across the front page; he was fascinated, but the paper itself was too bulky to smuggle under his clothes, and he was too shell-shocked from his arrest in the Green County Library to tear out the long article that continued to the last page of the first section. Instead, he tried to memorize the interesting, livid details of thirteen apparently connected murders and six other persons missing.

"Even if I couldn't see," Floyd said, "it wouldn't make me any better a pianist." He lifted the wired board off his lap. "This here's like I always rebuild." He carried it across the shop and drew back the curtain on an adjacent room. "You remember player pianos? I get them from all across the country. Bought one in Nebraska for twenty-five bucks. Sold it in Sausalito to Sally Stanford for you wouldn't guess how much." He pulled the curtain closed. "Nossir. Seeing or not seeing would be all the same to me pumping at one of my players with both feet."

Robert looked out the window. Down in the street the ticket left by the triumphant meter maid flapped in the ocean breeze sweeping down 18th Street to Castro where men, he never would have thought it, walked arm in arm. They were strangers, maybe dangerous strangers, but he recognized them all the same. "I should've locked my car." He thought of the .22 caliber handgun stashed under the seat and he laughed because it's impossible for someone on probation to get a permit for a handgun, but it's no way impossible for that same person to get a handgun, especially when that person's daddy dies and leaves it loaded in a bedroom drawer. "Damn," he said.

Floyd moved to the window, wiping his hands. "That your Chevy?"

He admired the Chevrolet gleaming all red and white with hardly a speck of any road grime Robert had wiped off every time he stopped to gas up. He had bought it, restored and cherry, the day he turned sixteen, paying for it with insurance money his mom had given him as his share of his dad's policy. Those had been the days! The draft had been lenient to neglectful. By 1973, the draft was carnivorous for red-blooded all-American boys. He told Louise Yavonovich, the gray-haired lady who ran the Green County Selective Service Board, that she couldn't draft him because he was leaving for California.

"For school?" she asked.

"Yes, a school" he said, "for becoming a minister, a Quaker minister," but his *yes* revealed itself for the lie it had always been before he had driven the first five hundred miles west. He knew he'd never sit in another school in all his life. He knew enough to get by in the world. And more. Even though he was no way, José, one of those spineless conscientious objectors, he vowed he'd never let anyone take him to some hellhole place like Vietnam, or even to prison for dodging the draft.

By no more than impetuous instinct, he had hopped into his car that day and worked out his plan about heading toward the coast, with its beaches and sex and drugs and rock 'n' roll, leaving fat old ugly Louise, no more the wiser, and a little the worse for wear, sitting on her cellulite in the sprawl of her manila alphabetical files. Even before the fierce rainstorm he had sat out in his car west of Omaha he had laughed. He was just another missing person out of millions. The old bitch would never catch up with him. He had no way of knowing that Louise had rather fancied him, and had let him make good his escape, because, in her heart she knew the war was a sad cause, and that Robert was all that was left of the Place family, his dad dead all those years, and his mother gone six weeks.

With Floyd looking down with him at his Chevy parked at 18th and Castro, he saw every mile of the 89,787.3 reflected back at him in the late sun of a thin Pacific afternoon. A wave of depression suddenly washed over him. It always did, right after he felt good about getting his own way. He wished to God he had been drafted. They'd have given him a uniform, an M-16 rifle, and his own chopper, and then turned him loose so he'd have had no choices to make about anything, but shoot it and screw it!

"Nice car," Floyd said. "And nice arms. You got real nice muscular arms."

"Thanks," Robert said.

"You work out a little?"

"Naw. I'm just naturally strong." Robert pulled up his sleeve and flexed his right arm, cocking his fist near his face. "You want to feel my bicep?"

Floyd rubbed his hands together and cupped his right palm over Robert's peaked arm and his left under it.

"Is that okay or is that okay?" Robert said.

"It's better than okay."

"You can let go now."

"So," Floyd said, "whyn't you drive your car over to my place? We can work us out a deal. You do something for me. I'll 'restore' it for you."

"Restore it?" Robert said. "You said you weren't blind! Are you crazy? That car doesn't need any restoring." He climbed into Floyd's barber chair. "Just trim it."

Floyd fastened the striped barber cloth tight around Robert's neck. He folded the tissue strip down neatly over the cloth. Wrapped and swaddled, Robert felt his body become subject to the barber. His mother had spent the entirety of his boyhood diapering and scarfing and lacing him in and out of clothes. One fall she had taken him after school to find a winter coat. She had wanted to shop at Penney's, but he had fast-talked her into a better buy at the Army-Navy Outlet. She had thought of her husband, a strict man Robert did not know was not his father, who had said the boy's last year's parka would fit well enough this season. Robert thought only of the brown leather bombardier's jacket he and his buddies had stared at through the plate glass window. They had pledged to form their own squadron. His blood-buddy Stoney named himself command pilot. Robert was to be head bombardier.

"This is the size," Robert had said, handing the jacket to his mother.

"That's too large, I'm sure."

"The boy's probably right." The clerk, whose name tag read *Nigel,* had spoken archly over the perfect knot of his stylish silk tie. "He really ought to know. He came in here several days ago with a gang of boys who disturbed the manager no end. I remember your boy especially. We caught him wearing this very jacket in the shoe department."

"I was trying it on."

"As a mother," Nigel the clerk had said, "you ought to know. We don't favor unattended young boys roving through our store."

His mother had been cowed. "Thank you," she had said. "I'll talk to his father."

Robert had ignored Nigel. He pulled the desired jacket down from the clerk's tight hand. He slipped in his arms and pulled the zipper. "I like it."

His mother had looked nervously at the clerk. "It does have windcuffs." Then making an unconvincing counterattack, for a moment she stared the clerk in the eye. "Well, Robert," she had said, "we'll take it. That's what we'll do. We'll buy it right now. No sense shopping around and then coming back right where we started." She looked Nigel the clerk dead on. "I think this will be fine," she had said. "Do you take charge cards? I'll have to put it on my charge card."

Back in the neighborhood, though the evening was warm, Robert wore the brown leather jacket out to show his buddies.

"Take it and shove it," Stoney had said. "Who needs a crummy leather jacket."

Robert Place could have taken them, maybe, one by one, but all of them together were too much. An older boy with light-blond down on his upper lip knocked Robert to the ground. Stoney picked up a piece of broken glass. He straddled the small of Robert's back and cut up the shoulders of the new leather jacket.

Robert escaped and ran and ran until he could run nowhere but to his mother's kitchen.

"I'm furious," she said. "After all I went through for you with that pansy clerk! Just you wait till your father gets home!"

Robert's father took one look at his bruised face and sent him to his room, shouting after him: "I'll be up to take care of you, sissy-boy!"

Robert sprawled across the bed. His head throbbed from the kicking. Angry voices rose and fell in the kitchen below. He dozed in pain and missed the tread of his father's boots up the stairs. He started when his door opened and light from the hall thrust an awkward rectangle across his bed.

"Take off the jacket," his father had said. "It goes back."

Robert wrapped his arms tight around his chest. The leather was warm.

"Take it off."

Robert glared up at the big man silhouetted in the doorway. "No," he said. He folded his arms tighter, holding on to himself as he had never held on to anything in his life.

"Then I'll take it off for you." His father pulled at the jacket.

Robert would not surrender.

His father pulled off his belt. He was a short, powerful man whose veins rose in anger as he twisted the buckled end of his belt around his fist. "Don't tell me *no*, you goddam kid." He lashed out. "No goddam pussy-boy is going to tell me *no*." His belt struck across

Robert's chest and arms. The boy rolled defensively to his stomach. His father saw the scuffs and tears on the jacket. "Sonuvabitch!" he said. In fury he tore Robert's corduroy slacks down below his slim haunches. His left hand shredded his son's worn cotton shorts. The blows from his belt welted across Robert's flesh, until finally, his father, hardened in rage, fell across him. His breath had the copper tobacco smell of Camels. "You tell your ma any of this," he whispered close into Robert's ear, "and next time I'll kill you. Make it look like an accident and kill you. Just hang you up by your neck in the attic and kill you. Just knock over a chair like you did it yourself, and kill you, you little sissy suicide, just like all faggot suicides. Send you straight to hell!"

"My old man was a real bulldog lady-killer," Robert bragged to the barber. "Everytime I come into a barber shop it reminds me of him. The way he used to smell once a month of all that Fitch Hair Tonic and rosewater. Once a month I could smell him coming."

"You don't say," Floyd said.

"He got himself killed in a fight on an oil rig in Louisiana."

"That a fact." Floyd combed and clipped at Robert's head. "Getting kind of thin on the top."

"Yeah," Robert said. "So it goes."

Floyd clipped at one small hair growing in Robert's left ear. "Do you suppose," he said, "that they put out their eyes when they're kids?"

"Who?" Robert looked up from the magazine in his lap.

"Those pianists on TV. The ones that can't see because it makes them play better."

"I don't know," Robert said. "Most people'll do most anything."

"Sometimes in India they put out a kid's eyes so he can hustle more from tourists. Hear the Mex do that too."

"Sounds to me," Robert said, "something like the boys who sang soprano for the pope. I got an article I tore out of some magazine at home on that. They'd take these altar boys and, you know, sort of spay them, operate on them, you know, down there, so they'd keep their real high voices. Their families were happy. Even the kids were happy. A kid with a real high voice could make a fortune in those days."

"That a fact," Floyd said. "Maybe then that's why they do it. Just so 'Mr. and Mrs. America' can sit at home in front of their 'T and V' and watch those black boys who can't even see play the piano." He reached for the talcum. "Dagos really did that stuff, huh?"

"Lots of people do lots of things that sound cruel to us but not to them. Anybody who's not an orphan knows that." On the shelf, between Bach and Liszt, Robert spied a fresh half-eaten deli sandwich. He shifted nervously in the chair.

"Hold still," Floyd said. He reached for the shaving cream. "I'm finishing up around your ears."

On the end-table next to the chromium-and-leatherette couch lay a second half-eaten sandwich. Blood sausage, the same color as the burgundy couch, hung bitten out of the white bread. In a Coke with no more than two swigs out of it, small bubbles fizzed noiselessly to the top.

"One of your customers left his lunch."

"Some customers leave stuff. Some take it. There's losers and there's claimers. You want it?" He arced his razor in a smooth crescent above and behind Robert's ear. The downstroke scrape flourished into a fast, thrilling swoop down his neck.

"I feel like my life is in your hands," Robert said.

"It is," Floyd said.

"I don't know if I like that." Robert hated the nervous laugh in his own voice. "I only started back to barbers about two months ago. Before that it was nearly five years, being a hippie and all, I had hair down below my shoulders. Then something, nothing really, happened, and this guy, this judge, made me cut it. When I was a kid, barber shops always gave me a headache.

"So. Just a little scrape with the law," Floyd, W. C. Fields, said. He swooped his razor over and around Robert's other ear.

"I never liked anybody fussing over me that much. Besides, this barber shop my old man took me to had pin-up pictures of really big girls and I wasn't a very big boy. I mean now it wouldn't matter."

"The bigger the better, huh?" Floyd rinsed his razor. He knew enough to humor his customers ambiguously. He met all kinds at the corner of 18th and Castro. "Never kid a kidder," he said.

"I kid you not," Robert said.

For years Robert had been titanic cruising among icebergs of females in his hometown. At the age of four, innocent of all need for cover, in the driveway between their homes, he had compared himself to the lower half of a giggling little Judy Esterbank. One month later, a modern doctor, new to small-town practice, had sold his mother an introductory twofer on the latest big-city hygiene and had wheeled him through white double doors to pull out his tonsils and slice off his foreskin.

He never really trusted her ever again.

At the age of ten, playing Lewis and Clark, he had tripped over a tent peg catching the strapless halter of twelve-year-old Joyce Gillette. One flawless white breast popped pert and eager into view. He stared and she smiled. He stepped forward and she stepped back tucking herself away as neatly as she packed her camping equipment. He stared at the veil of her halter. She stepped to him and cupped his groin in her hand. It felt good. "I ought to kill you," she had said. But her hand felt warm through his jeans. Three years later she kissed him there. Repeatedly. Up and down.

"Indeed I do love the little ladies," Robert said to Floyd. Screw Judy and screw Joyce. He hated himself for continuing the elaborate lie he had intended to leave back in the Midwest.

"And that's why you moved to San Francisco." Floyd dusted Robert's neck with clouds of talcum. "That's why everybody moves to San Francisco. They say it's the weather. They say it's the restaurants. But it's the sex that brings them. San Francisco's the place where when you go there you get laid."

"I'm interested in that Coke," Robert said. Brown air bubbles rose in slow chains up through the mocha cola.

"It's second-hand and half-dead," Floyd said. He handed Robert the bottle. "Just wipe the cooties off the top."

Robert toasted Bach and Liszt. He wished Floyd's magazines were better. Even a *National Geographic* with naked natives would help him swallow the dying Coke and the whole afternoon a lot easier. "You know," Robert said to distract his train of thought, "that a '57 Chevy is the best car GM ever put out. That's why I got it. That's why I still drive it."

"That a fact," Floyd said. He unwrapped Robert's neck, took two swipes with the talcum brush, and flapped the green-striped cloth with a whipcrack. "Being's we're finished, let me show you something."

Robert remained seated in Floyd's chair. Now maybe he would find what it was that had caused him to pull the Chevy to the curb, forget his meter, and endure a haircut and a Coca-Cola he had not desired. Floyd disappeared into the piano repair room. Two single swipes zithered across a dusty piano harp behind the Fifties' floral-print curtain.

Robert waited for Floyd as he had waited beside his mother's hospital bed. Her name was Isabel and his father always kidded her, saying like it was the first time, "Is a bell necessary on a bicycle? Is a bell necessary at all?" And she always laughed even though she hated him making fun of her.

For months she had lain wasting away with cancer in the depths of white sheets. He looked down at her remembering how all through his youth she had sized him up and encouraged him saying, "At least you're tall." She warned him that no girl likes a short man. "Short men," she had said, "are impossible to deal with." She should have known. Robert's father was short. But Robert had felt tall, standing next to her shrinking form. For an hour at the beginning of her last week, he had stood by her bed with the plastic tube of the intravenous fluid pinched tight between his thumb and forefinger. Mercy or no mercy, he had hoped to kill her, but his hand had cramped even before the nurse almost caught him.

In Floyd's piano room a large cardboard box grated heavily across the gritty floor. Robert heard Floyd say, "Ah, there it is."

"I suppose they do," Robert called to Floyd who was dragging the huge box into the shop itself.

"You suppose who does what?" Floyd panted with the exertion, but his face was triumphant.

"I suppose they do put out their own kids' eyes." Robert had read more than he even wanted hanging out in libraries, slicing pages out of magazines. "There's all those operas about Greek plays where the kids get turned into mincemeat. Some parents kill their young. Maybe they're no more cruel than nature is cruel. People wouldn't pay good money to go see that sort of thing if they weren't naturally interested."

Floyd began to dig into his box. "Now, don't you laugh at me," Floyd said. He was matter-of-fact. "I have these treasures I don't share with everyone."

"I understand," Robert said. But he did not understand as much as he thought he did, and he was about to understand a whole lot more.

The box was neatly packed with magazines, picture albums, and loose photos of the kind most adult men keep to themselves. At first glance, Robert Place knew, almost faster in his groin than his head, what kind of illustrations these were. They were the kind Robert had tried all his life to avoid, but could not. They were the kind who called to him, from the flat pages of magazines, to breathe into them his life. They were seductive, attractive, flowers of evil. They were, somehow, an occasion of sin. They were young men more stripped than dressed who posed as sailors and athletes and construction workers. They were the kind of pictures of men Robert had sliced from certain physique atlases in St. Louis bookstores to take home to lay with him on his bed, until he blacked out, saying, "Whoever you are, I want to spend eternity with you," waking up as if coming to, jumping from his bed, furiously destroying the evidence of his love for this kind of thing. He would crush the sticky pictures into tiny paper balls and burn them and flush their ashes down the toilet. They were bad boys and worse men and he was not one of them.

"Take a look at this," Floyd said. He offered a magazine to Robert.

"Very nice," Robert said. He fanned the pages from the back cover forward and made bits and pieces of bodies flip in crazy motion from the last page to the first. Couples began in orgasm and ended in foreplay.

"You know," Floyd said, "when it comes right down to it, your Chevy and my pianos show up for what they aren't." He scooped up a stack of magazines.

"What do you mean?" Robert asked.

"It's a lie what everyone says. That there's other things in life besides sex and money. Your car and my pianos aren't a hill of beans when it comes to getting laid. Down there at that intersection it's all bodies and sex. You could have the hottest car in town, and I could have the grandest grand piano, but unless you have a face and a body, which you at your age certainly do, and unless I have some extra cash, which at my age I have a little, no one's going to touch us."

Robert studied Floyd's pinched face. "What about love?"

"What's love got to do with it?"

"Hell if I know," Robert said. "I don't even care. I never loved anybody and nobody ever loved me. I'm not even looking for love. I got no expectations except of the worst kind."

"I'm a realist," Floyd said. "The only thing to be in life is twenty-one. Forever. After that, it's all hustlers. Everyone who comes through my door is selling something. Don't ever grow old."

"I've always looked young for my age," Robert said.

"So you don't know yet what I'm talking about."

"Yes I do."

"The devil you say!"

Floyd thrust a dozen magazines named *Young Adonis* and *Mars* and *Physique Pictorial* at Robert who immediately judged their covers. They made him covetous. He wanted three or four of the magazines, contents sight unseen.

"I'd really like one of these," he said, holding a copy of *Tomorrow's Man*.

"Money can't buy them. Some of these I've had for fifteen or sixteen years. When I page through them, it's like with dear friends. When I'm eighty, they'll still be the same age, the same dear friends, and I'll still have them and they'll be a comfort."

"They're a comfort right now," Robert said. As he paged the magazines, he felt his spirit rise inside him. He was in the room but he was not part of the room. He sat between the mirrors. The men in the magazines sucked his very essence into themselves, coming alive to him, whispering secret words he could not make out. He gasped for breath like a man being dragged down a drain.

Floyd pulled the yellow shade down over the glass door. Two years before he had painted in orange hippie Day-Glo the words SORRY CLOSED on the shade, and the paint had not faded at all. He had some rising hope that his strange customer was hinting, the way first-timers so often hint, that he wanted to become dear friends with him.

Robert, in fact, sat helpless in Floyd's barber chair. He made small gurgling noises as he turned the pages. Back in Canterberry, he had only imagined what he would find out west. But he had not found it; it had found him. His hand clutched his throat as his breath finally, totally, slid out of him. He suddenly saw how life was going to be with him. Really be with him. Really in control of him. The thought took root like mandrake in his heart. He had never considered until that minute that everything he was about, had always been about, had masked the slow flowering fact that he was not different from all those men and boys cruising arm in arm in the street below. The same wild lemming call that had summoned them from everywhere had summoned him from the south-midlands to them, to this city, to this very intersection, to this catbird seat in Floyd's Barber Shop looking down on something that was totally new to him, but also totally known.

He was not sure he liked the convergence.

What the fuck was Rainbow County?

The summer before, when he had fled south on a trial-run from Canterberry to St. Louis, Cleo Walker, with her brilly bush of flaming red hair, had walked right up and taken control of him. She had spied him sitting at a small table in an outdoor cafe in Gaslight Square and after she had scooped him up, she stripped him down in her sun-splashed studio on Delmar Avenue near Forest Park. He had not felt awkward standing nude before her. For years, naked exposure had been his urge, so he had slipped, a true exhibitionist, easy and erect from his clothes. Without meaning his words, he apologized for his thing, his *thing*, standing at attention. Cleo refused to dignify his apology with the benefit of a real reply, so he had stepped toward her, reaching for her breasts. That was the script, wasn't it? But Cleo had refused his advance for reasons he could not fathom. Wasn't painting only a high-toned excuse for getting naked and looking at nudes?

"I want," he stammered low, "I want...I want...."

"Don't reach for something," Cleo said, "you don't know you want."

"What do you mean?" he asked.

"You're a virgin, aren't you?"

He said nothing.

"I'm not a virgin," she said. "So I know things."

"You mean it shows?" he said. "I'm a book with blank pages?"

"You're a book with no pages," she said.

"I like the way you talk."

"Fuck!" Cleo said the word he had never heard a woman say. "You have an excellent body and an interesting face. You have a sexual energy I don't care to release. I only want to paint you."

He was crestfallen. "You can see faces like mine hanging in the post office."

She felt a sudden sorrow for him. "Look, *Roberto, caro Roberto,* there's nothing wrong with you. I'm a painter. I want to paint you. I don't want to have sex with you."

Yet, in Cleo's studio, he stood insistent, his pouting mouth silent, his lower part as straight and to the point as a declarative sentence. "I'm sorry," he apologized again, this time half-meaning it. "It doesn't have anything to do with you."

"I didn't think so," she said.

"This always happens when I take off my clothes, or think about taking off my clothes."

"It's no big deal," Cleo said. "I'm a painter. I look at you. I don't see your precious dick. I see light. I see shadow."

"Light and shadow," Robert said. He tried to concentrate on a pile of littered art magazines; but even they, so far across the studio, could not slow the excited flow of his blood. He had never shown himself naked to anyone, and he was embarrassed at how much he liked it.

Cleo ignored his excitement. She poured him a small glass of blood-red wine, and squeezed white and tan and browns across her glass palette. "I'm in my sepia period," she laughed. "I'm glad I'm no devotee of Freud, who I wish had been otherwise employed. Who said that?"

"Mrs. Freud?"

"Lean against the wall, Robert. Relax. Move your head to the left. Fine. Hold it. Just relax. I'm brushing in your basic line today. Later on I'll work in the tension."

He had leaned motionless against the doorway and then, finally, leaned against her for the next two months, because, one rainy August afternoon, when she had lost the light, and poured them both some more wine, she had said, "When I told you I didn't want to have sex with you, you silly goose, I didn't mean I didn't want to fuck you. At least once."

Go figure, he thought.

Their love-making confused him. All love-making confused him.

"Was I okay?" he asked. He had not been able to keep from asking that question even he knew was ridiculous.

"Who were you thinking about?" Cleo asked.

"You," he said.

"Liar!"

He could have cheerfully killed her. She had him pegged. She polarized him the way all women did. She was all women. He knew he was supposed to desire them, but he had no feeling for why. They filled him with an empty want they could not slake. They took his coloration and line the way Cleo's sidelong look, her brush-hand resting on her mahlstick, had day-by-day transferred his face from his head to her canvas. He was the primitive and she was the sorceress capturing his spirit. Transfixed, he could not move from the pose into which she had enchanted him. His naked body trembled visibly.

"Get it together," Cleo had said. "Take a break."

She handed him a book of prints and text. Absently he leafed through page after page of what seemed to be the *Life and Hard Times of Andrew Wyeth*. Not one of the reproductions tempted him to pull his single-edge razor blade from his wallet and start slicing.

"That's why I like to paint you," Cleo said.

"Why?"

"Your face hides nothing. You're bored. You're light years away. From here. From me. From everybody."

"I don't care for cartooning." He tossed the Wyeth book to the floor and resumed his pose.

Cleo strode across the studio and retrieved the book. "Wyeth isn't exactly Norman Rockwell," she said.

"Same school." Robert hated the nasty sound in his voice, but he didn't care.

"What would you know about art anyway," Cleo said. "It's about order. You're all chaos."

"Is that so? I know plenty. I've read articles."

"So don't throw Wyeth down. Read it," Cleo said. She shoved the book hard against his naked belly. "And you better not tear a goddam page out of it."

"I confess my secrets and you refuse to forgive me?"

"Fuck you and your sins." She said it flatly and marched back to her life-size canvas. "Tilt your head to the left."

Robert obeyed. The Wyeth book hung in his right hand. It felt cool against his thigh. Holding his pose, he raised it and fanned once more through the pages. Print after print of paint-brushed faces peopled Wyeth's decaying afternoons. One painting, an immense field, contained a solitary male figure. Everything was brown and dead and spun out of sorrow. Wyeth had painted it the winter of his own father's death. The editor's note explained the painting as an exorcism of sadness. Robert stirred slightly from his pose. He caught the sense of the painting, but he could hardly see the face of the man in the field. Somehow Wyeth had lost his own face along with the lost face of his father. The canvas was full of nothing so much as his own grief.

Deep inside Robert that thin tensile strand of generations snapped. In a moment of his own infinite sadness he realized that he too had lost the face of his father. In the stead of the man who pretended to sire him, and had really abused him, stood only shadow images and half-remembered sounds of the sweet times: the wet-lipped kiss from that unshaved face in the dark over his bed. It was all reduced to that: the memory of his father, home from the late shift, leaning over to kiss him goodnight. As if he were again half-asleep in his little boy's sleep, Robert could feel his father's ghostly kiss on his face. He could not forget his father's love, but he could not forgive that one night of his father's drunkenness.

Robert realized that he had been losing everything despite his desperate collecting of folders of stolen clippings and magazines purloined from under the eyes of cheery dental receptionists. In the glory days of the large magazines, he had tried to save the images of the week by swallowing up the sleeves of his school jacket whole issues of *Look* and *Life*. Finally, when he had been caught with his single-edge razor blade in the Green County Public Library, his mother had said, "I hope you're satisfied. You now owe me a hundred dollars more." Her face looked screwed with pain that he thought was no more than her embarrassment at his conviction. "Bobby, Bobby, Bobby. What do you expect me to live on? When will you ever grow up and settle down?" Six months later, she was dead and he had fled to San Francisco. He was fed up to his eyeballs with personal relationships. He had a need for a city of strangers.

Floyd, like most barbers, could hold a one-sided conversation with a corpse and was finishing up his long monologue when Robert remembered where he was. "Old Sammy Davis, Jr.," Floyd said, "only got one of his eyes put out. That's because his folks wanted him to dance. Be kind of hard to poke out both your eyes and dance too. Might fall off the stage. But before long, you'll see, someone'll show up and try it big as life on network TV." He handed Robert another magazine.

"And they'll be tapping out something in code, those dancers will." Robert took the magazine and laid his line on Floyd. "That blind guy you say'll be dancing on CBS will be tapping out in code something everybody ought to hear. Something like SOS." Robert considered his words. "Just like SOS," he repeated, and he wanted to cry out, not for help, but for something else, "because we're all in danger and we have to save our souls."

"That a fact," Floyd said. He passed a perplexed look up through his thick glasses. Should he make his move? Was this guy wanting it, or was he all talk and no action? Were the magazines, dragged out to arouse him, missing their mark?

"But not everyone will understand it." Robert slowly turned the pages of the last magazine.

"Maybe you shouldn't bother trying to understand what you do. Just do it," Floyd insinuated.

Robert looked up straight into Floyd's eyes through his thick glasses. "I have a gun," he announced. "A .22 caliber handgun."

"You don't say." Floyd backed off.

"Does that make you scared of me?"

"Do you have it on you?"

"No."

"Then you don't scare me. Your gun scares me. I don't like guns."

"Sometimes you have to scare people. Terror's the only thing they respect. If you scare them, you get their undivided attention."

"Whyn't you finish up," Floyd was changing the subject, "reading that magazine."

"Sure," Robert said. "So far I like it fine. It's your best one yet."

Floyd took a last few snips here and there around Robert's ears, then tried to gentle him down, and sidle on in, seductively rubbing Robert's neck with an electric massager. He was surprised to find very little tension in Robert's neck and shoulders. "You're a cool customer," he said, "as cool as a cucumber."

Suddenly, Robert sat bolt upright in Floyd's barber chair. He held it in his hands: a black-and-white photograph on an un-numbered magazine page. It was the picture he had spent his life looking for: magazines in one hand, razor blade in the other. The photo was of a man seated alone. On either side of the photo were separate single shots of athletic women. The one on the left held a golf club. She was set to putt and her breasts hung down between her stiffened arms. The naked woman on the right held a jaunty tennis racquet. But it was the naked athlete in the middle photo who mesmerized him as much as if he'd found a snapshot of his real father, the original missing person, whom he had never seen.

He was seated, stretched slightly back straddling a locker-room bench. He was a little older than Robert, and bigger, very blond, with a fully developed chest over his washboard abdomen. His thick wrists connected his athlete's hands to his powerful arms. He wore football pads across his broad shoulders, and a football helmet, and, between his casually spread legs, he was erect. His eyes looked directly from the helmet into the camera and directly out of the page into Robert's face. The face-guard on the helmet covered his mouth. No New Testament word of mercy could spring from those Old Testament lips that Robert knew were set, mean and hard and without mercy. He looked directly out at Robert. He was erect and Robert knew he faced the powerful, inevitable Face of God.

"I must," he said to Floyd, "have this." He rose out of the barber chair. "Ask any amount, anything. Only let me buy this from you."

Floyd thought to press the trade for sex, but the young man seemed too volatile. Besides, a quick flash of looking down the barrel of a handgun made him think better of it. "That one you can have," he said.

"I can't just take it. I learned my lesson about that the hard way."

"Then trade me something, anything," Floyd said. "I won't take your money." He stared into Robert's ecstatic wild eyes and suddenly, more than he wanted him, he wanted him gone.

"I don't have anything," Robert said.

Floyd laughed nervously at him. "Everybody's got something."

Robert mentally searched his car. He had his clothes. He had the loaded handgun. "Nothing," he said.

In the room, he seemed volatile.

In the mirrors, he looked vulnerable.

Floyd, fighting his rising lust, chided himself for being a cautious old fool. He threw risk against the wind. The boy was right. Danger was aphrodisiac. He put his hand on Robert's knee and slowly smoothed his palm up the inside of his thigh.

"Not that!" Robert watched the hand slowly advance up his leg like a giant spider. "Not that!" Robert said.

Floyd's heart jumped with a rush of adrenaline. "Then what?" Floyd stood straight up. "You said I could have anything for the picture."

"Not that. Not here. Not now. Not you."

"See what I told you about your car and my pianos?" Floyd

worked the only logic he knew in situations like this. "What if I pay you?"

"For what?"

He thought to say for sex, but he said, "To take the picture. I'll give you money to take the picture," Floyd said, "and then you can leave."

"Don't go inverting everything."

Invert? Invert. Floyd had psychology books from twenty years before when *invert* meant only one thing.

"Then take the picture for godsake and get a move on."

"I told you, man! I can't take it for nothing."

"As far as I'm concerned, you can," Floyd said. "This is getting old. I want to close up shop."

"Wait," Robert said. "I got it." He pulled out his wallet and reached inside. He handed the folded-up paper to Floyd.

"What's this?" Floyd asked. "The number of your Swiss bank account?"

"No, you asshole," Robert said. "It's the combination to my gym locker."

"I'll bet."

"Go on. Read it!"

Floyd unfolded the smudged slip of paper. "I need my reading glasses."

Robert stared down at the picture of the blond athlete, but he barked his order at Floyd, "Read it."

Floyd hooked his half-lens bifocals over his ears and read the word "Postmark."

"That's the title," Robert said. "It's a poem. A short poem."

"Good," Floyd said. "Short and sweet." The afternoon had not gone the seductive way he had hoped and he regretted missing lunch as much as he missed lunching on Robert. "I have low blood sugar."

"Read it, please. No one else has ever seen it. I wrote it on my way out here. To send back home. To everyone back home."

"'Postmark,'" Floyd read. "'Dear God: You created me, then you hated me....Dear Folks: You conceived me, then deceived me.... Dear Teacher: You taught me, then you fought me....Dear Boss: You hired me, then you fired me....Dear Lover: You painted me, then you tainted me....Dear Death: You embraced me, then erased me.'"

"Well?" Robert asked.

"It's not...bad."

"Not bad?"

"It's pretty good."

"You think so?"

"Yeah," Floyd said. "I like it like really a whole lot."

"Good," Robert said. "We just made a trade. My poem for your photograph. Strange, isn't it? I came in here not knowing why I came in here. I didn't want a haircut and you cut my hair. I got a parking ticket. You handed me a magazine and I found a picture of the face that's always been in the back of my head."

"What's that?" Floyd said.

"Never you mind. You wouldn't understand."

"That's three bucks for the trim," Floyd said.

"Here's four," Robert said. "Keep the change."

"Don't insult me," Floyd said. "You never tip the owner."

"I do."

"Suit yourself."

"I'm leaving," Robert said. "It's been real."

Floyd slipped full into his W. C. Fields routine. "Never give a sucker an even break. Here's your hat. What's your hurry? Don't let the door hit you on your way out."

"You calling me a sucker?"

"No," Floyd said. "Take it easy. Where you headed?"

"To the beach," Robert said. "Land's end at Land's End." He walked to Floyd's cash register counter.

"It's been a slow day moneywise," Floyd said nervously.

"Hasn't exactly been a stampede, I'd say." Robert pulled the single-edge razor blade from his wallet and expertly sliced the magazine page so that the athletic girls disappeared, leaving only the 5x7 of the handsome football player. "Tonight's the full moon and the summer solstice. I've never seen the Pacific. I'm taking this picture and I'm going to watch the sunset and the moonrise."

"You want maybe instead to use my john?" Floyd slipped the four bills directly into his white nylon pocket.

"What for?"

"What all little boys use it for when they've stolen daddy's dirty magazines."

"I never did anything like that."

"No one ever does, according to them, when it's always the thing they do most," Floyd said. "Do you have anyplace to stay for the night?"

"What's it to you?"

"Nothing." Floyd backed off. He slept single in a double bed. "It's nothing to me."

"I'm going to the ocean. I'll roll up my jeans and I'll walk in the surf and I'll listen."

"To what?

Robert held up the photograph. "To him," he said.

"To him?"

"To him. I'm old enough to see if he'll ever speak to me."

Floyd wanted to roll his strained eyes back in his head. All these people, all these immigrants to San Francisco were getting stranger than strange. "So," he said. "What if he doesn't speak to you."

"He'll speak to me alright."

"But what if he doesn't?"

"Either way it makes no difference since he never has anyway."

"So if it doesn't make any difference, why you so hot to go?"

"Because that picture is the Face of God."

Floyd stopped W. C. Fields from cackling: "The Face of God. You don't say." He didn't say it; instead he said: "You got to be kidding."

"He'll tell me, if he wants to, everything I need to know."

"What's that?"

"Ways to keep me out of hell. Ways to get me into heaven."

"What ways?"

"Ways you could sell like Salvation Coupons the night before Judgment Day. Ways those men and boys down in the street probably know. Old ways. Ancient ways. Ways so secret only a few men, and maybe a few women, know them. But there's more of them out here that know than back home, or anywhere else ever before in one place on this whole earth, right here, I figure, in your Rainbow County. They know the ways. I know they know the ways."

"You mean sex," Floyd said.

"Sex?" Robert said. "Sure, why not? Sex must be one of the saving ways, but the way has to be right. Just right. Or else sex is just like everyone says, the way to damnation." He bored his stare hard through Floyd's thick glasses. "And guess what else?"

Floyd guessed what else was he had himself another one of those religious sex nuts trying to break out of his shell. He wanted to take a step back, but he was too proud to show Robert any fear; he remembered Robert bragging that terror was the only thing most people respected once it got their attention.

"Besides sex," Robert said, "guess what else."

"I can't guess."

"Damage."

"Damage?"

"Just a little damage."

"Why damage?" Floyd said. "What damage? What to? Who to?"

"To you," Robert said. "To me. To everybody."

"What kind of damage?"

"Big damages," Robert said, "and little damages."

"I could call the police."

"By the time they got here, my razor blade could cut your face. I could make you blind so you could go on TV. By the time they got here, I could cut my throat. Slice right through my jugular. None of it would make any difference to anybody but you. I don't care.

I might die or I might go to jail, but you'd still be blind, trying to cut hair and play your pianos."

"I get the picture," Floyd said.

"No," Robert said. "I got the picture." He held the photograph up and out at arm's length. "He'll tell me what to do. In my life I know life does damage to you." He looked down at the swarming men in the street. He had his looks. He had his car. He had his gun. "So I figure I might as well inflict a little of the damage myself."

"I never quite thought of life that way."

"Well, you sure are the slow one. Everybody else thinks so. Doesn't that explain the evil that people do to themselves, smoking and drinking and whoring and taking drugs and driving fast and fighting and killing and raping and molesting, because that's the only way they can make the world that damages them everyday make any sense is if they do some of the damage themselves. Everybody but a fool knows when you can't beat it, you join it."

"You expect him, the guy in the picture..."

"God."

"...God...to speak to you and tell you what to do?"

"I expect he'll tell me if I should do any damage for him and if I should, to who. Maybe to you. Maybe to me. Maybe to anybody he tells me to. Nobody ever went to hell for that." Robert smiled and took a step forward. "Take it easy, Floyd. Relax."

Floyd pasted a smile on his face but his heart was racing.

"See what I mean about a little scare getting your attention?" Robert broke into guffaws of snorting laughter.

"You were putting me on?"

"I bet I had you so scared you had a bone on."

"You were putting me on!"

"If you think so, Floyd, ol' buddy! You should've seen your face, a hundred times over, scared sure as hell, curving off in those mirrors, which, by the way, could stand a bit of washing. Shoot, I was just kidding you, wasn't I? 'Don't kid a kidder,' you told me, but I did and you took it hook, line, and sinker. You wait awhile and you'll get to know I got a real killer sense of humor."

"Never mention killing."

"Hey!" Robert said. "That's a figure of speech. Nothing is what it seems. It's all mirrors. One thing's always meaning some other thing besides what a person thinks it means. You know that, being a barber, standing between your mirrors in all those parallel universes. I'm not dumb, you know. I've spent most of my life in recent years reading all kinds of the strangest things so the inside of my head's like an encyclopedia. My second-cousin, Ollie Thomas, who's madam librarian back home told me so."

"Perhaps you have," Floyd said, "low blood sugar. I myself often experience strange mood swings."

"Naw. My blood's fine and my sugar's better." Robert winked the way his father always winked. "If you catch my drift."

"Sounds like," Floyd pulled his ear, charading, working Robert toward the door, "like we've circled back to sex."

"Have you noticed that too? How everything sooner or later always comes back around to sex?"

"You are sure going to have a good time down there on 18th and Castro," Floyd said. "That intersection is laying on its back with its legs in the air just waiting for you."

"I ain't done it." Robert's face reddened with anger. "I told you I ain't done it! I ain't never done it when it was my will. But when I'm good and ready, I just might, and I just might be the best at it."

Something, some *thing*, in the room ground suddenly to a halt between them.

"What?"

It could only be one thing. Floyd wished he'd carried a little hand fan, something petite and operatic from the eighteenth century, to hide the smirk on his lips.

"I ain't done it. Not yet."

"Done what?" Floyd was intent on forcing Robert to say it.

I love it, Floyd thought, all this talk and no action has been the braggadocio of a male virgin with very blue balls. "Done what?"

"You're going to make me say it, aren't you?"

"Robert, I bet no one could ever make you do anything."

"My mother always said that." Robert's eyes kind of crossed in his head.

"You haven't done what?"

"I haven't had sex. Okay? So laugh."

"And risk another wrinkle? Never. My God, as it is, look at my face. If wrinkles hurt, I'd be screaming."

"I'm serious, goddam it. I haven't had sex. Not really. Not ever. Not unless you count the time I didn't want to, and the time I thought I had to, but I never count those two times and I never talk about them."

"Some experiences are too painful to recall," Floyd said, "but I can't recall any."

"Shut the judas-priest up. I'm not dumb. I can do sex. I know what goes on out there on those streets. I told you I've read and forgot more stuff than you ever even thought of." He held up the picture of the blond athlete. "I know what he's going to tell me, but I want to hear it from his own lips, me lying in the dunes at twilight feeling the warm breeze from the ocean."

"This is summer in Northern California," Floyd said. "What warm breeze? You'll die of exposure."

"He'll tell me. And they'll tell me."

"Who?"

"The fellows down there in that intersection. One at a time. And I'll listen. One secret at a time. That's how to make sense of it. One after another of the men who know the secret ways. One after the other. They'll all whisper to me and when I've heard them all, I'll know all about life and damage and death and the ways to stay out of hell."

"Are you sure, really sure, that's what he wants?"

"I don't know what he wants. That's why I'm taking his face

with me to the beach. So maybe he will talk to me first the way the others will talk to me later."

"Maybe you should forget him and them and figure out what you want."

"I just want one SOB and one SOS one right after the other. I want some of the pleasure of all of the danger if I'm going to suffer the damage anyway."

"You're talking crazy," Floyd said. "You're going to fit right in with all the fruits and flakes. You're a nut."

"No, I ain't," Robert Place said, "but so what if I am?" He held up the picture like a holy icon. "Only he can tell me."

"Sure," Floyd said, "you've got that pornographic picture."

"It's the Face of God!"

"I've seen London," Floyd, W. C. Fields, said, "and I've seen France. I've seen the queen in her underpants."

"Are you making fun of me?" Robert said.

"I wouldn't dare make fun of you," Floyd said. "My blood sugar's too low to keep this up. My prescription for you is to get laid twice before bedtime, and don't call me in the morning."

"What does all that mean? Everything means something."

"It means," Floyd said, "you've come to the right place. It means, Welcome to San Francisco. Welcome to Rainbow County."

"That's better," Robert Place said. "I like that attitude much better."

"Have you ever thought," Floyd said, raising his SORRY CLOSED shade and opening the door, "about maybe swallowing something you can buy on the street to lay yourself back some, about letting your hair grow long again?"

"Why, Floyd," Robert said, halfway down to the first landing, "You surprise me. I would never have figured you to be one to turn away business. I'm going out and I'm staying out..."

"You're coming out."

"...until he talks to me. So you'll see me again. A real regular. Plan on it. I intend to show your Rainbow County a thing or two.

I intend to stay a close-cropped soldier until all of them down there in that intersection talk to me, and you're going to keep me ready for him and for them, barbered and groomed like I just stepped out of a bandbox."

The Unseen Hand in the Lavender Light

REEL ONE
His life was a silent movie

His mind craved flickers the way his mouth watered over salt-grit popcorn. In the early nineteen-forties, while the World War raged from Europe to the Pacific, the doll-faced waitress who was his mother snapped her gum in downtown Peoria's famous Bee Hive Cafe while she fielded her counter tips into an issue-by-issue collection of *Photoplay* magazine which he read between the daily double features.

Each afternoon she paid his nine-cent admission to the Apollo Theater. Each dinner time, after the matinee double bill, he left the balcony to eat supper on the last counter stool at the Bee Hive, and thought it not at all odd that his mother's regulars called her "Countess Betty" because she never waited tables, always working the faster turnover of the counter.

She flirted with the men from the County Court House across Main Street, and the factory workers from Caterpillar. She turned nickel tips into quarters. The War Department had retooled Caterpillar Tractor Company into a defense plant. Peoria, in the middle of nowhere, became strategic. Landing Ship Tank Boats, built up the Illinois River, cruised downstream past Peoria, with soldiers waving, sometimes coming ashore, headed for the war. The nightly blackouts and air-raid drills made everyone feel important. The Caterpillar men, exempt from the draft, built Army trucks and heavy equipment. He liked them—more than he could say—calling his mother "Betty Grable." She was their very own Countess of the Counter Stools.

She was the star of the Bee Hive Cafe. No one even knew her real name was Helen which was the only name she let him call her, and only in private in their rented room in the Flatiron Kickapoo Hotel above the Pour House Tavern where, tired from gabbing all day long under a war poster warning "Loose Lips Sink Ships," she wanted no talking at all, taking off her shoes and her makeup, and watching out the window the soldiers and sailors leaning in the lamplight and whistling at the girls going in and out of the Pour House.

His mother, a take-charge arranger nobody dared cross, saw to his free meals the way she arranged his evening admission to the Apollo with the manager, a young man come downstate from Chicago to learn the ropes of the movie-theater business. His weak eyesight kept him from the draft and kept the movies on screen out of focus. One way or another, his mother was sure, even with a "Four-Eyes" 4-F man, a living was to be had in the movies, if not on the screen, then behind it.

Beggars, she shouted over her busy shoulder to her customers, and she meant herself, can't be choosers. Some people, he had heard her say to new waitresses, are born to be actors and some are just plain born to be the audience.

She never spoke directly to him.

Anything she had to say to him he overheard her telling someone else.

He got the point. He looked like his father.

She knew their place in life, his and hers, and she vaguely shamed him, too old for baby-sitters and too young for the draft, fending for him until he could fend for himself. He knew she wanted to divorce his father who was somewhere off in the war, but she was too patriotic to write him a "Dear John." So she acted, vague, like she was no longer married, and ambiguous, like her husband was dead, which was a convenience of war and the real hope behind her pretty doll's face.

No matter. He got the point his father had probably always missed. His mother, only fifteen years older than him, was a star, but despite her Hollywood longings during the endless war in Europe and the Pacific, none of the slick succession of young managers ever took her away or even convinced the home office in Chicago to install sound in the silent grind-house of the Apollo.

He longed to walk around the corner of Main and Jefferson to the brightly lit jewel of the Rialto Theater where big Hollywood pictures blazed across the silver screen in Technicolor and thundering sound. But his mother could not arrange things at the Rialto.

So he had sat, stuck in the Apollo, staring at the mute screen, out-of-fashion, out-of-sync, under the clack of the silent projectors. Even before he could read the dialog on screen, he had learned, without even trying, to read lips. He found no contradiction that the written dialog often said one thing while the actors said something else. He began pretending he heard words coming from their moving mouths, not knowing his mother was making arrangements and cooing sounds, with whoever was manager that month, behind the tatty screen where pigeons perched on the high dusty beams of the tired old anachronistic Apollo that everyone said was a tax dodge for a Chicago gangster.

Then quite suddenly, because of the war shortages, everyone said, the Apollo went dark. He was the last one left standing in the empty lobby. At the Bee Hive, his mother sighed something almost grateful about the end of that flea pit that should be torn down for scrap, but within a month the Chicago owners had sent in what his mother, leaning close into her mirror to tweeze her arched eyebrows, called, with a sneer, a Rosie-the-Riveter team of women painters and carpenters who remodeled the old girl, because movies, with the war and all, were bigger box office than ever.

Sitting alone in the balcony of the new Apollo the night of its grand reopening, he thought he had died and gone to an Arabian palace in heaven. The handsome new manager, another 4-F flat-footed floogie with a floy-floy, so his mother, always scoring laughs at the Bee Hive, reported, turned on the new projectors, and with the blaring sound track came the 1944 *Pathé News of the World*: a blitzkrieg montage of world leaders, beauty pageants, faceless troops, crazy inventions, atrocities, circus acts, advice on spotting saboteurs and spies, and fashion-ration tips, narrated by a man's enthusiastic voice, showing pretty young women drawing a line with an eyebrow pencil straight up the middle of the back of their long bare legs to create the illusion of a hosiery seam in a world that had run out of nylons.

Everyone was war-crazy.

He was too young to be of any more use than collecting tin cans and lard from patriotic housewives even in the last desperate year of rationed gas and food shortages. He lived out the world-nightmare in the balcony of the Apollo, the hundred lights of its marquee strategically blacked out. He liked the friendly way the newsreel soldiers, who danced wild athletic jitterbug contests, hugged each other. But the violent exploding newsreel battles scared him. The bombed rubble of destroyed cities frightened him. The long lines of refugees in rags, trudging icy roads past burning tanks, shocked him because they looked like him. The tortured children hung up by their thumbs terrified him. The shot, grotesque, frozen dead bodies petrified him. Each week the newsreels grew more bloodcurdling.

The audience around him was weeping.

The Apollo was sobbing.

Women and men.

And him. Alone in his seat. Crying in the balcony.

He felt there was only one finale to these real news movies between the feature movies. In the mad world of war, both sides were going to kill each other until no one was left. He was so scared the exploding World War, no one could end, was about to spin out of control, about to leap off the screen, leap out of Europe, leap out of the Pacific, that night after night he woke wet with dreams of breathless gagging sickening panic.

The news from the front was so bad, the patrons of the Bee Hive grew strangely quiet.

Behind the counter, even his mother shut up. Then, as if by force of collective will, the terror ended.

Suddenly, in the next wet April spring, the war in Europe was over. Even more suddenly, the following muggy August, the war in the Pacific ended with a surprising blast of radiant energy that made grown-ups cry with gratitude. People, screaming, laughing, joyous, crying, dancing, drinking, celebrating, filled the streets of Peoria, crowded shoulder to shoulder, traffic stopped, tossed toilet paper unrolling like ribbons out of office windows, horns blaring, singing, hugging, kissing, walking across cars stalled in the human surge of happiness into the streets, delirious, unlike anything he had seen, so happy, they were, he was, the fear gone, sitting by himself on top of a car under the marquee of the Apollo Theater whose lights in broad afternoon blazed away in rolling electric waves of American glory and joy and freedom with one word the Apollo manager himself had hung in huge letters: PEACE!

Then one suppertime, later that hot August after VE Day and VJ Day, he sat eating alone at the Bee Hive. It surprised him not at all that the waitress who was his mother just upped and casually vanished.

The last he saw of her she was carting a tray of four lip-sticked soda glasses through the double-doors of the sweltering kitchen.

She disappeared deeper into the cooking steam each time the doors, one fanning in as the other fanned out, clipped each other to shorter and shorter arcs.

Finally, the energy of her push evaporated and the doors seamed to a halt.

It made equal sense later that evening to find a new manager at the Apollo, a stern-faced woman whose steely-clipped hair told him without being asked that she had never heard about arranging his admission. He stood back from her and considered that since he at fifteen knew nothing of life, he must watch the movie-shows to find how people lived. The waitress who was his mother had never talked to him and all that was left of the man she named as his father was an eight-inch red vinyl record with sounds of someone laughing and whistling and trying to sing "Amapola" like he was dying drunk at long distance in a far-off phone booth.

Through the box-office glass he saw the stern-jawed woman point to him under the marquee, as if he were skulking, which he wasn't, not till she pointed at him, and then he could not help starting to skulk he was so embarrassed, because no one had ever pointed at him before, not even his teachers.

No one had ever noticed him.

The woman, who looked like the woman who had been foreman of the Rosie Riveters, said something he could not hear to the ticket girl who squinted her eyes to look at him. She said something back to the woman who pursed her lips, raised her chin, and humphed approval that someone at least knew his face.

He wasn't nobody. He was the audience.

She smiled at him.

Embarrassed, he shoved his hands into his corduroys, but he could not turn his back on the celestial bright of the marquee. He was one of those people who belong inside a movie theater.

In that moment's pause he decided he must arrange things for himself. The woman smiled again and he walked toward her the way a camera approaches a movie actor. The patrons in line, had they watched, could have seen them talking behind the heavy glass doors of the lobby. The woman led him across the new red movie carpet into her office. Ten minutes later he emerged in black slacks striped down the side with satin. He wore a maroon jacket which was a size too large and he carried a flashlight. The woman touched her hands to her hair and pointed him toward the balcony. A living, the waitress who was his mother had said, was to be made in the movies.

REEL TWO
Transformations

He was a bumper, a toucher, one of those kids who can't make it through a store without fingering every pencil and pen and magazine within reach. He grew to expect the clerks to follow him. He wanted one of them, particularly the one whose badge read "Mr. Coates," to collar him and take him to the security room of Clark's Department Store, second-best to Block and Kuhl's Department Store. He wanted desperately for Mr. Coates to accuse him of shoplifting. He wanted the police to be called and he wanted to be stripped down to his fifteen-year-oldness and searched and proven innocent. He wanted people to look at him and see he had never taken anything that was not his, or even laid claim to anything that was. But as it was, no one thought he had anything that was stolen, or even somehow remarkably different, and the very distinguished Mr. Coates never said a word. He simply shot his cuffs efficiently down over the black hair on his thick wrists and ignored the boy he knew as the usher from the aisles of the Apollo Theatre.

He spoke to no one except the moviegoers who asked for the time of the next feature or the direction to the loge or the lounge. Every night of his life with the waitress he had spent at the movies, so it had never occurred to him to ask for a night out when the manager herself made the suggestion. He did not argue. He pulled off his maroon jacket and hung his flashlight in the cabinet inside her office door. She smiled at him and handed him two passes.

"Perhaps," she said, "there is a pretty little someone you can take to the show."

He shook his head. She was deliberately confusing him. He knew she was right, suggesting that he ought to do what other people do. He had watched a million movie dates and it ought to have helped him. But somehow he hadn't the click for it.

He was no dummy.

He had ushered the balcony long enough to watch the back

rows while on screen two lovers kissed in the evening mist and the world stood still except for trains rushing into tunnels and trees bending in the wind and waves crashing on shore. Enough glow spilled from the triangle of light shooting from the small window of the projection booth down to the screen. He had orders to stop anyone from getting fresh in the balcony, but he could never bring himself to flash his light into the snuggles of couples who learned fast enough that when he was the usher no one would bother them. From his station at the top of the balcony aisle, he watched over the audience and stared down at the screen.

During the rolling credits at the end of each feature, he opened the doors. Slightly disheveled couples pulled themselves together, whisking powder off suit-jacket lapels and patting hair into place. They filed out through a long gauntlet of new couples held back by his red velvet chain. Some customers entered the balcony alone. One, a woman who reminded him of his waitress, regularly tipped him ten cents for showing her to the seat he saved for her each Tuesday for the last double feature.

An evening to himself threw him for a loss.

He lingered longer than usual at the Bee Hive, where the owner, sorry for him that the waitress who was his mother had disappeared into the steam of the kitchen, had allowed him to arrange his own discount meal ticket.

He pinched three paper straws from bottom to top. He alternated the pinches at right angles one above the other. He said she-loves-me and she-loves-me-not and never once wondered who the she was as long as she did more than she didn't. He reached for a fourth straw, but the waitress, who was not at all like his mother, playfully slapped his hand.

"Those cost money," she said. She pulled his empty plate away. Her name was Crystal. "More java?" she asked.

He looked at her and felt the two passes in his pocket. He smiled and she poured the strong boiled coffee up to the green ring around the outside lip of his heavy china cup.

She looked possible.

A wisp of blonde hair escaped from her black snood. Her lips were red as Technicolor. She looked like she could use a movie.

He smiled again.

"Want some pie?" she asked, knowing he missed her teasing double meaning.

He decided to ask her. He could take her past the box office, through the lobby, and up the stairs to the balcony. Unless maybe she wouldn't go to the balcony. Unless, maybe, this first time, they ought to sit in the loge.

"Well, do you, or don't you?" she said. Her hand made a petulant little fist on her aproned hip.

He smiled and held up his passes.

She stepped toward him. "Gee," she said, bussing up his glass of bent straws.

He handed them closer to her.

She was definitely balcony.

"You work there, don'tcha."

He tried staring directly into her eyes, but she looked straight at the passes. Like a hypnotist, he waved them back and forth and closer to her face.

She blinked, took the passes from his hand, and kissed them a light hello as she breezed them into her pocket full of tips. "Thanks," she said. "Here I always thought you were a pretty odd guy, always standing in the back of the balcony, watching everything that goes on up there. Shows how wrong a girl can be."

He felt the blood rush to his face. He wanted to say that was not what he had meant at all. The passes were not her tip. His breath seemed gone and the walls of the Bee Hive seemed to split at the seams and fall back and she kept wiping the counter around his coffee cup as if he were her best customer ever.

"I spent my last dollar on this really cute gold ankle bracelet at the dimestore," she said. "It was a dollar-nineteen, but I split everything with my best girlfriend Angela."

He reached for his coffee to hide his face and make it small behind the cup as he tilted it to his mouth.

"I'll get to wear it tonight since I got these two tickets to the show."

He set his cup down in the saucer and wished for a director who would yell "Cut!"

"Here's a piece of pie," she whispered, sliding a fork into his fingers. "I'll forget it on your check."

He slid backwards off the counter stool.

"You don't want the pie?"

He pulled the correct change from his black usher's slacks and laid it on the counter. He slipped from the Bee Hive into the street.

"Brother, what a jerk!" she said, just loud enough for him to doubt he heard it.

Down the block, under the Apollo marquee, the crowd from the early show eddied out to the sidewalk on Main Street. Men with girls on their arms paused in mid-stride to light up. Couples swirled out the doors around the obedient row of patrons waiting entry to the next double feature. Clusters of moviegoers slowed him. He pushed his way through. He saw a man in a gold gabardine sport shirt. He accidentally on purpose bumped into him. The man said, "Watch it, kid!" Overhead two bulbs had burnt out in the marquee. They broke the illusion of the long running line of light.

No one ever noticed that he walked into people he needed to touch. Bumping was his only intimacy. Since his mother had disappeared into the kitchen of the Bee Hive, no one had come up the stairs above the Pour House to their small room with the single sink, the In-a-Door bed, and the old horsehair sofa where he had slept before she had vanished. No one touched him but the barber at the Barber College where he sat high in a chair every Saturday, between mirrors curving off to infinity, watching his hair clippings fall onto the sheet pinned tight around his neck and draped over his shoulders and arms and knees like a tent hiding his hands in his lap. So he had settled for bumps, as if could nudge off anonymous elbows and backs atoms and energy, as if he could learn through a bump, which strangers thought the accident of a clumsy boy, how it felt with someone else. His eye was a camera snapping fantasy people for footage he projected in his head late at night, laid flat out and alone between the sheets of the Murphy bed, listening to the shouts and singing downstairs in the Pour House, holding his private self hard in hand.

But this night he purposely touched no one. He darted through the doors of the Apollo, waved to the doorman, and headed straight up the stairs to the balcony. He folded himself into the last row of seats. He slouched down on the middle of his back and hooked the indentation in each kneecap onto the curved back rim of the seat in front of him. The empty screen reflected the soft glow of the intermission houselights. Every ten feet down both side walls hung amber globes, each with a hand-painted lady, bathing identically, her towel draped like bunting across her torso.

He had never seen the balcony so empty. A good double bill kept the few Monday night moviegoers on the main floor. He heard them settling into their seats. The murmur of their conversation climbed up the moorish lattice stenciled on the walls. Their voices gathered to a vast hum under the domed ceiling where violet light hidden indirectly behind the lip of the lower circumference of the dome mixed their human voices into a breathy whisper. He fixed his eyes on the hypnotic purple light that grew iridescent as the other house lights dimmed. The sharp light from the projection booth cut over his head, but the movie that night held no interest. He did not even take his eyes off the violet dome to look down at the screen as the violet and purple dome melted to lavender.

Some sense in his body told him he was about to defy gravity.

Only the crick in his neck and the pressure from the inner-spring cushion under his back seemed to hold him in his seat.

He wrapped his arms through the arms of the seat.

Staring up at the soft lavender light, he lost time and direction.

A moment of panic swept through him followed by ineffable pleasure.

He imagined himself falling up, up, up into the pool of violet light, floating unnoticed above the moviegoers, lazy and dreamy, until the intimate unseen hand, inflating and then letting go the neck of a balloon, reddened the violet, shocking the audience who craned their necks and pointed to see him ricocheting insanely off the ceiling and walls, growing smaller and smaller until he disappeared.

He had never been chloroformed but he felt it was much like this.

The unseen hand lifted, and a dark mass next to him, almost invisible to his eyes blinded with the dome's lavender brightness, rose softly and moved, he could not be bothered in his swoon to remember, either up or down the aisle. He woke from what he had recognized as not sleep. Like a man who starts suddenly during a sermon, he looked left and right to see if anyone had noticed.

He did not know how much time had passed or even the difference between what might have happened and what he might have imagined. The balcony was still nearly empty. He untangled his arms and sat up straight in his seat. The second feature had begun, and he felt with little curiosity that the sticky wet on his undershorts was growing chill near the open zipper that he had not opened. Ten rows ahead of him sat the nearest patron. It was the lady who usually tipped him the ten cents. Five seats from her he spied Crystal and, he guessed, her friend Angela. In the first row, his feet propped up on the balcony railing, he was sure he saw Mr. Coates sitting in a blue halo of cigarette smoke. When had these people arrived? Then he remembered the door at the top of the aisle opening and closing during his doze, and he thought no more about it, because he was used to the way people appeared and disappeared.

REEL THREE
Some nights you wake up screaming

After he graduated from school and his job at the Apollo, he found other theaters, other cities. He moved upstate to Chicago. The movies widened from 35mm to 70mm Cinemascope. They left him breathless. He panicked the first time he noticed it. He panicked and gulped in a quart of air. He had sat through a feature and a half before he realized that he was forgetting to breathe. He had thought everyone breathed automatically, but somehow he was forgetting and he panicked. He stood up in his balcony seat and walked up the steps of the long carpeted aisle. He felt he would never make it. He vowed he must stop going up to the balconies. He pushed open the doors to the lobby with a great effort and brushed the arm of a blonde woman carrying a medium popcorn and a large Coke. His gasping lungs filled with her raggy scent. He felt sick. How could he forget to breathe? He had sloshed her Coke. He left her damning him in his wake. Outside, down the street from the running lights of the marquee, he leaned against a mailbox and looked up at the cold moon rising over Lake Michigan. He wanted ten deep breaths, but he counted only six before the freezing night air hurt his throat. An elevated train rattled past overhead. He shivered and turned from the moon to the marquee.

An usher had climbed up a tall wooden ladder with a box full of large plastic letters. One week's bill gave way to another as the usher slid the letters around on their wire tracks. While the usher struggled with the film titles, gibberish hung on the Bryn Mawr Theater's glowing marquee. He remembered that a couple years before it had been himself up on such a ladder, spelling and spacing words for everyone to read. The flush of altitude sickness from the balcony burned in his gut and he turned, on that barricaded edge of not-knowing that is the edge of self-revelation, and walked away.

"Moonlight," he wrote on a scrap of paper in his pocket, "has the same believability as black-and-white film. The moon washes the color from everything. Landscapes and faces lose their tint. Everything becomes believable within the range of gray."

Even one's self.

As a part-time projectionist, living on popcorn, he had worked his way through college and into graduate school and had taken to writing while he walked, insomniac through lonely nights, hanging out in tiled coffee shops with fluorescent waitresses. Sometimes when there was snow blanketing and silencing the Near North Side of Chicago, the night waitresses would have mercy on him and for his dime pour him bottomless cups of coffee and call him Shakespeare because of his books and his glasses, but he would not really think of them as real until later when he thanked them ever-so because the air was cold on his shivering hand as he emptied his bladder under the El, signing his melting yellow autograph into banks of pure white snow. What he wrote on paper was secret and wonderful. He kept it, at the coffee-shop counters, covered with one hand and only read it himself when back in his rented room that was not unlike the room that his mother the waitress had so long before abandoned.

He could no longer remember her face and it disturbed him slightly, because the face of anyone named Helen should have launched a thousand ships. He could identify the profile of a long-since-dead Hollywood star at a glance, but her face had given way to his last shot of the back of her head disappearing in the kitchen steam of the Bee Hive.

"Movies," he wrote thinking of his life and her, "are spun out of talking heads. The way the physiological eye prefers light to darkness, the psychological eye selects face over scenery when contained in the same frame." He tucked that note into the drawer with the layers of his random writings. "The camera-work provides the psychology of the movie."

He hoped someday he would start bolt upright in his balcony seat during an *Eyes-and-Ears-of-the-World* newsreel when he would recognize her face modeling clothes in a New York fashion show. Or maybe her face would come back to him as she straddled a horse diving into a tank at Atlantic City. She would surprise him that way and she would be immortal. He was sure she would remember that a living, and more than a living, could be arranged in the movies. She was out there among the stars.

REEL FOUR
Somehow between features he became a teacher

Time passed. Cinema was everything. He had touched no one and no one had touched him, not counting that warm hand under the dark lavender light of that balcony. In his mind the fear had loomed large that he would live only to thirty, but he was five years overdue and no longer bothering to wonder why he hadn't been taken or why he had not made love. He seemed veined and delicate as a night-blooming orchid. His eyes, which in childhood had been a deep blue, had faded into the uncanny washed-out hue usually found in beach people and ranchers exposed to constant brightness. Light from the silver screen had burned like radiation into his sockets.

Voices told him, advised him, "You can always teach," so for years he taught literature and creative writing. In his lectures, *Leaves of Grass* was a shooting script and Whitman's montage esthetic anticipated Edison's technology; Dickens' editing style generated Eisenstein's; and his punchline for *Ulysses* explained the novel's fluid complexities by revealing that while writing his masterwork, Joyce worked in Dublin as a projectionist. In his writing classes he argued his hippie peacenik students out of turgid undergraduate melodramas about stolen sex and repentant suicide and death in Vietnam. He tutored them into screenplays personal in matter and disciplined in technique. His colleagues regarded him indulgently, urging him over an occasional sherry to invent courses with titles like "Film Interpretation," "Novels into Film," or "Movies and the Liberal Arts." But always he shook his head.

"Why not?" they always asked. "Is the novel any less pleasurable when read as a class assignment?"

Always he smiled pleasantly and excused himself from the hearty company of them and their cheery wives. He was an alien they tried to corral. If he would not invent their courses, then they would have him married, and when married, they would have him father children. Somehow he had given no hostages to fortune; no wife begged him, for the sake of the family food and shelter, to capitulate his secret cinema pleasures to their university schedule. He was a private person and his privacy kept him free. No one could exploit what they did not know. His privacy was, before all, his right.

"Perhaps," one faculty wife whispered, "he abstains from the sexual revolution entirely. There is that rarity called chastity, I believe."

She had glimpsed something of the ideal fire deep in him that gave color to his cheeks.

The wife of his Department Chairman took his arm and pulled him aside. "My husband," she said, "finds you amazingly droll. We're so happy you joined our little group of eccentrics. I mean, that's what teaching is all about, isn't it?"

He watched her tilt her glass to her lips. Her drink was gone but for the ice which stuck for a moment to the bottom of the upturned cylinder. Her braceleted wrist jarred the glass sharply to break the wet freeze. The cold avalanche of cubes slid toward her lips which parted and bit off the advancing ice.

"You know," she said, "you are the still water that runs deep."

So he became water and flowed away from her, in flight from all the pursuers of his life.

REEL FIVE
In mummy movies, every diamond has a curse

Waiting in the box-office line of the Campus Theater, he worried about himself. He was older, not suddenly, but slowly as in a series of dissolves, conscious that the youth culture, wild in the streets, trusted no one over thirty; but he hardly looked middle-aged, he was sure of it. His hair had thinned a bit, but nothing that some artful combing and men's hairspray wouldn't fix, unless he got caught in a headwind; and the skin around his eyes had wrinkled no more than to a moviegoer's permanent squint. His boyish weight had maintained under the discipline of popcorn, no butter and no salt. He was vainly prideful he had not gotten fat. Perhaps he was, like Monty Clift, one of those neurasthenic cases he had read about.

He no longer climbed up to the balconies. With each paid admission in newer and stranger theaters, he sat closer and closer to the silver screen, not trying to find once again, he told himself, the unseen hand in the lavender light. He sat absolutely alone always staring at the screen, never looking left or right, no matter who came and went in the seats around him. Sometime, he feared, he would walk into a theatre, glide to the front rows, and be sucked up into the screen, lost forever in the 2000-watt glow of the Cinemascope feature presentation. Only his notes, theory on cinema scrawled in the dark, would remain strewn between the seats. No one, not even the janitor, would be curious enough to read them or wonder where the man in the first row had disappeared. He panicked and felt his breath go shallow. He shed his coat and retreated back into the lobby.

The small Campus Theatre was an art house co-featuring foreign films with experimental underground films. The hippie audience was intense, even reverential in the lobby, intoning the names of drugs and directors, congregating around the pot of free coffee. He waited behind a petite young woman who blocked his way to the cups. A wreath of flowers crowned her long blonde hair so straight it looked ironed. She was all bracelets and beads and madras. With her middle finger she dabbed repeatedly at the surface of her steaming cup. He grew impatient. The next feature, Bertolucci's *Last Tango in Paris,* was about to begin. He cleared his throat. He coughed.

"Something's floating in my coffee," she said, turning to him. "Like wax or oil or something."

She was really quite lovely in her motley layers of scarves and beads.

He smiled coolly and placed his own cup in its plastic holder and held it under the tap. He pulled the spigot down and the coffee bubbled black in the cone-bottom of the cup. He teased it to the rim. His hand was steady as he raised the steaming cup to his lips.

"It's wax," she said. "Definitely wax from the cup. It won't hurt you."

He looked at her. He was embarrassed. They seemed to be standing together as much as the other couples in the lobby. Three of his literature students passed by. "Good evening, Professor," one of them said. The other two smiled. He moved away from the woman, who was hardly more than a girl, and nodded to his students over his coffee. She moved with him. He moved again. She followed. They seemed to be dancing in the middle of the lobby. The students pretended not to notice.

"I'm NanSea SunStream. It's a mantra. I'm an Aries. I chant. Enchanted, I'm sure." She extended her hand, reaching for his which he did not offer. She recouped with so gracefully circular a gesture she seemed always to have intended to pull her lustrous blonde hair back behind her ear. "Something tells me you're a Gemini. With a moon in Leo. And, maybe, a Scorpio rising sign."

Music from the screen sounded the Main Title. He turned nervously toward the door, turned back to her, shrugged and smiled and left her standing. He found his way down the aisle to the front. This was his fourth viewing of the movie unreeling on the screen. He knew exactly what would happen from beginning to end and he found comfort in that. Occasionally a film might break or the reels become confused, but overall he enjoyed an order in cinema he did not feel with people. On the screen everything was arranged and directed.

"Here's some sugar," NanSea said, slipping into the seat beside him. "Better take one lump since you half-drank it."

Behind him someone shushed them.

She whispered. "How can you drink that varnish? I couldn't sit back there thinking of you drinking that. I couldn't keep my mind on the film. I've seen it before."

He set his coffee cup on the floor. He knew people like her added lysergic acid to sugar cubes.

"What's that?" She pointed to his notes. "I'll bet you're a movie critic. Wow! I should be quiet so you can concentrate. It's like I understand. I mean, one of the places I hang out is the campus. This is so far out!"

He tried to will her away, but her blonde presence shimmered luminous next to him. Her flawless young face glowed in reflections from the screen. She could have been in the film. He leaned to the opposite arm. He could not help studying her profile that was so like the winsome Gish sisters. She leaned forward, cupped her hand around the lighter she held to a half-smoked joint. "Want a hit?" she asked. He shook his head. "More for me then." She inhaled in short, sharp huffs, and exhaled in measured puffs. He, who had to remember to breathe, envied her even as she relaxed down to perfect silence.

He wished her gone and gathered his notes together. He long ago had ceased bumping into people to discover how it would be with them and he certainly had no recognizable desire to be with her.

"Hey," she said. "You going?"

He was already near the end of the row.

"What would a girl like me," she said loud enough for him to hear, "want with a square like you?"

As he neared the aisle seat, a large old woman sitting in a pile of shopping bags said, "Why don't you two fight at home!"

He escaped to the men's room and locked himself in the middle stall. No one could reach him or see him. He sat and lamented the broken sanctity of even this small neighborhood university theatre.

"Somehow," he jotted into his notes, "the shrines are all broken and my Lady Cinema is dead." For a long while he sat, not hearing the door banging open and closed, nor the sound of the urinals flushing. Finally he looked to the stall wall and saw his initials written on an earlier visit. It pleased him that proof remained that he had been there before and saddened him that he would never come there again. He wet his finger and rubbed hard on the ink of his signature. The rubbing made a squeaking sound and caused a shoe in the stall next to his to tap up and down, moving toward him.

He recognized the sexual Morse code. He gasped for air. He pulled himself together and escaped quickly up the stairs, through the lobby, pulling on his coat—Oh, Mr. Coates!—in the middle of the street. He was miles and cities and years away from the arrangements made for him at the Bee Hive and the Apollo and he could only go home for the night.

Behind him, he heard NanSea SunStream calling after him. "Hey! Wait! I didn't mean it. You're cool. You're different. You want to come over for some wine..."

He took a deep breath.

"...some music..."

He walked faster.

"...or something like whatever."

He ran.

REEL SIX
The man who loved movies

Why he wondered, do people believe that a man who is not married is available to anyone? No one understands vocation anymore. No one accepts dedication. No one believes in chastity.

He sat upstairs in the old house he had bought, locked safely behind the door of a closet large enough to be a small study. Snippets and yards of film footage clipped on fine wires were strung the length of the room: movie millimeters of eight and super-eight and sixteen and thirty-five and wide-screen seventy. The air was acrid with acetone editing glue. Its smell intoxicated him. A twelve-yard sequence of a Technicolor musical-comedy was wrapped around his neck, its ends trailing down his front like a priest's ritual stole. The hot light of his hand-editor had dried the moisture in his nostrils, chapped his lips, and wrinkled his forehead. Its glare threw his shadow huge against the wall-size screen that pulled down over the only door to the hidden room. Nightly he illuminated his celluloid strips the way monks once lovingly tooled manuscripts in lonely cells. He had only to arrange the sequences snipped from this movie and that movie into his own unreeling vision of what a film should be. Life, his waitress had told him was to be had in the movies, so he had waited, waited his whole life, for the return of the unseen hand in the lavender light.

REEL SEVEN
The transfiguration of the spieler

In his own time and by his own decision, he approached his colleagues. He smiled and was almost deferential as he made appointment to lecture in their Departmental Colloquium. Late nights he brooded in the very auditorium where in no time at all his much anticipated talk would be given. As the hour approached, he gathered his reels about him and taxied to the university theater. The seats and aisles and stairs were jammed. Students mixed with faculty. Even people from the local Town-and-Gown society arrived to hear him speak.

When he walked to the podium, the audience hushed expectantly. A slight murmur washed through the balcony and died. He raised his hand. The projectionist dimmed the lights and rolled the silent film.

His movie, ten-years-in-the-editing, was a montage, no, a barrage of hot light, choice sequences, brilliant frames, subliminal images, and remix snippets of found footage he had carefully scratched with pins, streaked with bleach, and hand-colored with multi-hued dyes.

Facing his audience, he stood in the center of the silent screen, looked, in fact, to be part of the screen as the images reflected off his pale skin and white clothing. The audience shifted and whispered in their seats. They expected from him something new, *avant garde*, possibly weird, maybe shocking, and hopefully wonderful. Somewhere an undergraduate girl giggled nervously.

"The silents," he began to speak into his lavaliere mike, "were never silent. Prosperous theatres featured orchestras. Small theatres had pianos and the clack of the projectors. Ethnic theatres hired monologuists to translate the written English titles for the neighborhood. The spielers, as they were called, freely ad-libbed, very freely ad-libbed, many a dull title and plot into gracious wit and good humor. They added dimension to the flat screen."

Only the shadow cast by his body on the screen helped differentiate him among the fast flash of images from Edison, Lumiere, Melies, Lange, Von Sternberg, and Riefenstahl to Brakhage, Anger, Deren, Warhol, Lean, Wilder, Hitchcock, and Bergman.

"In sixty minutes of film," his voice boomed through the theatre, "you actually watch twenty-seven minutes of total darkness. But the mind chooses to see only the remaining thirty-three minutes of light. I want to know what is between those frames, what is in that twenty-seven-minute darkness, what secret of life lies just out of reach in the flickers between those frames."

He began to pelt the audience with data.

"The very form of cinema is absurd. No picture moves. Still frame connects to still frame. The eye cancels the darkness, cancels the stasis. The brain aches for motion. The body aches for life."

He no longer heard the doors of the theatre auditorium opening and closing.

"The first movie audiences in Paris screamed and stampeded as Lumiere's train rushed toward them."

He dropped his arms to his sides and stared up directly into the projector light beaming down hard as grace upon him.

"We each," he said, "make our own movie."

He no longer turned his head. He panned it left and right. He no longer walked toward the stage edge. He tracked. The blink of his eyes became the click of a single frame. He blinked them quickly and the audience became a flicker. His talking became a whirr and his tongue turned to film feeding out of his face.

The gallery of his colleagues and the audience of his students rose to their feet cheering his passion. The applause continued at the reception arranged by his department.

"Very nice," the chairman's wife said, "very nice indeed. You really should develop that film course my husband wants so much. But come," she said, arranging the knot of his tie, "you simply must meet everyone."

Silent Mothers, Silent Sons

Nanny Pearl, whose name was Mary Day, was eighty-four years old on October 2, 1972. When she was sixty-five, her husband, Bart, who had been a teacher in St. Louis when they married at St. Roch's church, smoked his last cigarette and died at sixty-six, the night before Saint Valentine's Day, 1954. When she was born in St. Louis in 1888, the priest baptized her Mary Pearl Lawler.

When she was seventy-eight, her son who was a priest, shaved himself for early Mass in his rectory bathroom, clutched at his chest, and fought for the heart inside him. She was his parish housekeeper. She heard him fall. He died in her arms.

He had been a military chaplain in World War II. *Life* magazine, documenting heroes, had published photographs of him administering the Last Rites to dying infantrymen during the Battle of the Bulge. He was famous. His name was John Bartholomew Day. When he was buried, Governor Otto Kerner led the dignitaries to his gravesite next to his father, a hundred yards from President Lincoln's Tomb in Springfield, Illinois. He was fifty-four years old.

By then she had two real names. The parishioners of St. Cabrini's Church called her either Father Day's Mother or Mrs. Day. Close friends called her Pearl. Eight months later, when she was seventy-nine, her second son, Patrick, who was also famous as the owner of the swank Patsy's, "A Bit of Dublin Pub & Cafe" in St. Louis, turned yellow, perhaps from an ill-washed glass in his own kitchen, grew hepatic, and died. He too was fifty-four. That very same day, her grandson-in-law, a young St. Louis policeman, seated in his squad car accidentally discharged his own service revolver, and killed himself. He was twenty-five. Seven years later, when her youngest son Harry, who was not at all famous, died, he was fifty-four.

For a woman who survives her husband there is a word; for a parent who survives her children, language has no name.

Nanny Pearl lived through the unspeakable and when she was eighty-four years old, her three boys dead, her two daughters at odds, she was swept up by time and history.

*

The sign on the red brick wall read *St. Michael's Garden Floor Nursing Home*. St. Mike's Garden Floor was an ice floe of chrome and Kleenex and bathrooms close at hand. Simple solutions to complex lives. Old women were separated from old men. Deafness was a blessing from the sounds of ancient lips sipping noodles from cups of good hot soup. Blindness crept like a nun dispensing milky cataracts, blurring the veranda rows of former persons in whose mouths fear had replaced wisdom. "Please, just don't hurt me." Clarity was timeworn, lost, or drugged on schedule.

It was ten in the morning, November 29, 1972, when the Ace Ambulance Service, unimpressive without its siren, routine without its flashers, pulled up the long macadam sweep to St. Mike's. Inside the ambulance, swinging up the drive, being delivered, Nanny Pearl was mounded under sheets, swathed in them, re-babied by them. Her mouth was set. She said nothing. Her eyes knew all. She remembered kidnappings as famous as Lindberg's baby. She read about the new worldwide fad of skyjackings. Both were like rehearsals of this ambulance ride. She remembered full well what had happened to Katharine Anne's old Granny Weatherall, but this was personal, about herself.

"Hang on tight, Nanny," the young attendant said through the open rear door. He pulled her stretcher towards himself.

She thought two things: first, that with his kind brown eyes he was exactly like the young men calling and courting sixty-five years before, except he was colored that high octoroon that through a squint can pass for dark Italian; and, second, that lying down in an ambulance was like a ride in a hearse. "God, soon can't be soon enough."

The second attendant, groomed like a handsome Irish police cadet, helped unload her. Behind the disguise of his perfectly clipped moustache, he was very young, so young in fact that his previous job was stocking shelves at a St. Louis supermarket. He carried the number "466" carefully folded in the pocket over his heart because he had been lucky in that year's National Draft Lottery. With a serious job, if his number didn't come up, he might not be shipped off to Vietnam. He was too innocent to know that gaining paramedical training increased his eligibility.

"I shouldn't be here," she thought. The Receiving Nurse tucked the sheet tighter around Nanny's wattles of chin. A wave of claustrophobia sucked away her breath. She made little gulping noises. The Receiving Nurse seemed to understand. She pulled open the sheets, massaged the old woman's hands, and laid her delicate arms carefully outside the blankets. "There you go, Nanny," she said. The nurse, like the ambulance attendants, was very young. Everyone was very young. They were all strangers. They were not her family, not her children, not her grandchildren.

"Why didn't I notice? My children, especially my girls, kept me young. Until they didn't," she thought. Time had slipped into the future so gradually, then all those deaths so quickly. "My God! John. Father John, my son. Sweet Jesus, I was once the mother of a priest."

Her place had slipped, or her staunchly Catholic family had slipped, from the cold mists of Ireland to the breathless humidity of St. Louis. They had receded glacially, her grandparents and parents and brothers, evaporating into thin air, leaving her behind, alone, their dependable rock, ancient as the stone Burren her grandparents had left behind. Their nostalgic immigrant stories, often beginning in Celtic myth, always ended with the promise of one day taking her to Ireland. She had been born in St. Louis, but she knew in her soul's eye the vastness of the Burren's monumental swirl of limestone karsts, smoothed by ice and elements and time, east of Galway, northwest of County Tipperary, as familiar to her as if she herself had walked the rocks and furze of the Burren in her own bare feet.

Nanny Pearl was alone.

Her children and her children's children knew nothing, cared nothing, really, how the bridge of her life spanned from horse carts to jet rides. What did they remember of her own parents, her own four brothers, her husband's ancestors, her girlhood friends from St. Louis like Mary Hale who had given her a porcelain nut bowl on her wedding day?

Odd. But no matter. She held them all in her heart that would not not not quit beating.

She could not, would not be bitter. Had not the Blessed Mother survived her own Son's death? Through joys and sorrows, with her crystal rosary blessed by Pope Pius XII in her hand, she had held her fiercely independent head high with as much Irish pluck as luck.

Even with her men in so many wars, especially the one in Vietnam which she refused to discuss because she did not under-stand it, no one had died violently. Except for that policeman her granddaughter had married, they had all slipped away so quickly she could do nothing: not with all her womanly love of parents and husband and children.

"Don't bother about me," she had always said to her husband and children. "I take care of myself by taking care of you."

But time turned life into a vaudeville slip on a banana peel.

Quickly. That's how control is lost.

Slowly. Control is lost slowly too.

Slowly, then quickly. That was how her daughter, Nora, had gained the upper hand. That girl, herself sixty-two, had gradually, carefully, then quickly, at last, taken over everything. It had hap-pened so easily.

"Here, mother, let me do this."

Too polite to resist, she yielded—but secretly never surrendered to the tiny manipulations daughters contrive to coerce their mothers, as she had coerced her own—not to Nora's first persuasions after her husband Bart had died making her the widow all wives presume they'll be, but after her son, the priest, who was her very life, who was supposed to have outlived her and protected her and buried her, had died in her arms with the water in the shower still running.

"Mother, let me," her daughter, Nora, had said when the arthritis pained.

"Fool that I was, I let her. My God, John, I let her."

A second Receiving Nurse read efficiently through the old woman's charts. "Husband's name. Let's see, Nanny," she tested. "Can you remember your husband's name?"

"You fool," she thought. "He's deader than a door nail."

Suddenly, for the first time, she realized her sweet sweet husband had been gone so many years that she no longer talked to him. Instead, it was to her son John, the parish priest, with whom she had lived until he died, that she addressed her plaintive whispers. She felt herself blush. "God forgive me! How I loved you, Batty," she thought.

"Bart," she said. "My husband's name was Bartholomew. Everyone called him Batty." His name came hard to her throat. "God took him a lifetime ago." The wife she had been remembered the husband to whom she had gladly given up her first control when she gave up loving anything more than him, and then for him, loving his children, their children, more than herself.

"And the number of your children?"

"Will you call them for me?"

The nurse cocked a curious look.

"That's a joke, missy. I may be old, but I don't have Old-Timers' Disease. When you x-ray inside this haggis-baggis, you'll find a girl who's still seventeen."

"We're very busy today." The nurse smiled crisply. "How many children? You remember, Nanny."

You don't forget your children, she thought. One way or another you always remember them. The good things and the bad. The youngest, her baby, with his secrets, so different from her two older dead sons who had been so close, born ten months apart, so good as boys, definitely easier to raise than the girls, her two daughters, odd in their relationship as sisters.

Nora was three years older than Margaret whom everyone called Megs.

Evenings, double-dating, her daughters would return from a dance and lie across her and Batty's bed telling stories about their best friend Beulah Draper and how smoothly Joe O'Riley danced, and arguing who was cuter Nora's beau, Bill, or Megs' new boy-friend, Georgie, who earned four letters his senior year at Routt High School in Jacksonville.

Under their gaiety, even then in the hard times of 1935, she had sensed Nora's careless way of borrowing Meg's clothes, the easy way Nora slipped out of the supper dishes to sit before her vanity playing with her makeup. She had always told her children, "Think good of yourself or no one else will." But Nora only invoked the first part of her advice.

"Nora," Beulah Draper had once told Nanny, who had been "Mrs. Day" then, "certainly can shop for a bargain."

The three girls had been selling hose at Woolworth's Dime Store at ten cents an hour.

"Nora knows," Mrs. Day and her husband liked to quote the Irish, "the price of everything."

"And the value of very little," Mr. Day added. He made no secret, spoiling both his daughters, that he favored his younger.

Megs, much to Nora's chagrin, had been born on her parents' eighth wedding anniversary, July 12, 1919. Megs had made that date an even higher family feast by marrying Georgie on July 12, 1938. Nora was her bridesmaid and Harry, Georgie's best man.

Her brother, ordained April 24, 1938, officiated at the wedding at Our Saviour's Church. It was Megs' nineteenth birthday and their parents' twenty-seventh anniversary. Nora, always in competition, couldn't top her younger sister's timing. Nanny stood back from the rivalry. She trusted Megs to invent ways to outwit Nora, usually with the help of the three brothers who nicknamed Nora, Boss Lady. Everyone always said Megs was such a peppy tomboy and clever little miss as a girl and a woman.

Odd fate and bad luck: she had lost that younger girl too. Good as she was, Megs, vowing through sickness and health, had become absorbed into her own husband's chronic illnesses. Who would have thought that Georgie, so strong as a young man, so like another son to her, would be struck down so young and linger and linger, unlike her three sons who dropped dead without warning.

Maybe Batty had been right, always joking about an ancient Druid curse on the Celtic descendents of the High Kings of Munster. Nanny had laughed him off. She had heard the same blarney from her own grandfather. "I'm telling you, Mary Pearl Lawler, a hundred and fifty kingdoms there were and Ireland hardly bigger than Iowa and much more interesting."

She finally stopped laughing the year Batty was diagnosed with a brief blood affliction, an episode of Blue Blood, "Hemoragica Purpura," that Dr. Carrier said, quite seriously, usually ailed only people of royal ancestry, but then, Dr. Carrier, flipping away his diagnosis, said, "Try and find a Mick who doesn't claim royal blood."

"Five children," Nanny said to the St. Mike's nurse. "Two boys. Two girls. And last, another boy." She studied the starched young woman who had yet to learn the gamble of parenthood.

Nanny examined her conscience about her last and only remaining son, the one Batty had named Harry after a hunting dog he had once owned. "Crazy Harry." She said the name and hated herself for laughing at her baby the way they had all laughed in parochial school and high school at "Crazy Harry," the life of any party, fox-trotting with a lamp shade on his head, a practical joker who would do anything for a laugh. She loved him immensely because her mother's heart knew all the Whoopie Cushions in the world couldn't assuage his hidden pain. Five years after the war, in 1950, she found she had lost even him, just as his wife and children lost him, living at the bottom of a bottle where he hid the big secret he covered with his antic, diverting looniness.

Somehow it was all linked to the way Harry had wrestled with his boyhood chums. She hadn't known that his affliction, as she had always thought of it, had even existed out in the world, much less in him, until she grew older and wiser about the world's silence and secrets.

She knew finally.

Deep down she knew he knew.

Maybe Batty had been as right about the Druid curse as he had been about the Blue Blood affliction on kings and queens, blood sweating out of their pores.

"God, forgive me if I caused it."

But, between them, between her and Harry, the knowledge went unspoken so long it became impossible for either of them to speak of it. Not all sins are committed; some silences are sins of omission. She skirted the secret, wanting advice, but Harry's secret was a word that could not be said, even by her son, the priest who, despite years of hearing confessions, would say nothing to enlighten his mother how she might help her youngest son.

She regretted that she had never had any control there with Harry. Mothers didn't discuss then what mothers, like her grand-daughters, discussed easily what they watched on their endless television talk shows and soaps. She, usually so outspoken, regretted she had let Harry's secret, remaining unspoken, cut distance between her and her baby. If she had only said something, maybe something positive about making the best out of the bad deal of it, maybe Harry would not have turned to the real Irish curse of whiskey.

Maybe it was fate.

"If you believe in luck," she thought, "you have to believe in fate."

The St. Mike's staff was rolling her gurney again.

"I shouldn't be here."

Ceilings of corridors. Light fixtures. Sounds of efficient care. Lives prolonged at all cost. She found it impossible to see above the rail of the gurney which wheeled down the hallways. Straight. Right. Right. A left turn. She had to remember the directions so she could escape. She could walk slowly but well. Again the claustrophobia sucked the air in tight past her lips. She felt the fear of the foreign. She recognized in herself the fears of her grandparents, shipping out from Cork in 1838, seven years before the Potato Famine, from County Tipperary for "Americay."

She was headed for the final emigration to parts unknown.

Her grandparents and her parents had been young enough to invent new lives in St. Louis. Her four brothers had worked building the Eads Bridge across the Mississippi from St. Louis to Illinois. They, all of them in her family, blessed with blarney, knew how to talk their charming way in, or get out fast if they had to. But in those earlier days of fine vigor, none of them was old the way she was.

She had lost her gift of gab when she could not speak to Harry. Her silence then had cursed her later.

Her spirit was willing. She truly felt herself no more than seventeen. But her flesh was weak. Her once-beautiful hands ached. Her arthritis was worse. Her twenty-eight finger-knuckle joints had turned crooked as stone cold pain. In the mirror, she feared time had turned her into an old Irish hag. In truth, because, weekly at the hairdresser's, and nightly, anointing her skin with Pompeian Olive Oil, she had cared for herself with more pride than vanity, she had aged into a dignified beauty who had risen as high as a Catholic woman can aspire: she had been the mother of a priest.

In the summer of 1910, long before she was Nanny Pearl, when she was still the cheery young Mary Pearl, she had taken the river boat up from St. Louis to Kampsville, Illinois. Her cousins, the Stillbrinks, had invited her to visit for her last summer before her marriage to Francis Devine. But something uncontrollable, an infinitesimal intuition, heading north up-river made her unsure that her love for Francis was deep enough for a lifetime bound in the sacrament of marriage.

At the Kampsville Landing, Cecilia Stillbrink, with her new husband, Cap Stillbrink, had noticed. Something. Mary Pearl seemed flushed, pinker than usual to her pink cousins.

"Pearl," Cecilia said, "Mary Pearl Devine. Mrs. Francis Devine. Oh! Mr. and Mrs. Francis Devine request the pleasure of your company...." Cecilia chattered on hoping to tease small virginal gossip from the first of her cousins to be engaged to be married.

Nanny remembered how odd she felt upon arriving at Kampsville.

As if something unusual were about to happen.

Cecilia annoyed her about as much as a fly.

Yet a fly could spoil the ointment. "Not now, Cecilia dear. I promise to tell you everything."

"Hurry then," Cecilia said. She climbed hastily up to the wooden seat and Cap Stillbrink, proud as a banty, gathered the sorrel horse's reins. The clutch of girl cousins climbed in, eager for gossip about St. Louis. Mary Pearl held them at bay to protect her feeling that lightning was about to strike.

Like an answer to an unasked question, what Mary Pearl felt unreeled like film in a Nickelodeon.

Riding in the Stillbrinks' open carriage, she spied a man walking across a field. It was not the Burren, but it could have been. He had red hair and she had always hated red hair. Despite herself, as if self-control evaporated into the summer humidity, she announced to her cousins, "That's the man I am going to marry."

Years later, after she married Bartholomew Day, she told her own children. "I always hated red hair, and when I told your daddy I was going to marry him, he said he hadn't planned on marrying just then, because he was taking a trip to Oregon to visit his granduncle, John T. Day, who had come directly from Ireland to the Gold Rush and done quite well moving up in the Northwest. So I said to him, 'Bart, you just go to Oregon, and if you come back, I'll marry you.' He said, 'If I come back, we will.' When he came home, his red hair wasn't red anymore. My prayers had been answered. His hair had turned black. It was a sign for true and for sure he wanted to suit me and marry me. That's how a true suitor acts. We were a match made in heaven."

*

It was her favorite story to tell her grandchildren when they got to be that curious, but brief, age when children ask their parents and their grandparents how they met and how they fell in love, and were they ever really young.

She wondered whatever happened to poor Francis Devine. "I was a willful devil of a girl back then."

A voice strained over a tinny squawk-box calling a nurse from one station to the next. "Hijacked," she thought. "Old people should never give up their own homes. I don't regret I lived with Father John. I had my son, but I should never have given up my home."

She wanted to shout a warning.

But she did not shout.

Dignity is control.

Pure and simple.

Of oneself.

Silence was the only dignity left her.

She could not control growing old. She knew how haggard and repulsive she must have looked at the Northern Pacific Railroad Hospital where first, before Saint Mike's, they had admitted her immediately into Intensive Care when she was too ill to care at all about anything.

She had wanted to see all her grandchildren, but the world had flung them far, even farther than her own family of Lawler's and McDonough's, and Bart's family of Day's and Lynch's, who all had been launched from the emerald green of Ireland. But better they did not see her wired to machines and tied to tubes that pumped into her, and out of her, measured amounts that were charted and examined by well-meaning strangers who were someone else's grandchildren.

"That's a good girl, Nanny Pearl," the nurse said when all she had done was sip some water through a bent straw to swallow one more pill. Did she look like a circus act? Did she need applause? What's the difference between an old-folks home and an orphanage? Nothing. They both treat you like kids they'd rather be rid of. She resented St. Mike's making her into a child-thing fed and emptied and washed and moved under their pale-green control. She resented the other residents whose age was a reproach to her that she too was as old as they. She had always preferred the company of younger people. Their liveliness energized her.

*

Before she had been transported to St. Mike's, while she was still in the Northern Pacific Railroad Hospital, a grandson flew in to see her and brought her a single red rose.

"Sorry. No flowers," a nurse said. "Rules are rules in Intensive Care."

So he had taken the rose away with him to his motel.

Several times in two days the Northern Pacific allowed him see her. Nanny knew these visitations were the last for them. She regarded everything with a longing, knowing everything was the last, a sweet last, so far off, so slow in coming.

This young man, who was thirty-two, was her first grand-child, Megs' son, baptized John by her own priest of a son, John. Yet Johnny seemed more like Harry whose flare he had without the screaming looniness. He seemed happy, as if Harry's secret had become Johnny's gift. They talked the way they always had. Johnny had a human openness she had never seen in Harry, who Johnny told her, oh so subtly, had been a sensitive man born into a time that couldn't understand him.

Johnny knew Harry's secret.

Johnny had the gab, respectful of her feelings, revealing nothing directly, but saying everything she needed to hear to right her final examination of conscience about Harry. She appreciated he knew she needn't be hit over the head with a frying pan, because he, of all her kith and kin, knew she wasn't stupid. She had always preferred tasteful honesty to secrets and deceit.

He leaned in over her bed, reaching over the high rails and around the tubes. He held her hand. She was conscious that her wrists had disappeared. Intravenous fluids had infiltrated her flesh. She felt puffed and lay back on her pillow, not comfortable, but satisfied.

It was the two of them together again.

They were related by blood, but they were special pals.

In 1943, thirty years before, they two, when she was young Johnny's Nana, had pacted a friendship beyond a grandmother spoiling her first grandchild.

She had been fifty-four herself when Johnny was two, and they all called her Pearl. Batty once, only once, dared call her Pearl Harbor because she'd changed his plans about Oregon. "Bartholomew," she had said, "I laugh at all your jokes, but there's nothing funny about Pearl Harbor." She was no longer remembered as the daughter of John Patrick Lawler and Honora McDonough Lawler who both had died in the 1918 Influenza Epidemic. She was Batty's wife and the tense mother of three soldiers.

The war raged in Europe and the South Pacific. It took her three sons and two sons-in-law from her into the faraway fighting. Nothing she could do about it. Nothing any of them could do about it.

Those years the world had a run of bad luck.

In the summer of 1944, leaving Batty in St. Louis helping Nora with her four babies, she traveled to Peoria on the electric Traction Railroad to visit Megs who was expecting. During the long warm evenings, she sat with Megs swinging on the front porch at the corner of Ayres and Cooper. They traded Johnny from lap to lap. Megs was due in three weeks. Georgie was an Air Corps ball-turret gunner stationed somewhere in England. Megs needed her mother's help with Johnny and then with the new baby who was to be baptized either Elizabeth or Robert, but called Betty or Bobby. On the sidewalk the air-raid wardens, men either too young or too old for the draft, strolled by, tolling the darkness of each house and calling night greetings to the neighbors rocking on their hot sprawling porches.

Next door, Mrs. Janet Blanchard played the piano in the dark: "In the Good Old Summertime," "Meet Me in St. Louis, Louis," "Sentimental Journey," "I'll Be Seeing You." Mrs. Blanchard's right hand tinkled treble notes with her strong thumb, index, and middle finger. Her left hand splayed out arcing rote chords from the middle of the keyboard down to the sad deep bass, and back, wringing the longing out of songs popular because they were about families and wives and husbands desperately separated by war.

In the evening darkness, Mary Pearl imagined Janet Blanchard's flabulous arms flying up and down and sideways giving all the syncopation possible to "It's a Grand Night for Singing." Some evenings, when only Janet's playing broke the twilight silence of the neighborhood, Pearl hoped for the overweight pianist, Janet, who was her age, to be bombed by the Germans, or, at least, to gain enough momentum on "Roll Out the Barrel" to knock her fat fanny off her own piano bench. Janet had beautiful hands untouched by the pains already sneaking into Mary Pearl's fingers.

What does anyone remember of the First World War, or the Second? No one remembers the longing loneliness, the aching fear, the terrifying reality. Everyone remembers the nostalgia of the songs, the movies, the dancing, the styles of clothes and hair. Pearl hated trivia. She had suffered through the bitter winters, fearful that a son's death in war might make her a Gold Star Mother. She hated the Gold Stars hanging in the windows of bereaved parents on every neighborhood block. She resented all the days and nights living in a world of women and children, when nearly all the men were gone for four years. Separation had been the hardest. She hadn't raised her boys to be soldiers.

Pearl was quietly proud that Ireland, despite controversy, stayed neutral, just like Charles Lindbergh tried who had flown his plane, "The Spirit of St. Louis," from America to France and then lost his only son to a kidnapper. Ireland had its own Troubles. Her grandson stirred in her lap. Not if she could help it would Johnny grow up to ship off to some new excuse for war. Words had begun to form in his mouth like butterflies. No one knew why he invented words he added to the words they taught him.

He refused to say Grandmother.

He called her at first Nana and then Nanny.

She knew the name wasn't original in the world, but she knew it was original with him. So she squeezed him, hugged him in thanks. Always she had hated the simplicity of her name Mary, which was not a grand old name to her, and secretly she recoiled, being a St. Louis girl, at the negroid sound of her name, Pearl. Names could be a curse. She felt stuck with Pearl for reasons she thought proper to keep secret, another unspoken secret, she could not tell her priest-son, because she respected his vocation, which she didn't see as hers, to save souls of all colors. When Johnny had so easily babbled Nana, she blessed his little soul, and fostered the change so quickly at home and in V-Mail letters, that within weeks, everyone, even Nora, giving in to Megs' little brat, called her Nanny.

Grateful to Johnny, she gave him a one-dollar bill and a small plastic pocket statue of the Virgin in a thumb-size carrying case. He kissed her and led her to the bathroom. He seated her on the edge of the tub and worked his short pants down his hips, the Blessed Mother in one hand and the dollar in the other. He was proud to show her how grown up he was in controlling himself. She found it oh-so-sweet: the two of them alone together, with the others arguing about Eleanor Roosevelt in the living room.

Suddenly, she realized she hadn't been listening when Johnny asked her a question. For help.

She looked up.

Too late.

He pulled the flush handle.

The dollar and the Virgin Mother lay in the Y of his tiny lap. The water swirled. The Y parted as he stood, and they both watched in fascination as the green money and the plastic statuette plummeted into the roaring swirling suction of the bowl.

Neither dared reach in as George Washington and Our Mother of Perpetual Help swirled around together finally to disappear in the last great gulp of the toilet.

At the same instant, Johnny began to cry and she began to laugh, both so hard that the others came running from the living room.

"It's alright," Father John, home on leave, said, and she, with her new name looked at both her John and her Johnny and kept on laughing.

"Nanny knows," she hiccupped. "Nanny knows."

She gave Johnny another dollar.

Those homey adventures, like flowers, except for this last adventure, were over for her now, she guessed. Not even that one red rose from her grandson could she keep in the Northern Pacific's Intensive Care, and even he would soon have to leave her for the last time.

She wanted a good look at him. She raised up, white hair flying and worn thin in back from her weeks in bed. She was satisfied with what she saw.

"What do you want, Nan?" he asked.

She lay back, taking his hand, and told him that her own mother, Honora Anastasia McDonough Lawler, had been laid out in St. Louis under a blanket of red roses. Her mother, she said, had been jealous of her. Honora had not liked the way Mary's four brothers and father spoiled her. But she had outlived her mother in quantity of years and quality of life and no longer begrudged

Honora her petulant looks that were so much like her own daughter she had named Nora to placate her own mother, Honora.

"I don't blame my mother," Nanny told her grandson. "Never blame yours."

"I don't. I wouldn't. What for?"

"Mothers always get blamed. Your mother is as good a mother as she was a daughter and she is a wife."

"Nan, I'm too old to need mothering."

"No one's ever too old for that."

"I mean Mom and I, since dad got so sick, have become friends. Like you and I are friends."

"Just never blame her. I don't blame her. I don't blame anybody. Not even Nora. That's why I know now I've been through it all, been through all of it, when you don't blame anyone anymore, not even yourself."

"That's some kind of peace," he said.

"Until someone pulls some new trick on an old dog."

Her grandson had left her sweetly, she, leaning up on her elbow in the Intensive Care Unit to receive his final kiss.

That evening she imagined she heard his flight pass over the Northern Pacific Railroad Hospital where she told Dr. Carrier in no uncertain terms she had been railroaded.

Johnny was flying over head, flying out of St. Louis Lambert Field Airport, where Lucky Lindy's plane hung suspended from the ceiling concourse, back to the university where he taught and led protests against the war. He was her only relative truly and constantly interested in her past, her present, her future. As she was in his, because, with her sons dead, her daughters old, he was her future. In him would lodge the only lasting detailed memory of her whose only sadness was he'd never have children to listen to her story.

She imagined him at that moment taking off up into the dark night sky. He would see all of St. Louis laid out in lights below him, just as she had marveled at the model "St. Louis of the Future" laid out in miniature lights at the St. Louis World's Fair in 1904 when she was a young girl and fighting a war of independence from her mother, Honora, who said no daughter of hers was spending every Sunday at the Great Exposition.

Honora had been no match against the five men who were less husband and four sons to her than they were father and brothers to her sassy daughter whom Honora herself always, after her daughter had won, called Miss Mary Pearl. Honora had been no match for Mary enthralled by the million dazzling Edison electric lamps, the new Ferris Wheel the barkers called "The Big Eli," the gondolas shaped like swans gliding through the grand "Canals de Venice," skimming past the glorious band concert gazebos and the outdoor waltz pavilions surrounding the myriad lagoons. Forest Park had never looked more beautiful.

Nanny warmed. She knew. She felt in her bones that her grandson high in the Ozark airliner would think to himself the words of the tune which that long-ago summer had become the theme song of the Fair: "Meet Me in St. Louis, Louis." She had sung the melody to lull him to sleep during the war. She and Megs had taken him to see the movie and he had asked if the girl singing on the screen was his Nana before she got old. He often asked her to sing the song. He even recorded her once on the tape recorder Megs and Georgie had given him on his fifteenth birthday. "Meet Me in St. Louis, Louis! Meet me at the Fair." The melody was forever her song. "...lights are shining...." The music made her young again. "...We will dance the hootchy-kootchy. You will be my tootsie-wootsie." He was gone and she knew she would never see him again.

Loss fisted her heart.

Her face grimaced in pain that alarmed the nurse who did not understand.

She reached under Nanny's hospital gown: "This won't hurt, Nanny. You'll sleep."

The needle-sting blossomed to a rose in her hip. *Ah.*

Don't tell me the lights are shining anywhere but there.

"My God, Batty," she thought, the ending is more confusing than the middle and the beginning.

We will dance.

This is the future and I shouldn't be here."

*

November 29, 1972, three days after Johnny's visit, the Northern Pacific Railroad Hospital packed Nanny into the Ace Ambulance that drove seven miles through St. Louis streets, passing nowhere near the rundown ruins of Forest Park, to St. Michael's Nursing Home.

"No, no, no," she cried. "You all promised I'd leave Northern for home. I know what St. Mike's is. Help me. Don't hurt me!"

"But, Pearl," Dr. Carrier said, "you need a week or two of convalescence."

"I need to go home. Just prescribe me something."

"Nora's made all the arrangements."

"Sure, of course, she has," Nanny said, "without asking me or Megs."

So Nanny Pearl was carted off, her thin lips set tight against the betrayal that no one whom she had repeatedly rescued from one thing or another could rescue her. Old age had made her their hostage. She took back her last words to Johnny. She blamed them all, even him.

At St. Michael's Nursing Home, they added new torture. Music from an easy-listening radio station was piped everywhere through the facility. They played instrumentals of all the old songs. She remembered all the words, against her will, all the words associated with times, sweet and bitter, and all gone, but for the sentimental memories she hadn't the strength any longer to entertain. The lyrics broke her heart. She pulled her pillow around her ears. In her bed, she heard the melodies; in the bath; in the hall; on the long veranda; even behind and underneath the music at morning mass. She complained of it the third day she was there when Nora finally came to visit.

"Ignore it, Nan," Nora said. "You'll only be here until you're well enough to go home."

Nanny Pearl set her lips. "Your home," she said.

"You know how much," Nora said, "Bill and I want you home with us. You'll be back in St. Louis where you lived your whole life."

"Till I made up my own mind to live with Father John."

Nora's lipstick, leaving her face behind, smiled. "You can live with us like you lived with him."

"He gave me a choice!"

"God forgive me," Nanny thought in sharp words she had never spoken, even though she should have, always knowing Nora, like Harry, had her own secret. "My daughter's a bitch."

Nora looked and sounded exactly like Honora: women who say *no*.

"You can't stay in Peoria with Megs. She has her hands full with poor sick Georgie in and out of the hospital like a revolving door."

"If your daddy was here..."

"Well, mother, he's not, and I am."

*

Nanny Pearl despaired again she had ever given up her own home. She had been dispossessed without notice. After the war, her priest son, with so many decorations for bravery, had been given his own parish by his proud bishop.

He needed a housekeeper.

"You can cook and clean," Father John had said, "and Dad can garden. It will be wonderful for the three of us."

She and Batty considered their son's offer for a week, and then packed up their small apartment on Pershing Avenue near Forest Park. Much they owned they gave away to young Harry and his new bride, Rosalie, setting up their own apartment three doors down on Pershing. After that first move, their life had been a round of parish after parish as their son rose through the ecclesiastical ranks. In each place, she had lost more of her household belongings. Somewhere, even her grandmother's Irish linens disappeared.

Batty had said, "No matter. Better to leave everything than move it."

She had let her men let her things slip away from her.

Then Batty slipped away the eve of Valentine's Day, 1954. He dropped dead in Father John's Mother Cabrini parish house in Springfield.

"God's will be done."

Then for years, it was she and her son who ran St. Cabrini's, until he too fell dead in the early morning of May 9, 1967, showering and shaving to say Mass.

Without him, she had no claim to live in the parish house. She had seventy-two hours, the Bishop had said, to move. "Seventy-two hours," she said. "God's will be done."

"Mother," Nora had said, "Let me help. Megs is so busy taking care of Georgie. Who'd think he'd outlive John and Patrick? Megs can't take care of you both."

"What makes you think I need taken care of? I've run Father John's house perfectly well, thank you. Besides, I can help Megs with Georgie."

"Come back to St. Louis and live with us."

Nanny Pearl looked up from her rocker. Her knees pained constantly, bone on bone. She was angry. "Why did He take my boy? Tell me, Nora. Why did God take two of my boys?" Her Irish was up. "Why is Harry always drunk? Why has Georgie been so sick so long? Why has Megs had to suffer so? Can't God give us a weekend off?"

"You're talking nonsense," Nora said.

"How many of your brother's sermons did you ever listen to?"

"St. Louis is your home." Nora packed Nanny's bag. Everything fit into one gray-blue valise.

"Why has nothing ever happened to you, Honora?"

"I'm Nora, mother."

"What's the difference. You tell me, Nora, why has nothing ever happened to you? This wasn't supposed to happen to me."

The bishop's new pastor was arriving at St. Cabrini's the next day.

"What will I do now?" she cried.

"Nan, don't you worry," Nora said. "John had lots of insurance."

*

Long nights in St. Louis at Nora and Bill's she lay awake. Over her bed hung, almost the last of her possessions, a Holy Crucifix, built thick enough to store inside its metal crossbeams the candles and oils for the Last Rites of Extreme Unction. After a lifetime of father and brothers and husband and sons, she lay alone in her small room under her daughter's chenille spread. Next to her bed was a photo album. One of the oldest pictures was of Honora, yellowed and fading. "Batty was right about the Druid curse. He was right as rain about my witch of a mother."

Through the heat vent in her room, she could hear Nora and Bill drinking at the knotty-pine bar in the basement rec-room with Harry and Rosalie. She could hear them arguing about elections and what the Negroes were doing to Forest Park and the Jews were doing next door and how the St. Louis Cardinals were the best team in baseball because Stan Musial belonged to their parish.

She heard their friends come and go.

She was hungry, but it embarrassed her to ask Nora to bring a tray. It embarrassed her more to walk slowly into the kitchen. It embarrassed her that her failing eyes caused her to make crumbs on the cabinet in Nora's spotless kitchen. Anyway, she had small appetite for anything. Crackers. Just crackers. And maybe some warm milk. Dr. Carrier had said she must eat more, but crackers were all she wanted. Something to tide her over. Anything to tide her over. "God, in the name of your Blessed Mother, let it be soon!"

Late one evening through the vent, she heard Nora's voice, husky on Jim Beam, say, "Harry, you can bet your ass I'm claiming every last penny. You and that Megs can go to hell. You don't know what I know. Megs either."

Against her soul, Nanny Pearl cried that she hated Nora as much as Honora. She hated them all. They preyed upon her. What hadn't been taken by life they schemed to take away. She had lied to Johnny: she couldn't forgive any of them. She couldn't go. She couldn't stay. She couldn't die. She had stayed too long at the Fair.

She should never have come back again to St. Louis. She should never have gone anywhere on someone else's terms into someone else's house. No matter what any of them said, she was a guest, a paying one at that, who was staying too long, long enough for Nora to add insult to injury.

She had even managed a small smile, apologetic, and broken-hearted, when Nora told her in no uncertain terms that she always left the bathroom untidy, that, in fact, she who had been pristinely clean and proud of her appearance all her life, was herself dirty.

Nora won.

She had cut her like a knife stabbed precisely into the last vestige of her personal pride.

"Perhaps it's true," Nanny said.

"I can't take care of you, mother, not like that. I can't wash you and feed you."

Silently, Nanny vowed never to eat another bite in Nora's house again.

"I bathed and fed five of my own kids. I'm sixty years old myself."

"You're sixty-two," Nanny said.

It was only days from that remark to the Northern Pacific Railroad Hospital, and then weeks to St. Michael's Garden Floor Nursing Home.

"Bill and I," Nora said, "truly want you very much back at home again with us."

"Then get me out of St. Michael's," Nanny pleaded. "Get me out now."

"When the doctors say you're ready."

Lies. Lies. Lies.

*

Megs came to visit her mother on her fourth day at St. Mike's. She had left her invalid husband and flew to her mother's side. She manicured Nanny's nails and brushed her hair. They drank tea in the dining hall and ate all the crackers on the surrounding tables. Megs was her only hope, but Nanny wouldn't tell her about Nora, because Nora's victory meant her failure as a mother. She hated that she finally had become another one with an unspoken secret.

"Get me out, Megs," Nanny Pearl begged. "You live far away, and Georgie is so sick, but you must get me out." She was embarrassed at the tone in her own voice. She had never begged, but these children with their lives defeated what she had always called her "Irish." They had her surrounded. Her control was gone completely.

"I can live with you and help take care of Georgie."

Megs held her mother tight and close. "My plane is leaving soon."

"Get me out."

"I'll talk to the doctors."

"Dear God," Nanny Pearl said. "Give Georgie my love and prayers."

"I will, Mom."

*

Seventy-two hours after Megs left, on her seventh day at St. Michael's, Nanny Pearl awakened and looked at the ceiling. The phone had not rung. She had received no mail. "No one will ever come," she said.

The old woman sharing the room asked, "What did you say, dear?"

Nanny Pearl, resolved, said nothing else.

She rose from her bed, crossed to the small table where her

breakfast had been set and ate in silence. The piped radio music broke for an announcement: "Today is Tuesday, the sixth of December. The temperature is 38 degrees. The time is seven AM."

*

At that exact time, Megs, driving her car, with her son, Robert, Johnny's younger brother, riding shotgun, as much passenger as accomplice, sped down the snow-cleared highway from Peoria toward St. Louis, their radio tuned into the seven AM news right at the tone. President Nixon was in the fast-breaking lead story the announcers called Watergate.

Robert asked to stop for coffee.

Megs said, "I brought the thermos."

Robert reached behind the seat and pulled the thermos off the pile of blankets folded ready for Nanny Pearl's escape. Dr. Carrier had said Nanny was stubborn as a mule, but strong as an ox, and if she could sit all day long at the nursing home, she could sit in the car while Megs drove her from St. Louis to Peoria. In the right environment, Dr. Carrier had said, she'd be better off taking care of herself, especially if she felt useful attending to Georgie.

The radio news of Nixon finished and Megs had heard none of it.

"Legally," she said, "Nora can't stop me." Her foot pressed heavy, speeding the car down the Adlai Stevenson Highway toward St. Louis.

"Mom," Robert said, "let me drive." He had served two tours of Vietnam with the Marines.

"No," she said. "I'm doing this."

*

Nanny swallowed the last of her breakfast.

She neatly wiped her lips with the paper napkin.

She looked at her fingers gnarled with arthritis.

"No one will ever come," she thought. "So my will be done."

She rose from her chair and smiled at the woman in the other bed.

"Who is she?" Nanny thought. "Who am I? We're the same old lady. We're the same old, old, old lady."

An infinite sadness...*Don't tell me*...filled her...*lights are shining*...and as she walked...*anywhere but there*...toward the bathroom, she stepped...*we will dance*...out of herself: part of her floated away with more relief than surprise, and part of her crashed to the cold tile floor, while the stranger in the next bed screamed and screamed and screamed at death working so close to her.

*

St. Michael's Nursing Home was efficient and neat, set up with Christmas trees, and carols playing on the Muzak.

When Megs arrived, not sure exactly of anything but how swiftly she and Robert might pull off the legal kidnapping, Nanny Pearl's bed was neatly made up.

The pillow was in place.

Her crystal rosary was gone from the bedside table where the clock read 8:12 AM.

It was as if no one had slept the night there.

Even the other bed was empty.

Megs ran down the hall to the nurses' station. She held out the legal papers. "I've come to get my mother. Where is she?"

"What is your mother's name, dear?"

"Mary Day."

"You're not Nora are you? You must be the other one."

"Believe me," Robert said, "she's the other one."

"Let's us see," the nurse said cheerfully. She punched her computer which lit up the typed words: "Mary Pearl Lawler Day; female caucasian; 84; admitted November 29, 1972; deceased December 6, 1972; cause of death: internal bleeding."

The room crashed down in a wind-shear of shock and embarrassment. Dead!

The nurse stood bolt upright.

She spun the computer screen away from the counter.

Too late.

Megs, always the quick sister, had read the screen.

Her face, reddened by the excitement of her dangerous drive through the snow, blanched whiter than white.

"I'm sorry," the nurse said.

Blankness filled the space between the two women.

"Perhaps," the nurse said, "you'd like to sit down. Perhaps some coffee while I page Dr. Carrier.

"You fucking careless bitch," Robert said.

"Sir, I'm sorry. I just came on duty."

A second nurse, Nanny Pearl's nurse that morning, ran apologetically up to them. "We're so sorry. I called your home myself."

"You told my husband?" Megs said. "He's so sick you could have killed him."

"He sounded very weak. We told him. He knows. He said, 'Why Pearl? Why not me?'"

"Oh, Mom!" Megs said. "She didn't know we were coming to get her."

"Your husband called the Highway Patrol to try and stop you to tell you."

"Oh, my poor Mom," Megs cried. "She got out the only way she knew how."

"You people," Robert, the Marine Sergeant, said, "are real fuck-ups."

*

Winter that December, 1972, in St. Louis was early and fiercely cold. In Forest Park, snow capped the soft curves of what graceful buildings still stood from the 1904 World's Fair. Small floes of ice clung to the piers of the Eads Bridge. Automobile traffic across the span was more choked than usual as the hearse, and the cars following in cortege, their antennas flagged with mourning ribbons, headed away from St. Louis, across the Mississippi River, back to Illinois, to Springfield, to the cemetery where Batty and John lay waiting patient as the ancient Irish dead in the burial cairns of the Burren.

Perhaps only the dead can be trusted.

The car radios, the sound breaking up crossing the steel bridge, said, "...and that's the President's latest statement about Watergate. In Vietnam, heavy fighting was reported today near Da Nang. Local news after this message from Double-Good Double-Good Double-Mint Gum."

"Why would Nora make such a lie," Megs cried, "about codeine, five years of codeine."

Johnny held his mother's hand. "Doctors will give anything to the mother of a priest."

Off the bridge, the announcer's voice, fading slightly as the cars headed north into Illinois, reported that a mystery pilot had become the talk of St. Louis, baffling police and aviation authorities. Repeatedly, at odd hours on odd days, he arrowed his small plane under and through the great Gateway Arch causing delighted crowds of tourists to cheer. The radio editorial denounced the pilot's lack of respect for the new public monument and his disregard of the common good.

The Story Knife

After Skagway in Alaska, in the long arctic light of the last summer solstice of the millennium, Brian Kelly, heading north, heading toward true north, realized the twilight of the gods must not be desperate. On his American cruise ship, docked against the granite mountains of the North Pacific, he had caught himself catching the eye of a cabin boy from Genoa.

The boy was, in fact, freshly tipped over the cusp of adolescence, a young man, the Italian kind who gives occasion to sonnets, whose innocence beguiles, whose dark curls and darker eyes and supple-shouldered body cause notes of invitation, of assignation, accompanied by a cabin number and a hundred dollar bill, to be written in hope and then crumpled and thrown away in confusion.

Sex was not the quest.

Beauty was.

Love was on dangerous times.

To touch a stranger put life at risk, but the need to touch beauty, to trace the curling hair of the head and thigh and foot, even more than the groin, bit into his fifty-year-old heart.

He himself had always worshiped beauty.

Never was sex itself his purpose. Sex was the hook to distract beauties in their own tracks long enough to savor beauty itself incarnate. Brian Kelly, Chicago-born out of a Dublin Dempsey come over to marry a Boston Kelly, was not some feckless rover traveling ignorant through the world. He knew what some people are for. The young man from Genoa may have hired on as ship's crew. But he was not for that. His beauty was his true vocation.

Daily, the cruise ship, which had embarked from Vancouver, swirling in colorful serpentines of merriment, heading north up the waters of the Inland Passage, washed away the anxiety which had become Brian's habit at home. He traveled alone. He was happy keeping to himself. In San Francisco, at the jammed Bloomsday Fleadh Festival in Golden Gate Park, he had stood separate from the sunburnt crowd cheering Van Morrison and Elvis Costello singing out the anthem of the "thousand miles of the long journey home." On the cruise ship, he gladly avoided the endless programs of entertainment and distraction. He made himself invisible.

As the ship cruised northwards, he walked the wooden decks, sometimes warm with June sun, sometimes cold with pelting arctic rain, purposely neither smoking his cigarettes nor saying his rosary, leaving himself open to what flow of smell or thought or feeling might come from the sea, the passing blue ice, the mountains.

Always his *Daybook*, full of scribbled notes, was in the pocket of his long Australian slicker that flapped like a cassock around his ankles.

Always he carried his Camcorder, shooting with exotic angles the wake of the ship, the rain dripping on the decks, and the empty chairs and empty tables of the piano salon.

The Reverend Brian Kelly purposely kept people out of his rectangular video frame. His footage, viewed and re-viewed alone in his cabin, made the classic ship, built in 1957 and never done up for disco, look empty of the present, and so reminiscent of romance he wondered that no Hollywood location scout had exploited its varnished wood decks and steep stairs and vintage carpet in the long hallways below that led to the perfectly preserved period staterooms and cabins.

Films, he mused, because films had been his late-night refuge alone, lonely, celibate, in the rectory, were no longer about romance on the high seas. Hollywood had turned to crash-and-burn adventures with action scripts that would have no use for the venerable ship but to blow it up.

His camera zoomed in on the ship's nooks and doors and rails, and tracked down the gangways, with an aching nostalgia. His blazing blue eyes searched for imagined forbidden trysts of sophisticated passion from those romantic times past when, as a young priest sitting in the dark confessional, whispered sin had once been interesting, before the limp whinings of neurotics, seeking reconciliation face-to-face, had caused him to laugh out loud, because he was only a priest, not a psychiatrist.

Other passengers nodded to his head of red hair haloed by the bright summer sun, nearing solstice, but could not penetrate his aura of privacy. He protected himself from the presumptuous privilege of strangers thrown together for a week, eager to make new acquaintances, and tell their life stories.

His cabin stewardess, a worldly little blonde from Strathchyde, Scotland, hardly surprised him with her openness. At first he had been uncomfortable with her constant attentions, making up his room, turning down his bed covers. He felt viscerally the class distinctions of the world. He, no aristocrat, had never felt comfortable with the parish housekeeper, because he always empathized with the people who cleaned other people's bathrooms. But his stewardess put him at ease. She was on top of the roles acted out on shipboard.

She too knew what people were for.

He figured she knew what he was for.

His stewardess, pretending the black-and-white roman collar that tucked out of his suitcase was for the final night's costume party, told him what no one else would tell. She told him how passengers, perhaps pursuing some metaphor of life's voyage in a ship, boarded to die, how one or two each trip died, how they were quietly taken away to refrigeration below decks. Old people, ancient ones, and sickly people, terminal ones, invisible among the fiercely robust breeders and feeders determined to have the good time they had paid for, had boarded the ship to die. That was not what the cruise ship's frenetic television commercials had promised, not the way they promised shipboard partying, sports, and fun.

Father Brian Kelly, after twenty-five years in the confessional, was not surprised at her tale.

But he had not expected the dark surprise of the cabin boy from Genoa.

He'd thought he was beyond temptation.

The young man slept well below the passenger decks with the crew. Brian's stewardess told him of their small rooms with no windows. "This is a prison for us, it is," she said. His own cabin had a porthole whose three brass bolts he had unscrewed to let in the cool North Pacific air. Small icebergs flowed south past his porthole north of Ketchikan in the Inland Passage. He kept to his cabin surrounded by his books and papers and cameras.

The other passengers feasted, gorging themselves from breakfast to midnight buffets, orgying through croissants and custards, each day appearing in new clothes brought on board in incrementally larger sizes as they ate their way northward, intent on getting their money's worth. The wives of businessmen and contractors and doctors were continents unto themselves: plump, pink, bejeweled members of the charge-card classes, cruise-ship women, towing what was left of their silent husbands, impatient wives of living male mutes, waiting for the man they had married to collapse leaving them at last free to enjoy all the riches of insurance dividends that funded the cruises of the real widows on board.

None of them, old or young, husband or wife, bothered him, because, between the fat and the dead, he found the silent thin thread of his own individual life so sweetly unlike their straight coupled contempt for each other. Anyone who thought priests should marry could be cured listening to the confessions of married people. Their marital boredom rather amused him. They had replaced athletic lust with guileless gluttony, but they seemed so ordinary, so harmless, so nice, he wondered if sins any longer actually existed, because God could hardly take offense from such poor creatures. If the old traditions and taboos had evaporated, was he himself, as a priest, irrelevant?

The ship, mercifully, and mercy was all he found himself want-ing at home in Chicago, from where he'd fled, was carrying him away from his daily life, his daily things, his daily routines of Mass and prayer and counseling. No priests of his acquaintance could telephone him from the Archbishop's office with gossipy updates on who was doing what to whom, on who was drunk or dying or dead. He read no news. He watched no television. He attended no films. The less he saw and heard, the more visible he became to himself.

In his *Daybook*, he wrote: "Zen and the Art of the Priesthood." His Jesuit spiritual director had warned him he read too much for his own good. Reading had colored his thinking.

He stood naked alone in his cabin with the sea breeze from the open porthole cooling his athletic body and his Camcorder recording his solo movements. Once, after a port-of-call at a lake where he had helped row a canoe with twenty other passengers, picnicking on Tlingit reindeer sandwiches, he returned to his cabin and danced for his camera, a slow undulating male dance to ancient music no one but he himself could hear. The hypnotic rhythm of the ship's engines, way below decks, was a white noise broken only by the splash of waves against the ship.

He was more than naked.

He was not his telephone ringing. He was not his car driving. He was not his Roman collar. Not his sermons. Not his books. Not his face smiling kindly at the sick, blessing the children, comfort-ing the widows.

He was, stripped clean in the cold North, becoming himself behind his smile, behind what breezy conversation he sometimes felt impelled to make as a reality check, behind his gentlemanly stroll among strangers quietly, expectantly, waiting to be spoken to, eager to be ignited by someone who had not yet heard the story about themselves they had told a million times.

He was himself in his cabin. Despite his abiding grief that his priestly life had turned into a disaster, because no one needed priests anymore, he was overflowing with ironic energy, laughing at the ship taking the sick and the old from his tribe into the ark sailing toward the ice floes. He admired their bravery. They no longer bothered to ask any priests for Last Rites. They sailed free-choice straight into Death's cold waiting embrace.

Love and death.

The death of love.

The love of death.

He had fled everything familiar at home because his personal telephone Roladex of priests who were friends read like the Tibetan *Book of the Dead*. He could no longer cry when a classmate from the old seminary died. His grieving had run out of tears. So many priests died so young. He had bought passage on the cruise to be alone for healing.

He had to think over his Jewish doctor's advice. Was it cynical or not?

"Father Brian," Dr. Bernie Wiegand had said. "When your test comes out negative and you know what *safe* is, then the plague is over for you. Keep safe. Keep your act together."

What act he had was driven by beauty more than lust, but driven all the same.

"What do I know?" he wrote in his *Daybook*, "I'm a burnt-out case."

The third night, his stewardess pulled him aside. "A man must have jumped overboard."

He was as fascinated to listen to her as she was insistent to prove to him what she had said was true.

"Overboard. Many do," she said. "They come up here to die." Her Scottish burr gave a credible chill to her voice somewhat the way his Dublin-born mother's soft lilt still entertained him with conversation. "He's nowhere on ship. The crew's looked everywhere. It's not unusual. Jumping is better, for me, it is. Better than finding them in the morning lying their in their beds. I leave them till last. The dead ones. Clean the other rooms first, I do."

She was certainly progressive enough, and Protestant to boot, not caring a fig for priests, but he could not bring himself to ask her about the cabin boy from Genoa. He could not profane to a woman the secret way the young man's eyes met his own, the way the young man smiled knowing full well what was wanted, and what he was for.

Remembering their first exchange of looks, that first look, Brian could not deny the rush in himself. He had no poker face. He knew the boy recognized the look.

The boy knew what the man was for.

Brian could not tell the stewardess about the looks men sometimes exchange. He was confused, unfamiliar with shipboard etiquette, uncomfortable with the pinched confines of class distinction that made the boy and him virtually inaccessible to each other.

Was the boy's look really beauty smiling back?

Did the boy really know what he was for?

Or was his the coined smile of a Mediterranean hustler, hot for business in the North Pacific?

On the fourth morning, the ship docked at Skagway. The other passengers stampeded for the curio shops that were the same as all the other curio shops in all the other ports.

Brian, instead, stood quietly in the center of the village to listen for the sound of hammers, following the sound, finding the local men, talking with them, telling lies, pretending he was a teacher, saying his principal had made him promise to bring back to his students some documentary truth about the people of Alaska.

The men, accustomed to cruise ship tourists, chatted easily and kept working as the priest knelt before them recording them with his Camcorder.

Only minutes before returning to the ship, he approached a mountainman sitting in a beat-up van with a canoe strapped on top, a stove pipe jutting through the rear roof, and a large Husky panting on the passenger seat. The mountainman talked angrily about big government and oil companies and clear-cutting and how stupid the voters of Ketchikan had been to allow a nuclear warship to homeport in their fishing waters.

His Camcorder worked like a magic confessional.

The lens sucked in people eager to spill their opinions and their secrets.

Everyone wanted to be on television.

The mountainman, shilling into the Camcorder like a TV commercial, showed him, through the driver's window, objects he had crafted while snowed in the previous winter.

Brian was fascinated by a small knife, its blade an ancient smooth mammoth tooth, its six-inch handle a beautifully burnished willow twig, honey-colored, accented with dark woodknots. He instantly liked the delicate object held in the mountainman's hand.

"It's a story knife," the mountainman said. "When the Tlingit or the Eskimo elders tell a story, they use this knife. They smooth out the snow and with the knife they draw a rectangle. The children watch the knife draw the story in the snow. They understand better when the knife draws the image of one person or two in the rectangle. As the story moves on, the storyteller wipes out the drawing, smoothing the snow, drawing a new rectangle for the next part of the story."

Brian turned his Camcorder off, hung it from his shoulder, and reached into his deep oiled canvas pocket where he kept his money in the flap of his *Daybook*. "I'd like to buy it."

"You want to know how much?"

"You made it. You tell me."

"At those shops over there, it'd cost you twice as much. Me? I don't have any overhead. I can let you have it for a hundred."

Brian wondered how people arrived at a price for beauty.

"I'll take it," the man said.

"No haggling?"

"I don't know how to haggle," Brian said. "I don't usually shop at all."

"Then I should've said two hundred."

"Okay. I'll haggle. Here's a hundred."

That easily, he bought the story knife which he planned to keep next to his laptop computer. He imagined himself teaching *Bible* stories and *Catechism* and the *Lives of the Saints* to children in a whole new way. He'd tried everything else.

The fourth night at sea, the evening of the day at Skagway where he had videotaped the men building fences, he stood in the lobby outside the main dining room, purposely leaving the table a bit hungry, smiling at a group of Australian doctors who were inviting everyone to come hear the papers each had written prior to sailing.

"We'll give any other health professionals on board a letter saying you attended our seminar. For tax purposes."

Standing in the midst of their lucrative laughter, in that carpeted lobby, on the main deck outside the Purser's Office, surrounded by the tax-evading doctors and their cheerio wives, he saw the cabin boy, all innocence, so dark and young, come passing toward him, his angel's face smiling a smile more genuine than the polite smile crews thrive on.

Brian smiled.

Their eyes locked.

The boy cut courteously through the clutch of doctors straight toward him.

Face to face, neither having spoken to the other, the young man crossed all bounds. He placed his right hand on Brian's left shoulder in a quick flowing gesture noticed by no one but Brian himself who said nothing in his flush of surprise.

It was the boy who spoke.

He used his deep voice lightly, as if the upper register of speech would promise more than threaten: "How are you this evening, sir?"

Brian Kelly, born with the gift of gab, could say nothing. His fair skin blushed red as his hair.

As fast as he had appeared, the boy was gone down the stairs.

In years past, before the world was scared sexless, Brian might have dared follow the boy down the stairs to some private place.

Pacific whales would have spouted in the northern sea.

Brian, that night, could not, would not, by a conscious act of will, follow. Assignation required discussion. A thousand doubts of language and reason and vexed passion sent him careening down the long, carpeted, sloping passageway to his cabin.

In the long-ago Dreamtime, on one of his trips to the Greek isles, before the viral horror, this boy could have made his heart sing. He threw open his porthole to the cold midnight air. He braced himself against the force of the wind.

Desire beat his brain with lust for the boy's beauty.

He had been careful so long, he would be safe if he continued his care, but the only care he knew for himself, because he had taken vows he had only rarely broken, was abstinence.

He loathed his own self-discipline.

He raged against the circumstances of contagion.

He sat at his desk writing furiously in his *Daybook*.

His face grew hard as his groin.

He slammed the book shut and wrote three notes, throwing all three away, not knowing how to gain access to the young man.

He walked from his desk to the open porthole. The June night-wind below the Arctic Circle blew silken and silent around him.

The Alaska midnight, at this longest daylight, was the constant twilight his life had become.

He slept fitfully.

The ship cruised northward fast.

He rose early for the docking at the village of Sitka. A Russian Church, filled with gold icons, sat in the town center. He hadn't come to Newcastle for the coal. He pulled away from the crowd of passengers flocking into the church and headed to the combustion-engine sounds of a hundred small fishing boats bobbing at mooring. The crews of one or two men in rubber waders, heavy jackets, and watch caps, smoking and talking, drinking their coffee from steaming paper cups, paid him no attention as he shot them close-up with his Camcorder's telephoto lens.

He could look and long for everything, but he could not touch.

How had he become so dead?

He was beside himself.

He became himself watching himself.

How had he become a voyeur of his own life?

At Juneau, Brian boarded the helicopter tour which set him down on top of the windswept ice desert of the Mendenhall Glacier. The tiny chopper lifted off leaving him and three strangers alone to wander for an hour.

He set his Camcorder down firmly on the ice, recording, in the distance, the mountains, and, in the bottom of the frame, the glacial ice running a rivulet of topaz blue water.

He walked into focus in front of his own camera.

He was his own best director.

Who else would bother shooting his private dances?

Who else would shoot his private rituals?

He was a lone pilgrim kneeling on the ice-cap at the top of the world.

He reached into his pockets for the dozen healing-crystal rosaries he had brought from his previous pilgrimage to the Shrine of Our Lady of Knock in Ireland. He immersed the clear-cut beads into the freezing blue trickle where they became indistinguishable from the ice of the glacier itself. If his priest friends believed the crystals to be curative, then his submerging them into the ancient arctic ice, melding them with the clear water in the bright light, might empower all the more the crystal rosaries he took back to the ones desperate for any hope.

Later, in his cabin, watching himself on screen, he realized his hands—the anointed hands of a priest empowered to call down the Body and Blood and Soul and Divinity of Christ under the appearances of Bread and Wine—looked very young for a man his age.

After Sitka, on the fifth night, heading from the smooth flow of the Inland Passage, out to the open sea, northwest, hundreds of nautical miles towards Anchorage, he realized the cruise was passing him by.

Only two nights remained. He had to decide.

He wrote lists in his *Daybook*.

If the young man found him a fool wanting to discuss safety, he would not have too long a time onboard to be embarrassed.

He was overheated and underventilated.

He felt unreasonable being safer than safe.

Was his life reduced to a search for safety?

What was living without risk?

He had always, almost always, disciplined his passion with absolute purity.

Had he no trust in his reason to govern his lust?

If alone with the young man, would absolute abstinence explode to absolute abandon?

It would be simpler to throw himself overboard.

He was not afraid to die quickly.

He was afraid to die slowly.

He felt sick.

He had not eaten all day.

He headed down the rolling corridors toward the main salons. He could not walk a straight line. He pitched from wall to wall.

The open sea of the North Pacific lifted, then dropped, the ship. The line at the buffet was short. *Mal de mer!* He fled back down the stairs to his deck. He skirted around two passengers with dangerously green faces. He noticed white paper bags had appeared, stuck every ten feet into the railings along the passageway going to all the cabins. He had willpower. He willed he would not be sick. He slammed his door behind him. His *Daybook* slid from the desk to the floor. The story knife flew through the air. The room was hot as a furnace. He pressed his hands to his temples. He was wet with sweat.

He opened his door to let the cold air blow through.

He was not prepared for the sudden spectacle.

There stood his stewardess. Her face wide-eyed in astonishment.

A gluttonously heavy woman, supported by two other women,

had just, as he opened the door to his cabin, thrown up on his stewardess's shoes.

"You bitch!" the stewardess screamed.

He ran past the four women, hitting first one wall, being tossed against the other wall, down the stairs to the Infirmary where the good ship's Doctor Marcello told him quickly of something new: "A shot of Promethazine will fix you in minutes."

He rolled up his shirt sleeve as three new patients arrived tossing at the tiny Infirmary door.

Calmed almost instantly by the injection, he felt suddenly superior to the rough seas. He lay on the gurney smiling, relaxed, freed, his blue eyes staring up into the bright light, feeling thoroughly himself, floating up, out of his body toward the light.

Always in his life he had decided what he would do; and what he had decided to do, he decided he could undo.

He returned through the deserted passageways to his cabin. He was no longer at sea. He was on the sea. The self he had felt the first days alone onboard seemed anemic in comparison to the sense of self-purpose he had suddenly gained.

He stripped off all his clothes.

He paused once, only briefly, to consider if the Promethazine might be affecting his judgment.

He opened his porthole, and thrust his slender upper body out into the air, a pink human torso with flaming red hair sticking out from the port side of the white ship. The waves made by the prow spread out on the topaz water like foaming epaulets into the never-ending summer twilight.

It was June 20, the solstice, the year's longest day.

He felt chilled by the wind. He could not afford to catch a cold. He pulled himself back into his cabin. His white teeth chattered. He had never intended to jump, but he laughed at how easily he could have flung himself into the freezing sea when he realized that many had made their exits through open portholes. The scenario offered so perfect an exit it was ridiculous. He was getting pleased with himself. That was a good sign.

He had the luck, he did. His mother and father both told him so.

The ship's engine throbbed its white noise in backbeat to the sound of the waves. His senses, soothed by the injection, shook themselves out. The rhythms of the sea and the ship played bass line to the melodic flow of the ancient Irish blood-sea inside his body. He felt the ship roll, seeming so lightly a rocking cradle, back and forth. An ashtray slid across his desk to his laptop computer whose gray screen lit the cabin.

The story knife rolled into his hand.

At that moment, so abrupt, so crystalline, it surprised him, he knew what he would do, how he would make the best of times in the worst of times. It was not the twilight of the gods. He congratulated himself that he and his kind, sacred and profane, were always so goddam clever.

He sat down at his desk and wrote in his *Daybook* of himself that he who had told a mountainman he could not haggle had actually perfected the self-haggling of a scrupulous, oversensitive, outmoded conscience into a lifestyle.

He took the story knife into his consecrated hands and felt the power of its nature.

He reached for a sheet of ship's stationery and printed very clearly a message, saying "1 AM, Cabin 336," and stuck a precious hundred-dollar bill with the note inside the envelope.

He rang for his stewardess.

"Did you see what that pig did to my shoes? Now she's off already to the midnight buffet!"

He was glad she was madly distracted.

She took the envelope, glanced at the name of the young man from Genoa, and smiled.

It was not her first *billet-doux*.

He gave her ten dollars, shut the door, and carefully placed the crystal-bead rosaries in the dob kit on the table next to the bed where he aimed his Camcorder into the soft light, framing the waiting rectangle of white sheet like a Tlingit elder smoothing snow for a story about to be told.

He sat in his chair, holding the delicate story knife, and waited.

His Camcorder hummed softly.

There were safe ways, ways as good if not better than the old ways, for savoring beauty and making it, always before so passionately fleeting, last forever.

Mrs. Dalloway Went That-A-Way!

Mrs. Dalloway each night decides to buy the flowers herself, on the *Mrs. Dalloway* channel on satellite dish. All *Mrs. Dalloway*. All the time. Twenty-four hours, reliable as a clock ticking up in the sky aiming down signal digital bits of *Mrs. Dalloway*, of Vanessa Redgrave being, acting, Mrs. Dalloway-being-Virginia-Woolf, she of the abiding presence, all the Mrs. Dalloways deciding to buy the flowers themselves.

In the last month of summer in the last year of the last decade of the last century of the second millennium, Mrs. Dalloway, the person, the novel, the film, the myth, not yet the play and not yet *Mrs. Dalloway! The Musical*, hanging the way she does in the framed film poster, (cadged from the cute gayish couple who own the arty Rialto Cinema), smiling, umbrella, promises of a life flown by, imaged with an airbrush on the cover of the paperback novel, *Mrs. Dalloway*, meaning Vanessa, her head, omniscient goddess, smiling down on two lovers; her younger self, as a remembered girl, holding a bouquet of flowers she picked herself, speaking as she does the lines in *Scenario* magazine printing the film script of *Mrs. Dalloway*, realized, written, by Eileen Atkins, wondering about La Atkins and La Redgrave, who have played Virginia Woolf and Vita Sackville-West on stage in Atkins' play, *Vita and Virginia*, holding a copy of a yet another parallax parallel Mrs. D in that prize-winning novel of Mrs. Dalloway impersonators, *The Hours*.

"My head is swimming. I can't keep up with them all," Huxted Daly said to his lover, Riley Daly-Thomas, mixing his media, widening his experience through page and screen, (Huxted Daly was a writer known for capturing *pastness*, his sketches of *pastness*), and dealing with Mrs. Daly, Virginia Daly, his mother, Mrs. D, or rather what was left of his mother, Virginia, realizing at the party, the party itself wobbling, the party for her eightieth birthday, born when Virginia Woolf was thirty-seven, born in 1919 during those five years, 1918 to 1923, that Virginia Woolf thought changed people's very look, surrounded by thirty-one of her ancient friends, (31x80 equals 2,480 human years), laughing at the party, or smiling through the pastness lostness of their glory years in the early mid-century; talking around monuments of old men, husbands really of the women who were the actual friends, the tissue of women the actual human connection through the years, not the men who early on had evaporated in their shoes, the way his father had evaporated, *poof*, long before he died, leaving him, Huxted, dallying his own way with his father's wife, Virginia, his mother, his own Mrs. Daly, the talker, the social gadfly, the conqueror, who was a Virginia not at all tremulous the way Vanessa made Clarissa Dalloway as fragile as, well, he presumed Virginia Woolf herself, given all the goods, jot and tittle, her anal-retentive nephew, Quentin Bell, had spilled about his famous family who could not stop writing diaries and essays and novels about one another, publishing one another, binding the books, entrepreneurs working at home in Bloomsbury.

At Mrs. Daley's party, of the thirty-one guests, twenty-four were senior women, 24x80 equals 1,920 female years, two female millennia, of wisdom he was himself trying to understand, because the male god, *oh, and it grieved him so*, this message, that this male god, the former god, God the Father, God the Son, God the Holy Ghost, the God of the Creed, "*Credo in Unum Deum, Patrem omnipotentem*. I believe in one God, the Father Almighty," was the avowed god of all these women, but not really the one they worshiped silently secretly.

Huxted could not, without shaking, think of the gender shift, the quake of one tectonic plate scraping over, under, another, theologically, feeling, mid-gender, a bit himself like Septimus, the red-haired man, Mr. Septimus Warren Smith, whom Virginia, pen in hand, had walked through the streets of London, parallel to Mrs. Dalloway, all day, on the day of the grand party seamed up seamlessly by Mrs. Dalloway who had bought the flowers for her party herself, richer, better flowers in the mind's eye, on the page, than in the film, squeezed, *oh yes*, "budgeted," Eileen Atkins told Todd Pruzan, so that although expensive ravishing sweet peas were called for in the flower-shop scene, less delicate chrysanthemums had to do, and what was to be done about it, about the low budget, in that movie, marginal, independent, a film by Marleen Gorris, but to go on, like life itself, to completion, shooting frame after frame.

So Huxted agreed, shaking his head, *oh, yes*, affirmatively over the texts of Ms. Woolf and Ms. Atkins and Mr. Cunningham and even Mr. Bell as well as the visual text of Ms. Gorris and the *gravitas* of Vanessa Redgrave's acting. All so sad, every night on the satellite dish that had fallen in love with endless running of *Mrs. Dalloway*, so sad that at the same time, 65:57 minutes into the film, (22:22 minutes into DVD Chapter 4), Rupert Graves jumps from the window, and, *oh, yes*, wasn't Eileen clever to have imagined him, Rupert, his face, all of Britain in his face, before even starting writing her screenplay, because even his pretty teeth act in his pretty face, waking on a couch, dreaming a dream, a nightmare of a soldier, calling the name of "Evans! Evans!" the way a man calls a lover, lost, or a god slipped away into the past, who cannot return, despite the promise of a Second Coming. "Ha, not on this millennium," Huxted said, arranging gorgeous roses he could well afford even on his writer's budget, because he had vowed, right before his father evaporated, to live seamlessly the way people live in movies.

Quite so sad, all this Woolfian loss, lost pastness, and every night, like a ritual play, over and over, Sunday through Saturday, and around again, Septimus, shaken, shell-shocked by the way the world, the century, life itself shifted under his feet in the trenches of the war, the first war, fleeing the doctor, feeling the power of others; (all humans are dangerous humans); what happens when others gain power over one? Not suicidal. Panicked. Poor Septimus, saying his last words, "You want my life?" Septimus jumping, falling, flying out the window, impaled below, *oh*, that sound of guts on the soundtrack, guts impaled, smackdab in the middle of what should have been a Merchant-Ivory film, but wasn't, and why not, the way his mother, Mrs. Daly, was not supposed to have fallen, kept falling, one time after another, that first night outside the Rialto Cinema where he and Riley had taken her to see *Mrs. Dalloway* on New Year's Day night, January 1, 1999.

In the dark, seventy-nine she was then, that first day of the first month of the last year of the millennium, Mrs. D had roared on ahead of him, leaving go of his arm, surged toward the box office, the warm light of the ticket window glowing in the dark January night, and she had roared, so much competition for such a tiny little shrinking body, denying it was growing tiny little shrinking, as if her body were not herself, falling flat down in the dark, on the pavement, crashing next to Huxted, at his feet, him looking up at the marquee letters spelling *Mrs. Dalloway*, and the posters declaring Vanessa Redgrave and Rupert Graves and Natascha McElhone and that adorable Michael Kitchen, directed by Marleen Gorris who seemed Sapphonic, roaring not shrinking, not falling flat, coming off winning the Oscar for *Antonia's Line*.

Why had his mother, Virginia, Mrs. D, actually always to roar and shove ahead, competing with everyone male and female, people standing in line waiting to buy tickets, why, and why him, since his father driven to death no doubt by competition, by losing, and by Mrs. D. He thought of her as she fell past him, always saying, as she fell past him toward the pavement, always saying, in the looped dialog of widowed mothers dependent on gay sons, "I'll never surrender," and he answered, "I'll never surrender," and she had repeated, quite primly, "I'll never surrender," more than once in her little porcelain Mrs. Dalloway house, a house of her own, covered in modern aluminum siding, with windows sealed closed and so barred against intruders no Septimus, not even he himself, Huxted, had he wanted to, could have thrown himself out of his mother's windows. His whole life he had resisted any waterlogged, slow, sinking of his will into hers. He would not snap the "snap" in Virginia Woolf or in Edward Albee. "Snap, Martha!"

Mrs. Virginia Daly said she would buy the movie tickets herself. Then she flew through the New Year's dark, toward *Mrs. Dalloway*, pushing around all the happy filmgoers shivering in line, and fell past him toward the pavement, making a little sound, *oh, Oh, OH*, crashing down in the dark; her wrist was broken and her chin was cut; blood; why blood on New Year's night, the first night of the New Year. *How dare bring blood into my year!* He knelt on the cold pavement and held her, his mother; a doctor came from the line of moviegoers; and a nurse; and the handsome young gay couple who owned the theatre, so young they gave Huxted (who thought *he* cultivated *them*), because he was an older gay gentleman, free movie posters, "*Mrs. Dalloway*, A Motion Picture Starring Vanessa Redgrave, Adapted for the Screen by Eileen Atkins."

His mother eliciting a child's greatest fear, a parent making a public spectacle of weakness, a what? A lapse of taste, a fall, *no, No, NO!* The instant guilt in his heart at her fall. Into their cell phones, a dozen moviegoers punched 911. The ambulance; the flashing lights; the cold from the pavement sucking the warmth from Huxted's kneeling legs. All the paramedics, handsome, efficient, no time for giving Huxted the mouth-to-mouth resuscitation, resurrection, he so desperately wanted, needed, taking her pulse, Mrs. D's tiny wrist; she was not on a fainting couch; she was not Ms. Redgrave acting. She was his mother. The 35-degree night temperature, her age, *Mom!*, the fall life-threatening.

"Where do you hurt?" the handsome paramedic asked.

"All over," she said, so typical, quite like her, hers not being the breathy voice of Vanessa Redgrave husking dialogue in a voice-over; real; panicked.

Familiar with long kneeling, from church as a child, from

bedrooms as a man, Huxted knelt on the pavement with his bare hands under her back, holding her fragile old body up off the cold, feeling himself, them, his mother and him, and Riley, his lover, the man who won him, who loved him, handsome blond Riley who was really the prize, kneeling there together, the three of them, a gay couple and the mother/mother-in-law, surrounded by paramedics and flashing lights, like some spectacle, some urban tableau of violence, as if someone had been shot; but not; the anger and competition exploding from within themselves; feeling themselves, a family tripped up, being stared at like something dysfunctional by the voyeur line of filmgoers finally shuffling off to admittance into the theater lobby, into the seats, to watch the screen, the opening credits rolling over the explosions of World War I montaged over the gorgeous face of Rupert Graves so ripe, so endearing, so unforgettable in movie-memory as the stableboy in *Maurice.*

"No," the paramedic insisted, "Don't tell me you hurt all over. Be specific."

Thank you, Huxted thought; the paramedic insisted his mother focus; finally; *thankyouthankyouthankyou.* The paramedic was a man, so handsome; *"Evans! Evans!"*; easy to imagine frontal, a male from central casting whom no one dared tell that the male gods were on the way out, as Huxted had been informed at rallies; headlines: "Extra! Extra! Read all about it! Rising goddesses oust male gods! Extra!" He still saw those male gods, knelt to them, especially when he looked at Riley, kneeling with him on the pavement beside Mrs. D, crying, being brave, blood running from her chin, her glasses askew, her white cloth coat reddening at the collar.

He knew that all their life together, his and Riley's, that in those twenty-five years he had seen the male god rise and rise and rise again triumphant, in himself, in Riley, in a thousand men, until this New Year's, this last pre-millennial New Year's the two of them, coupled, longing for marriage in Hawaii or Vermont or wherever a civil union might be recognized in a ceremony for which they would buy the flowers themselves, in a house of their own, brought down to the pavement by a woman falling, nude descending staircase, shouting, "I will never surrender."

A policeman came up, walked up, sidled up, himself, a frontal male god attending on the female deities that had fallen, temporarily, for the evening, like Mrs. D who did not drink, *not ever, no sir,* and, *if I were the IRA,* his mother had said to Huxted, had challenged him, two minutes before her fall, *and if you were England, I'd never let you win.* Win what, he wondered. What is the nature of resistance? What is it that people, women, resist, like Clarissa Dalloway resisting herself?

At least, he knew, Mrs. Dalloway had a past, savory with choices. Riley had the novel, Virginia Woolf's novel, *Mrs. Dalloway,* in his jacket pocket the way Virginia Woolf carried rocks in her coat pockets. They both, Huxted and Riley, not Mrs. D, had read it; and Huxted had moved on to *that novel that won the prize by that handsome writer, whose name I can't remember, who is on the best-seller list with that book whose title I can't remember,* Huxted had said in the bookstore, trying to buy the book from a half-remembered review, *that is not about Virginia Woolf but is sort of a spin on Virginia Woolf, you know,* but the bookstore clerk did not know, kept typing on the keyboard of his computer, hitting *search,* and kept insisting that they had *five copies of Virginia Woolf in the store, sir, "Orlando," "A Room of One's Own,"* and, and, and Huxted, frustrated, had kept insisting that Virginia Woolf hadn't written the book, but, *oh,* then, as part of his ritual abasement before the rising goddesses, so they would not be correct about one more angry male, he had apologized to the clerk recently graduated from MacDonald's saying, *I should have written the title down, everything whirls by so fast, the holidays, the internet, the satellite dish, I'm not sure where I am in time and space, in California, I know, but I mean where in time, memory and all that, yes, of course, but more, where exactly in time on the big clock, actual clock, to the theater-wide TV screen, virtual clock, which knows all time the same, because,* he laughed, *ha ha ha,* his voice like bright water rushing fresh over stones, at himself, *ha ha,* and Riley, his constant and true lover, had agreed, that *the speed of light doesn't seem as fast anymore,* when insomniac in bed at 2 AM in California they were seeing the future *simultaneously* in the early-morning *live* 5 AM wake-up news in New York, *live* 7 PM traffic reports from Tokyo, *live* 10 PM jumpers from windows in New Zealand, and *live* 10 AM stocks from England where over the head of the news anchor on location for the London weather in Regent's Park buzzed an airplane, noisy, flying over Bloomsbury, spelling out something in skywriting. "Nothing is more evanescent than skywriting which all writing is," Huxted wrote in one of his streaming critical essays which grew even more evanescent when his editor, at Riley's insistence, published them on the worldwide web and they went in digital bits of one's and zero's God knows where. Huxted adored the manifesto of the Swedish filmmakers of Dogma 95, proclaiming the way they composed film, handheld from the hip, budget zip, improvisational actors, shooting with available light, available props, freeing themselves of studio constraints, almost the way Ms. Redgrave/Mrs. Dalloway, night after night on one channel after another, stands in her own window contemplating her life in a monolog voice-over, almost the way Huxted himself folded time and place and words beyond convention: "There exists a future time when we are already dead."

Riley, the truly good son-in-law, had said, making conversation in the hospital emergency room, holding Mrs. D's hand on her unbroken wrist, how sad magazines and media, *All Diana All the Time,* had become since Princess Diana had been driven into that tunnel that August night in Paris, much like the August night when Huxted and Riley realized they were watching the *All Mrs. Dalloway Network, All Night, Every Night,* living through the slow-motion single-frame advance of the last August of the last summer of the century ticking toward the anticipated millennium midnight.

In fact, *Mrs. Dalloway* began reappearing on satellite television the exact last night of the last August, almost two years after Diana sped off from the Ritz not wearing a seat belt, and French doctors massaged her heart, her poor broken heart, as the ambulance, with her in it, moved (slowly) through the Paris night, *live* (as she died) (slowly) on satellite feed, as they watched the orange glow of Paris lights glow *live* on CNN, and wreckers hoist *live* the twisted Mercedes from the Alma tunnel and haul the car away *live* on a truck, while paparazzi sat *live* under arrest, having hunted Diana the Goddess of the Hunt to death, under suspicion, in a van while cameras *live* photographed *flashflashflash* them for a change.

We all make ourselves up; we make our own selves up, Mrs. Dalloway said on Virginia Woolf's pages. Diana had made herself up. Mrs. D had made Riley up insisting Riley, his beautiful fresh color, resembled her fair family more than the dark Huxted himself. Huxted had to laugh when the paramedic said to him, with his own hands freezing on the pavement under his ancient mother's back, and Huxted not as young as he once was, or ever as young as Riley still was, *oh, my, yes*, he had to laugh, when the paramedic asked him, "Who are you?"

The policeman asked him, "Why do you have your hands under that woman?"

The pair of man-gods, authorized by their uniforms, looked, demanding an answer, and Huxted said, weakly, trying not to sound weak, "I'm her son," as if that should have been enough to keep her from falling, and the cop flashed his light into Huxted's face, momentarily, just momentarily, but long enough, long enough to see Huxted's eyes had the intense stem-cell quality of gay; the key to the gene was in the eyes; the straight beam of light bright enough to hurt Huxted's eyes, as if he'd turned and looked directly into the bright light of the movie projector right that moment inside the Rialto Cinema where *Mrs. Dalloway* was unreeling, the younger Clarissa running and the mature Clarissa walking, two Mrs. Dalloways, two for the price of one, through the hallways of what Riley called a "furniture movie," trying to decide, she was, Clarissa was, Mrs. Dalloway was, (Virginia Woolf had been) whom to marry to be safe, secure, not perhaps to the one who loved her best, but to the one who made her safe, because, perhaps love was wonderful, but safety was better.

Huxted never thought safety was better than the risks of love.

Michael Cunningham knew that when out of his own hands he let his own draggy Mrs. D, Richard, sitting in a windowsill, exactly like Septimus, let him let go, spilling him, not letting him fall exactly, letting him fly down, full of HIV (neither love nor passion were safe), down three stories inside the window well.

"It was a window well, wasn't it," Riley had asked after they had finally found the prize-winning book, (bought it actually over the web, their first net purchase, searching Amazon.com for "Virginia Woolf" which led to "Michael Cunningham," a real writer winning real awards in the real world, not the velvet gay world), and read it the week of Huxted's mother's eightieth birthday party, and *The Hours* kept them excited, hearing the writer's voice. Dreaming of the strapping athletic author, Michael Cunningham, gorgeous as a Hurrell film star on the cover of *Poets and Writers*, working out his chiseled Los Angeles cheekbones in Manhattan, sweaty, buffed in a gym in Chelsea, kept them sane visiting in Mrs. D's aluminum-covered house where they tried to invent themselves (*re-invent* themselves, everyone was saying in the so clichéd new small talk).

In that dollhouse, Huxted had invented himself as a boy; then, coming back, returning for the party, as a man in longtime domesticity with another man. All of Virginia D's friends knowing what it was, but never saying what it was, as if, how dare you boys bring this into our party that you have paid for, but you haven't bought us, you *must* not say what we *must* not know.

You must do this! You must do that! Huxted's parents had told him that. Riley's parents had told him, also, *You must! Must? Must?* They both had grown up saying, *Must? Must?* What is this *must?* You *must* marry. *Must* marry. *Must. Must. Must.* So like Virginia Woolf herself, *must* marry, *must* marry, *must* marry whom? Lytton! Marry Lytton! Lytton who said the word, "Semen." Unbuttoning Bloomsbury. How could you; you can't; he won't; he might propose, but he *must* run. Lytton *must* run. Marry then, not passion, but safety. Marry whom? Leonard? Leonard Woolf? So very Mrs. Dalloway. Marry Peter? Marry Richard? Mrs. Peter Walsh. Mrs. Walsh. No. Mrs. Richard Dalloway. God, Huxted's mother, Virginia, Mrs. Daly, Mrs. D, who knew when she was fifteen whom she would marry, delivered by ambulance to the hospital's bright lights; the cold air of the emergency room; left waiting, waiting, waiting.

"Is my face cut? How is my face? Huxted? Riley? How bad?"

Mrs. D, a madonna; rosary, novenas; she was their lucky charm, praying for them, her two sons, one by birth, one by luck. Sweet old girl, not vanity; her face the only part of the old seventy-nine-year-old body turning eighty that still in its bones looked like the girl who at twelve, when planes were young, had defied her mother and flown up in the air, bi-planing, once, thirty minutes for a dollar she had earned herself, with a skywriter who for an extra quarter wrote her name in the blue. *How fast we are all growing old*; Huxted looked at his mother in the emergency-room glare, shied away from his own face in a mirror, looked at Riley; even Vanessa Redgrave could no longer play her younger self in films. There exists a future time....

Eileen Atkins was right lamenting the slow progress of films directed by women or written by women and, *oh, my, yes*, beyond all that doggerel and dogma, saying people, agents, send her women's books to adapt, figuring she must like them, because she's a woman—a cause-and-effect presumption which she can't bear; and she was right, but it was true for men too, at least for men who were stem-cell men the way Huxted and Riley existed in the genome of males, resisting especially even other men like themselves, too gay, ("straight-acting, straight-appearing" was the desire of all the Gay Personals ever printed), acquiescing only to frontal males. They had a *must* to marry, each other, and daily the news was about same-sex marriage, *pro* and *con*, but finally, thankfully, at last, a daily part of the national discussion in the press, on the internet, over the satellite dish. There was no old boys club for old boys like them, and no old girls club for the girls to get together, have a bake sale, and raise the money for shooting their little film about Virginia Woolf who was the original-recipe Mrs. Dalloway. How dare a budget interfere? How dare a budget enter art and politics; how dare a budget come into any grand little party and jar the music and make the flowers a bit less than grand, and make people stretch and say ridiculous things like "less is more," (when every gay man knows in his twist of XY chromosomes only more is more), when the budget causes the lighting to be too bright, to flood the screen to almost burn up the incandescent Redgrave.

Oh, God, Huxted and Riley, reassuring Mrs. D her face was fine, her chin was cut, (stitches), her wrist was broken, (a cast), but her face was fine, and, during the long wait on the gurney for the emergency-room doctor, Huxted could only imagine where in the unreeling *Mrs. Dalloway* at the Rialto the plot might be. This was the first showing of the first night of the New Year. Only 364 days to count down. Signs and omens were everywhere. How dare blood! Was this to be their luck for the last twelve months of the millennium?

During their last stay in London, in Kensington, Huxted and Riley had watched in awe as Princess Diana surged by on the sidewalk, in sweat clothes, running to her gym in the hot August, so humid, that Huxted's face had wept sweat as he shot video of the full moon over Kensingston from the window of their small apartment hotel at 7 Trebovir Street, (Earl's Court Station), not far from 22 Hyde Park Gate, in Kensington where Virginia Woolf had been born; the last full moon Diana would ever see, he had shot on video tape.

In London, a few years before that last visit, the way time was relative, quantum, folded, the hours before, seconds before in memory, they sent a note backstage saying they were friends of a British actor in Los Angeles, Peter Bromilow, who had been young in stock with Vanessa Redgrave. She had, herself, the Redgrave, invited them backstage after her performance in *When She Danced*, (a color photograph of the blue marquee of the Globe Theater lit with billboards and red-and-yellow neon letters spelling out *"When She Danced,* Vanessa Redgrave, with Frances de la Tour, A Play by Martin Sherman"* was the screen-saver on Huxted's laptop), greeting them on the stairs of the Globe lobby with her right hand extended, "Exactly," Riley said, "exactly the way she extends her arms at the end of *Mrs. Dalloway* to dance with Peter Walsh the man she loved but was afraid to marry," and *oh,* the two of them, Huxted and Riley, had lived on that (touched by Vanessa Redgrave) for years, going off to her party, swept off to a party by Vanessa Redgrave, a party in London, a lovely party.

"Save me," she said, "we're trying to raise money" for a play, a movie, something, (perhaps even for *Mrs. Dalloway* itself, or *Vita and Virginia*) and she, Ms. Redgrave, had signed her autobiography, new out that week, (the index alone a "www" meta-data *Who's Who*), and handed the book to them, wishing that they were, perhaps what she hoped them to be, angels, producers from the States, backers with money, when they were just theater queens died and gone to heaven watching Vanessa dancing Isadora Duncan, folding time, in the quantum writing of the script, making the older Isadora dance the younger Isadora by simply standing stage-front center, still, still as a still life, still as a human can stand, her shadow cast up enormous on the back wall of the bare stage by a light, the kind of low-budget light which theatre can make magic—and movies, which are light, cannot. "I have just spoken with Vanessa Redgrave," Tennessee Williams said. "She is the greatest actress of our time."

Spinning, Huxted and Riley had spent the Friday evening with Vanessa Redgrave playing Isadora, three nights before the Monday Princess Diana handed Vanessa the 1991 Olivier Award for Best Actress in a play, six nights before the Thursday Vanessa Redgrave, once Vanessa Redgrave Richardson, left the stage dark, because her former husband, director Tony Richardson, the father of her two daughters, was dying in Los Angeles, died November 14 in Los Angeles of the viral plague, leaving them, leaving the stage empty as a window from which someone wonderful has lifted floated flown away, run off in the loneliness of the long-distance runner. "You want my life?" What does the brain matter compared with the heart? Tony was to direct Vanessa in *The Cherry Orchard*. Virginia wrote through Septimus: "How the dead sing."

"I hope you slept with him," Vanessa Redgrave said to Huxted, meaning her old friend, Peter Bromilow, with whom Huxted had a short affair and a longer friendship, until Peter, so elegant with cigars and leather and T-cells, died and *Variety* printed his obituary, "...played Sir Sagramore in *Camelot* to Vanessa Redgrave's Guenevere." Vanessa and Glenda Jackson, both in full queen costumes, (posed together for *Mary, Queen of Scots*, in a huge black-and-white photograph), had hung, framed, in Peter's entry hall in Los Angeles, signed by both actresses, "From a pair of queens to a truly Big Queen."

Gods and civilizations rise and fall, plagues come and go, plays open and close, but what matters any of it, all night, every night, when the quantum clock of a 97-minute movie lights the wide-screen TV, lights the faces of Huxted and Riley, ticks out the digital bits of the satellite dish and *Mrs. Dalloway Mrs. Dalloway Mrs. Dalloway*—is the title, so insistently *wifely*, ironic?—repeats over and over, Septimus falls, yes, again, and yes, again, to bits in one's and zero's, and they read on in books, reading through the stunning, endless, bibliography of Virginia Woolf, reading *Orlando* out loud to the eighty-year-old Mrs. D who smiles her smile of "no surrender," seeming to more than understand a story of how a woman becomes a man becomes a woman becomes a being. Watching Tilda Swinton swing in DVD from Derek Jarman's *Edward II* to Sally Potter's, *Orlando*, Virginia Daly, asking, "Is that the woman, that actress, you met? I can't keep your friends straight."

"Vanessa Redgrave," Huxted said. "Not friends, actually; we met just once."

"Don't you criticize my senses; my memory."

"Why become so defensive, mother," Huxted asked, "why go on the defensive, all I answered was your question, why do you think everything is an attack, why do you think everything is a competition, how did I become the enemy, how does someone gain the power over another one, and you will not, mother, no one will be, the rock in my pocket. I'm your son, an adult, not your husband. If you want a yes-man, get married. I don't want your life."

Huxted only imagined saying little cruelties like that, spurred on by snipey magazine rhetoric. He was rereading Janet Malcolm's tasty article, "Bloomsbury, live" in *The New Yorker*, the same issue that Peter Conrad, paraphrasing others—others who had paraphrased Huxted, to sound informed in their own personal right—wrote about Robert Mapplethorpe, (who had once been part of Huxted's own private Bloomsbury), calling Mapplethorpe "The Devil's Disciple" and making bad puns, calling Huxted's dear, dead Robert, the "Prince of darkrooms" who died, throwing his life away, without knowing his own self; which was not true. Indeed, Robert had thrown his life away; Huxted, in fact, years before, when they were young together had predicted that Robert would throw his life away; but Robert, his own kind of Septimus Warren Smith, always knew his own self, and when he would jump.

Huxted knew Virginia Woolf's Bloomsbury had not all been sweetness and light; the Woolfs, censorious, frightened, bourgeois bohemians, refused to publish *Ulysses*; their strained relations with the painter Dora Carrington who ended up living with the writer Lytton Strachey who had proposed to Virginia then ran for his life. Huxted knew gay life was the same or worse; was, in fact, Bloomsbury; Bloomsbury, the very model for gay life, especially the gay literary life, where East Coast writers, *indifferent* and *hostile* VW would have called them, sniffed at West Coast writers, as if the geography of fags were literature, and in Manhattan, the Gay Mafia, the Gay Reich, friends publishing friends, reviewing each other, all living together in the same apartment building, giving each other awards at circle-jerk ceremonies, canonizing themselves, plowing pertinent academics, writing blurbs that caused *ha ha ha* in the country house which Huxted was pleased one day to hear Riley name their own "Monastery of Art."

Their house, their domesticity of twenty-five years, was a retreat from the violet Mafia Reich, because Huxted was a writer not comfortable in the purple company of other lavender writers who pontificated into their Cosmopolitans that AIDS writing was a genre, and gay writing was political correction, as if politics were literature, and social climbing, and money, and publishing contracts reserved for viral twenty-one-year-olds, and queenly expatriation to London (for twee unsuckable kveens) and to Tuscany (for young feckless fucks). They all seemed fundamentalist, very Miss Kilman, as righteous about lilac "literature" as VW's Miss Kilman about strict "religion," sectarian, carrying their violet violent grudges intravenously against each other, perhaps because the straight world marginalized gay writing into genre writing, reduced alongside "westerns" and "mysteries."

It was not them personally he disliked, it was the platonic ideal of art from which they had fallen, petulant, inbred, drunken, impotent, imperiously entitled. Huxted tried to liberate himself from competition and cliché. He was comfortable with readers who thought writing was sexual magic. A hard cock was the best review. Still, one wondered, really, "Why after all does one do it?"

With clarity, free of tree-based books, Riley was an internet biographer. He wrote, "The way Mapplethorpe was an artist who was a photographer, Huxted Daly is an artist who is a writer in his own private Bloomsbury, www.virtualgayliterature.com." They laughed together, poking fun privately, like married couples, which was their abiding dream. "Happiness is this, is this," Riley said.

They could not be separated against their wills.

Lone Woolf-like they manufactured biographical narrative, Huxted of others, Riley of Huxted, all tapped out on the internet, sent directly to satellite, by Riley himself, from a laptop in a room in a house in a vineyard in a valley in the country where at dusk the peacocks screamed. *"Evans! Evans!"*

Yet, Huxted found a certain esthetic incest agreeable. He took delight that in the international circle of Vanessa Redgrave's power, that she herself could star with her brother, Corin Redgrave, and his wife, her sister-in-law, Kika Markham, at the Gielgud Theatre in the revival, *Song at Twilight*, a play written by Noel Coward, once her own father's lover, with whom her father, according to her mother, had chosen to spend his last night prior to his enlistment in World War II. On eBay, the on-line auction house, Huxted had bid on, and won, a letter handwritten by Vanessa Redgrave to her father, and signed, age sixteen, and a first edition of *Mrs. Dalloway*, published 1925, on May 14, Riley's birthday, twenty-five years before his birth year.

Huxted wondered if in the long pastness in the Noel Coward clique of London *artistes*, the ever-widening pools of Bloomsbury, Vanessa Redgrave herself had been named by her father, Sir Michael, and her mother, the actress, Rachel Kempson, Lady Redgrave, after the fifty-eight-year-old painter, Vanessa Bell, Virginia Woolf's sister, and the mother of Quentin Bell. His head was swimming, which was the way he liked it, because he had no choice, born the way he was with gay stem cells and a queer genome spinning analysis on feeling. On a sudden entrepreneurial inspiration, with his laptop on his lap, he typed in the correct "www" to buy a website. What fun, he thought, to own www.VirginiaWoolf.com. For ninety-eight dollars, he might buy a piece of virtual real estate and sign it over to Vanessa Redgrave Enterprises Ltd. in perpetuity, with $5,000, to do with as she and Eileen Atkins might see fit to build a budget for a film whose rolling end credits would acknowledge Huxted Daly and Riley Daly-Thomas.

"It says here," Riley said, pointing at the DVD's "Interactive Menus," "Scene Access," and "Letterbox Format" showing *Mrs. Dalloway* on their theater-wide screen, "that Virginia Woolf in 1941, having experimented with suicide previously, knew enough, at fifty-nine, that on her final walkabout to the river, to the water, to pick up a stone, a big stone, to put in her coat pocket, so she could not fight the tide, the river's tide, and the will to live, which she no longer had, or wanted, but could not trust would not roar up in self-preservation at the last moment, except by loading her pockets with rocks to drown herself. Fifty-nine then was old. The new fifty-nine is the old thirty-nine."

"So the new eighty…"

"Is really the old sixty."

"Huxted! Riley!" His own Mrs. Dalloway, his own Mrs. D, his own Virginia, over eighty, grown stronger once she entered her new decade, came in the door, wrist healed, flushed from driving her own car, happy in her independence, ("I forgive you, Huxted."), she of the abiding presence, ("I forgive you, mother."), much happier and less angry with a knee replacement and two hearing AIDS which finally she admitted she needed after five years of telling everyone around her to speak up and stop mumbling. "Huxted, I bought these flowers myself. They're for tonight, for you, and for you, Riley, dear, for your party, for your engagement party…after all these years."

Why, and how escape? His own Mrs. D taught him the will to survive. Would they all live forever on stem cells, cloned parts, and gene therapy? Huxted's talent for pastness made him hungry for the futurity, the futurity, the futurity of the new millennium, standing at the window of the new millennium, the way Vanessa/Clarissa stood at windows, white curtains rising softly in the evening summer breeze, thinking his own voice-over. "Is death the only way? No. I won't go. Not falling, not calling, 'Evans! Evans! Riley! Riley!' Not the cliché of exit, at least not that exit cliché, not that very gay cliché, the *must, must, must* of suicide, *The Children's Hour* fate of every mid-century gay character—'You want my life?'—in every gay play or movie, not jumping out some window, not like Septimus Warren Smith, not like my father, best, bested, who's afraid of Virginia Woolf, who's afraid of Virginia Daly, not with rocks in my pocket into a river, not like Dora Carrington shooting a hunting rifle into her own heart, not like Diana flying arabesque unbuckled into a Paris tunnel.

"Why would I try to escape such sweetness as union with

Riley? What matters if a future time exists when we are already dead, if we are alive this moment. I shall live, and some day die, a happy man, a groom, a man who has had a wedding, happier than Clarissa Dalloway, no Sapphonic suicide like that Virginia Woolf, peacefully in my lover's arms in our legally licensed marriage bed in a new world in a new century with digital bits of *Mrs. Dalloway* written in the air like skywriting from a plane over a park in June. I will not surrender. Why should the male gods surrender? Why should anyone surrender?"

He saw his reflection in the window glass.

"Here I am at last."

He heard Riley's voice, coming from another room, welcoming guests, "Here we are at last."

"This millennium," he voiced, rejuvenated, feeling that sixty was the new forty, toasting the new forty, "is a new age of stem cells, web sex at www.toughcustomers.com, compact discs of one's and zero's, and books printed on demand and on-line"; he voiced in his inner voice, saying nothing, greeting their incoming wedding-engagement party, hearing someone shout "so *Four Weddings*, darling!" and, he vowed, "We will neither live nor die the past deaths forced on our kind of tender genome people: *non exeunt*, like Diana and Dora and Virginia, pursued by a bear."

Together, at their party, with the flowers Mrs. D had bought, Huxted took Riley into his arms, and Riley took Huxted, and they danced close to "Moonglow and Theme from *Picnic*," closer even than Mrs. Dalloway (on the *All Mrs. Dalloway Network, All Night, Every Night*) dancing in the final scene with Peter, Peter Walsh, her one true love.

Jack Fritscher is the sole author of the meta-screenplay, *Duchess: Berlin 1928*, as well as of its poster, its Vienna Film Restoration review, and its glossary of film terms. Naming the director of the film, he chose his Austrian immigrant grandmother's maiden name; other names of cast and crew are names of relatives, or friends, or are fictitious.

Austrian ReViviFilm Presents
A Hapsburg Films Re-Release
Duchess
Berlin 1928
Zuflucht in Berlin
A Film by
Amelia Haberman
Vienna Film Restoration Festival

VIENNA FILM RESTORATION FESTIVAL

DUCHESS: BERLIN 1928

(DRAMA – AUSTRIAN – B&W)

A Hapsburg Films (Vienna) release, in association with Restorische Films, with the support of Austrian Revivifilm. (International sales: Lu Lu Rodenfels DVD Ltd, Stamford, CT.) Produced by Isaac Gottlieb. Co-producer, Amelia Haberman from her original screenplay, *Zuflucht in Berlin*. (Sound. 1932) Restoration produced by Fritz Haberman and Maria Nagle, 2000.

Directed, written by Amelia Haberman. Camera (B&W), Bea Brooks; editor, Agnes Tschohl; music, Marta Jean Solomon; art director, Annya Deitwig; costume designer, Helga Kuehner. Original title: *Zuflucht in Berlin*. German and English soundtrack. Running time: 80 MIN.

With Nadja Hoenig, Hannes Mueller, Ilsa Pilvonka.

Now seeming an earnest period film traversing material recently settled (more or less) by DNA testing of royal Romanov remains finally buried decently by post-Soviet Russia, "Duchess: Berlin 1928," takes a forward-for-its-time romantic look at a woman's identity crisis. While moody with expressionist shadows, pic's story is uncomplicated, simple, and made on a low budget on the backlot at UFA by assistant scriptgirl, Amelia Haberman, whose feature debut lifted her damsel-in-distress material by direction and camera into a luminous complexity here restored by her grandson, Fritz Haberman and his wife Maria Nagle, for Austrian Revivifilm. (All original prints of the 1932 drama, reviewed at the Vienna Film Restoration Festival, were thought destroyed during Nazi occupation of Vienna and UFA.) Scripter Haberman evidently had a prescience about female history because she early on paid attention to Romanov identity rumors rampant in Europe in the 1920s. Haberman-Nagle's translation of Amelia Haberman's simple script make this restoration accessible as historical femme fest-fare and playable on satellite stations devoted to late-night romantic programming.

Is she or isn't she the Grand Duchess Anastasia, youngest daughter of the murdered Russian royal family? That is the question when Anya (Nadja Hoenig) turns up mysteriously in Berlin where Frau Teufel (Ilsa Pilvonka in a star turn) tries to exploit her suspicions about Anya's identity. Berlin itself is a character on screen in sets, lighting, and cinematography. The American reporter, John Wilson (Hannes Mueller), asks all the right and wrong questions. The plot is standard girl-meets-boy except that Haberman wisely directs her Anya towards the door like Ibsen's Nora. Film is no "A Doll's House," but piques interest because of female

p.o.v,. advanced for its time, but not sensational enough for today's taste. Haberman is courageous. She had one chance to direct in a film industry collapsing under Hitler. Film is a conduit of anxiety in a context of history that swept women and men into anonymity. By the end, pic gives creditable understanding of German film visuals reinterpreted by nearly all-distaff writer, director, crew and as much insight into female identity fears as contempo movies-of-the-week. —*Renalda Becker*

The Russian Imperial Family: Czar Nicholas II and Czarina Alexandra with their four daughters and son. Anastasia is on the right.–German postcard, 1913.

A Quick Glossary
SCREENPLAY TERMS

INT. means Interior, inside a house, room, etc.

EXT. means Exterior, out of doors

FADE IN means a dark screen turns slowly into a picture

FADE OUT means a picture turns slowly to a dark screen

FADE TO BLACK means the picture turns to a black screen; can also be **FADE TO WHITE**

DISSOLVE means one image gives way to another, as in, image A, on screen, is momentarily overlaid with fade in of image B, with both existing together, until A fades out, leaving only B

MONTAGE means a mixing and ongoing dissolve of two, three, or four images into a sequence

ESTABLISHING SHOT reveals in broad terms where the action takes place, say, the skyline of a city, a hillside in the Alps, the facade of a building, or a staircase, etc. where subsequent closer action will occur

FULL SHOT reveals a complete view, for example, of a room, showing actors feet to head

MEDIUM SHOT shows actors waist to head

CLOSE SHOT shows actors shoulders to face

CLOSE UP SHOT shows a face; or a thing, very close

TIGHT CLOSE UP SHOT shows features of face

INSERT SHOT is something edited quickly into the action, such as a close-up of a photograph, a newspaper, a hand with a ring, etc.

TWO-SHOT is a shot, medium or close, of two actors

ANGLE is the way the camera looks at the subject or person

ANOTHER ANGLE is a variation on the previous **ANGLE**

WIDER ANGLE is a change of focus moving from, say, a person, wider to include the person's room, surroundings, physical circumstances

FEATURING means favoring a subject/person in the shot

POV is the character's POINT OF VIEW, how something looks to the character

TRUCKING SHOT indicates the camera itself is moving one way or the other with the action

VOICE OVER: dialog spoken by an actor who is not on screen when the dialog is heard over the image that is on screen

Duchess
Berlin 1928

THEME

Caught in the turmoil of the Russian revolution, a young woman with post-tramatic stress syndrome, fights a Royal Family, political enemies, and an American lover to create her own identity.

24 CHARACTERS

In Russia, 9 characters

NICHOLAS: 50, former Czar of Russia deposed by revolutionaries, a gentle man suffering in exile; now a worried husband and father of five.

ALEXANDRA: 46, former Czarina, born a German Princess, and granddaughter of Queen Victoria of England, a religous royal remaining Czarina even in exile; hard, bitter, righteous.

The four royal teen-aged daughters, the Grand Duchesses, and the one son, the future Czar of all the Russias. Anastasia is the youngest girl. Murdered in the early morning of July 17, 1918, all had mid-summer birthdays.

OLGA: 21
TATIANA: 19
MARIA: 18

ANASTASIA: turned 17, June 18, 1918, 29 days before the murders.

ALEXIS: 12, the only son, the future Czar, often carried in the arms of his father, suffers from hemophilia inherited from his great-grandmother, Queen Victoria of England.

KARKOV: 28, the leader of the Cheka Guard; dark, brooding, mustachioed, burly.

EUGENEV: 20, a handsome Russian soldier, pressed into service by the Bolshiviks; bearded, romantic, and of interest to the young Grand Duchesses.

In Berlin, 15 characters

ANNA EISENSTEIN: 27; is she or isn't she a Grand Duchess? Her demeanor is ambiguity. She is a woman of perplexed mysteries. She is at cross purposes with herself and the world with her. She reads who-dun-its and histories of the Imperial Family. Is she ANASTASIA? Is she an impostor using reverse psychology? Is she possessed/obsessed by ANASTASIA's spirit? Is she Everywoman in search of her own identity, in flight from the identities forced at her by others?

JOHN WILSON: An American reporter for a New York paper; hard-boiled, at 35 he has been around; he has a leading man's smoothness with a cynical edge.

FRAU ILSA TEUFEL: 50ish, she has good bone structure; plump yet stylish; worldly-wise, she runs a sanitarium and she wants out. ANNA is her ticket. In German, her name means *devil.*

OLGA: A Romanov in exile, a Grand Duchess. She is ANASTA-SIA's aunt and godmother. She wants no Romanov resurrection; for her the past is past. In her 60's, she is short and sharp. She smokes stylish cigars.

ERNST LUDWIG: A Romanov in exile, a Grand Duke. He is brother of OLGA, and ANASTASIA's uncle. He is a short man; a typically aged Imperial officer: 60's and an old fool, but sympathetic.

KATHARINE: the former Imperial Governess and mentor to the five royal children; 40's; patient.

MALENKOV: the villain; a fat-faced Russian Soviet agent of the NKVD. He eats often and well. He speaks no lines. His face is everything.

BORODIN: an ironic male; former Imperial officer; 50ish.

NIGEL ROBERTS: a stereotypical British reporter; his shirt is stuffed and his lip is stiff.

LORRE: German reporter.
POLICEMAN: German, 30.
MONIKA: young German bicyclist.
GUNTHER: second young German bicyclist.
DESK CLERK: German, 25, Hotel Odeon.
MOVIE-GOER: Woman, 50.

SETS

In Russia, Interiors

Act I: THE HOUSE OF EXILE
    1. Bedroom of NICHOLAS and ALEXANDRA
    2. Hallway of the same old house
    3. Bedroom of the four young Grand Duchesses
    4. Stairway and landing
    5. Cellar

In Berlin, Interiors

Act II:
    1. ANNA's sanitarium room

2. A 1928 Rolls Royce: rear seat

3. Foyer of sanitarium, with hallway

Act III:

1. Berlin: a Russian Gypsy Cafe

2. Movie theater seats and aisle

3. ERNST LUDWIG's hotel suite

Act IV:

1. Hotel Odeon Lobby and stairs

2. Hotel Odeon ANNA's room

Act V: Public Hospital room

Act VI: Russian Church

In Berlin, Exteriors

Act IV:

1. Facade of Hotel Odeon

2. Dark streets and canal of Berlin

Act VI:

1. Facade of Russian Church

2. Railroad yard train tracks

3. Boat at dock

ACT I

FADE IN
INT. BEDROOM OF
NICHOLAS AND ALEXANDRA—NIGHT

SUPERIMPOSE logo:
EKATERINBURG, RUSSIA
July 16, 1918

ESTABLISHING SHOT

In the bedroom of the exiled Czar and Czarina, NICHOLAS

and ALEXANDRA, their son, the Czarevitch ALEXIS, 12 years old, sleeps soundly in a bed near them.

The shot PANS SLOWLY into a CLOSE SHOT of a black-and-white, formal photograph of the Russian Imperial Family. A TIGHT PAN moves to each face as the VOICE OVER, the same voice as the American reporter, JOHN WILSON, softly intones:

(Voice Over)

Wilson: In the summer of 1918, in the village of Ekaterinburg, in Russia, a murder was committed. At 3:15 in the morning, July 17, the Red Communist Guard awakened the four-centuries-old Imperial Family of the Romanovs: the father, Czar NICHOLAS II, and his wife, the Czarina ALEXANDRA; their four young daughters, each one a princess: the eldest, the Grand Duchess TATIANA, who volunteered as a nurse in a military hospital; the Grand Duchess OLGA, who danced long evenings at the palace of Peterhof; the Grand Duchess MARIA, who was shy and bookish; the Grand Duchess ANASTASIA who in that murderous summer turned 17; and lastly, the only son and heir to the throne of all the Russias, the Czarevitch, the Crown Prince ALEXIS, 12 years old, incurably ill with the bleeder's disease, hemophilia. On the night of July 16-17, 1918, on this summer night, the Royal Family, deposed and arrested by the Red Communists, were roused from their beds. The guards told them they were to be removed by truck from Ekaterinburg to a safer sanctuary...

The TIGHT PAN LOOSENS AND CONTINUES, PANNING from ALEXIS' portrait face to ALEXIS' real face asleep in the bed next to the bureau holding the family picture.

ALEXIS's face is flushed and almost beautiful in sleep. The PAN continues, discovering the sad royal attempts at making the room comfortable until it holds on a MEDIUM

SHOT OF NICHOLAS AND ALEXANDRA lying awake and distant in their bed. TATIANA opens the door to the room her parents share with their sickly son.

Tatiana: Father!
Nicholas: Tatiana?
Tatiana: I'm frightened, father.
Nicholas: Come in, my girl.
Tatiana: The noise. Outside. On the other side of the house. Trucks are gathering. The soldiers are drunk and shouting. We are all frightened, father. Anastasia is crying.
Nicholas: Again.
Alexandra: Anastasia cries enough for all of us. She is a silly girl.
Nicholas: Anastasia is young. Too young. For this.
Alexandra: You spoil our daughters.
Nicholas: (Chucking TATIANA's chin) As beautiful young Grand Duchesses should be.
Alexandra: You fill them with useless dreams, Nikki. The life we knew is destroyed. Gone forever.
Tatiana: Mother!
Alexandra: These are hard new times, Tatiana. Because of these drunken Red soldiers, I am no longer Empress and you are no longer a Grand Duchess.
Nicholas: (To Tatiana) You will always be my little Duchess.
Alexandra: God has told me in a dream. We are the last of the Romanovs...Tomorrow the soldiers will have us scrubbing their lavatories.

A second KNOCK on the door. It is ANASTASIA.
As the door opens, the SHOT PANS to a CLOSE UP of ANASTASIA.

Nicholas: (Voice Over) Anastasia! My Anya... What is it?
Anastasia: In our room. With Olga and Maria. Three soldiers.

ANOTHER ANGLE

Nicholas: I'll have them shot!

Anastasia: They ordered us to dress. They want to take us away.

Alexandra: (Sits up with a glimmer of hope) Perhaps our loyal soldiers are closer than we know. Perhaps we have hope yet. O my sweet Savior! To be rescued from this godforsaken place.

Nicholas: Away? Dare they? Away? Where?

ANOTHER ANGLE

Karkov: (Enters and pushes OLGA and MARIA through the door) Away! To wherever I choose to send you and your Duchesses, your "Excellency."

Olga: Father!

Maria: Mother!

Alexandra: Come to me, Maria.

Karkov: You will have one hour to pack together in one trunk whatever valuables and documents you wish to take with you.

Alexandra: One trunk for an Empress and four Grand Duchesses? One trunk for five royal women?

MEDIUM SHOT FEATURING
KARKOV AND ANASTASIA

Karkov: No longer "royal," Madam Comrade. (Karkov strokes Anastasia's face) Just women.

CLOSE UP NICHOLAS

Nicholas: Sir!

CLOSE UP KARKOV

Karkov: (His intonation dares a standoff) Sir!...

ANOTHER ANGLE FEATURING KARKOV

Karkov: ...One hour. One trunk. You will depart before dawn. (Exits)

Alexandra: (Rises and crosses to Alexis' bed and touches his forehead) My little Prince.

Nicholas: How is my little man?

Alexis: Is it midnight, father?
Nicholas: Hurry, children. All of you. Dress warmly.
Alexandra: Wear as many clothes as you can.
Alexis: Where will the soldiers take us, father?

MEDIUM ANASTASIA

Anastasia: They intend to kill us.
Nicholas: (Voice Over) Anastasia!

ANOTHER ANGLE FEATURING ANASTASIA

Anastasia: Outside the guard room. I heard them talking.
Alexandra: That will be, Anya, enough. God is with us.
Nicholas: Go, Anastasia. Go. Go, you girls. Dress. (The four
     Grand Duchesses exit)

MEDIUM NICHOLAS AND ALEXANDRA

Nicholas: ...Anya is right.
Alexandra: Never!
Nicholas: I've known all along.

ANOTHER ANGLE

Alexis: Why do the soldiers wish to kill us, father?
Alexandra: Because we are everything they can never hope to be.
Nicholas: Because they believe differently than we.
Alexandra: Communists! Atheists! Godless atheists!
Nicholas: They think to make a whole new world.
Alexis: When I am Czar and have 20 ships, I too will make a
     whole new world.
Alexandra: Oh my dear Alexei!
Nicholas: (Sadly) ...when you are Czar of Russia...

INT. DUCHESSES' BEDROOM—NIGHT

The FOUR GRAND DUCHESSES are in a flurry of dressing. Each is pulling on three and four dresses. ANASTASIA
accidentally rips the seam in a muff. Jewels spill out. The

others stoop to help her stuff the jewels back into the lining.

Olga: Anastasia! You are so careless.

Anastasia: Poof. I've decided not to care. When the soldiers drink, they say things they don't mean. When they drink, they sing.

Maria: Silly Anastasia.

Anastasia: When they sing, they dance. That makes me happy.

Tatiana: Foolish Anya. So changeable!

Olga: Soooo romantic!

Tatiana: Will you take along that gangly soldier Eugenev?

Anastasia: I know no soldier Eugenev.

Maria: (Giggling) The Eugenev who kissed you last week.

Anastasia: He did not.

Olga: Kissed you in the hallway.

Anastasia: Eugenev. Poof! I never heard of him.

Tatiana: He has black hair and dark eyes.

Olga: He has a beautiful black beard.

Maria: Does the beard tickle when he kisses, Anya?

Anastasia: I've never been kissed. Not by any soldier Eugenev. Not by anyone.

ANOTHER ANGLE

Alexis: (Enters on one crutch) Father says to hurry.

Anastasia: When will you learn to knock.

Alexis: Never.

Anastasia: After all, we're DRESSING.

Alexis: You are wearing three coats.

ANOTHER ANGLE

Karkov: (Enters with EUGENEV) Eugenev here... (The GRAND DUCHESSES giggle. ANASTASIA blushes. EUGENEV buries a private smile.) ...Eugenev here will escort you to your parents' room.

Tatiana: Where will you take us?

Karkov: To a secret place.

Olga: Is it safe?

Karkov: Very safe, *Comrade* Olga.
Maria: *The Grand Duchess* Olga is not your "comrade."
Tatiana: We are none of us your "comrades," Comrade.

ANOTHER ANGLE FEATURING
ANASTASIA AND EUGENEV

Anastasia: (Closes in a step on EUGENEV) Are we in danger?
Eugenev: For you...no danger.
Anastasia: For my family. You must promise.
Eugenev: As far as I am able.
Anastasia: Just as I thought. "As far as you are able." Indeed! So much for your talk of your "whole new world."

ANOTHER ANGLE FEATURING KARKOV

Karkov: You will follow Comrade Eugenev to your parents' room. From there you will be escorted to the cellar.
Maria: I don't like the cellar. It is stone and cold.
Anastasia: Why the cellar?

KARKOV smiles enigmatically, turns, and exits.

Eugenev: Outside the cellar a truck will be waiting... Follow me, please, comrades.
Olga: *Please.* The Red soldier says "please" and calls us "comrades."

They begin their exit.

INT. HALLWAY—NIGHT

The FOUR GRAND DUCHESSES and ALEXIS follow EUGENEV into the hallway.

REVERSE TRUCK SHOT

precedes the party down the hall.

SOUND

OUTSIDE THE WINDOWS: RANDOM
GUNSHOTS, SHOUTING, REVVING OF ENGINES.

Alexis: Guns. The soldiers are shooting.
Olga: The "comrade" soldiers are drunk.
Anastasia: They have their guns to protect us.
Tatiana: Anya. Why should they protect us?

CLOSE UP TRUCKING FEATURING ANASTASIA

Anastasia: Because we are who we are.

REVERSE TRUCK SHOT
AS ABOVE CONTINUES

The FIVE CHILDREN walk bravely toward their parents'
door.

INT. BEDROOM OF
NICHOLAS AND ALEXANDRA—NIGHT

Nicholas: Alex, I am afraid.
Alexandra: Hush, Nikki. We must pray and plan.
Nicholas: Even if they must kill me, they must spare you and the
children.
Alexandra: They will not dare touch us.
Nicholas: Women and children should not be political.
Alexandra: (Stroking the lining of her cape) The jewels are sewn
in safely.
Nicholas: Your cape is very heavy. (Puts it across her shoulders)
Alexandra: We will escape to Finland. Then to England.
Nicholas: (Adjusting the cape) Can you manage, Alex?
Alexandra: (Coldly) I have always managed, Nikki.
Nicholas: A better manager than I.
Alexandra: Slip these pearls into your tunic.

ANOTHER ANGLE

Nicholas: (Captures ALEXANDRA's hand, kisses it, looks
straight into her eyes) For once, and maybe for all, Alex...

Alexandra: Be strong, Nikki.

Nicholas: ...no matter what has been or has not been between us, I have always, in my way...

Alexandra: Oh...Nikki! I love you too, Nikki. You are my husband.

ANOTHER ANGLE

Eugenev: (Entering) Sir. Madame. You will come with me.

The CHILDREN pour into the room. The entire FAMILY hugs and kisses.

Eugenev: You will please follow me.

The FAMILY pulls itself together and proceeds out.

Camera PANS BACK and rests on the Royal Photograph, left abandoned on the bureau.

THREE BEATS

INT. LANDING AND STAIRWAY TO CELLAR—NIGHT

The FAMILY solemnly descends the stairs. Outside SOUNDS of GUNSHOTS and TURMOIL. SOLDIERS smirk at them on the landing. DRUNKEN SOLDIER #1 drops a bottle which smashes in front of ALEXANDRA's feet.

Soldier #2: Pardon him, Madame.

SOLDIER #3 restrains DRUNKER SOLDIER #1. SOLDIER #2 shakes his head and crosses himself as the FAMILY proceeds past them. NICHOLAS picks ups ALEXIS and carries him on his hip. They descend deeper into the cellar. EUGENEV ushers them to the door of the chamber.

INT. CELLAR—NIGHT, BEFORE DAWN

Nicholas: The cellar is damp for my son.
Alexandra: The Czarevitch is not well...
Nicholas: ...as you can see.
Eugenev: For me, I am sorry. But I have my orders. I can change nothing.
Nicholas: Many crimes are committed in the name of obedience.
Eugenev: You more than anyone know that, Sir.

ANOTHER ANGLE FEATURING ANASTASIA

ANASTASIA dislikes the exchange. She throws EU-GENEV a glance. EUGENEV shrugs. She takes her father's arm.

Anastasia: Come, father.
Nicholas: Thank you, Anya.

ANOTHER ANGLE

The FAMILY sits down to wait. They form a tableau arranged exactly like a living copy of the portrait upstairs.

CLOSE UP ANASTASIA
ANASTASIA is frightened.

SOUND

GUNSHOT

ANASTASIA starts. She clutches her fur muff to her breast. A shadow falls over her, reacting, as the door opens.

LOW-ANGLE MEDIUM SHOT KARKOV
FAMILY'S P.O.V.

Deeply shadowed, KARKOV reads from a paper. His moustache is great and thick. Five Cheka guards armed with rifles and handguns stand beside him.

SOUND

As KARKOV reads the death sentence, the REVVING SOUND of the trucks increases. Faraway LAUGHTER is heard.

SHOT PANS SLOWLY UP
to the face of KARKOV reading.

Karkov: For political crimes committed against the Russian people, the Committee of the Soviet sentences Nicholas Romanov of the Imperial House of Romanov, his family and heirs...

Although KARKOV's lips continue to read, his voice mixes and drowns in and under the outside SOUND of turmoil.

MEDIUM NICHOLAS

NICHOLAS seems not to comprehend.

ANOTHER ANGLE MEDIUM NICHOLAS
FEATURING ALEXANDRA

ANASTASIA stands halfway up in full realization.

MEDIUM THE FAMILY FEATURING ANASTASIA

The FAMILY is trapped, terrified.

CLOSE UP ANASTASIA

ANASTASIA reaches for her FATHER and her little BROTHER.

MEDIUM ANGLE SAME AS ABOVE

ANASTASIA continues to rise.

Alexandra: My sweet Jesus!

ALEXANDRA's forehead explodes.

ANOTHER ANGLE FULL SLOW MOTION

A volley of gunshots, the family rising, falling, exploding, caroming in slow motion in their white clothes, jewels spilling out.

ANOTHER ANGLE SLOW MOTION
FEATURING CHEKA GUARDS

They shoot coldly, blankly.

INSERT SLOW MOTION

The naked light bulb swinging in clouds of blue smoke. It slows.

SOUND

SILENCE. Then: a MOAN.

CLOSE ANASTASIA SLOW MOTION

Bloodied, ANASTASIA rises.

MEDIUM FEATURING THE RISING ANASTASIA
SLOW MOTION

A CHEKA butts her chin with his gunstock. She falls. He raises his bayonet.

CLOSE ANASTASIA'S WHITE HIGH-TOP SHOE
SLOW MOTION

GUARD bayonets her foot through her white high-top shoe.

CLOSE ANASTASIA'S UNCONSCIOUS
AND BLOODIED FACE

SLOW CLOSE UP KARKOV

Karkov: Cart the "royal" pigs out to the truck. At the mine shaft
is kerosene and lime. Burn them. Not one trace of them shall
remain. Not one splinter of bone. Not one relic. The Old
Russia is dead. This is the last of the stinking Romanovs.

KARKOV spits.

DISSOLVE

INT. BEDROOM OF

NICHOLAS AND ALEXANDRA—NIGHT

MEDIUM EUGENEV

EUGENEV stands before the photograph of the Family.
His eyes are moist. His finger moves, tremulously, toward
the photo. CAMERA TIGHTENS DOWN as his forefinger presses on Anastasia's face and rubs down to her chest.
SHOT holds on her smiling teenage face.

SOUND

MAIN LOVE THEME MUSIC SWELLS

FADE OUT

ACT II

FADE IN

INT. SANITARIUM. ANNA'S ROOM.
BERLIN—NIGHT

SUPERIMPOSE logo
BERLIN 1928

CLOSE UP ANNA's face

pulls back to FULL SHOT ANNA AND TEUFEL

ANNA's CLOSE-UP FACE is virtually a MATCH CUT from ANASTASIA's portrait in previous SHOT. CAMERA TRUCKS SLOWLY BACK from ANNA holding a pillow to her chest and chin as she reclines, half-sitting, in her bed. She stares blankly. The shot becomes a FULL SHOT to include a heavy dumpling of a woman, FRAU TEUFEL, shuffling about the room arranging things. A Russian icon predominates. FRAU TEUFEL lights a new candle. Outside the window, a heavy night rain flashes with lightning and thunder.

MEDIUM ANNA AND TEUFEL

The low-angle candlelight makes TEUFEL's face evil.

Teufel: I know something, Anna...you have a secret.

Lightning flashes. TEUFEL crosses herself.

Teufel: I know something. I know your secret. I won't tell.

TEUFEL moves in close to ANNA.

Teufel: I know who you are.

ANNA seems not to hear.

Teufel: Anna! I said I know who you are.
Anna: I am nobody.
Teufel: A clever nobody.
Anna: I am Anna Eisenstein.
Teufel: *Ja.*
Anna: I am no more, no less.
Teufel: Your secret is safe with me.
Anna: Let me alone, Frau Teufel. Please.
Teufel: At night you cry out in your sleep.
Anna: No!

Teufel: You call for your father. You cry for your sisters and your brother.

Anna: No. Those are your dreams, Frau Teufel, not mine.

Teufel: ...but you never call for your mother.

Anna: My poor mother is dead. My father is dead. My family: all dead.

Teufel: Some there are, they say, who want you dead as well.

Anna: My father was a farmer. He died of hunger.

Teufel: Your father was Czar Nicholas II of Russia.

Anna: You read too many fairy tales.

CLOSE TEUFEL

Teufel: I read only the newspaper. You see. Here. A story by an American journalist. He too writes of rumors running rampant throughout Europe that one of the Czar's daughters, one of the Grand Duchesses, escaped the cellar at Ekaterinburg.

MEDIUM ANNA AND TEUFEL

Anna: Ffff! Everyone knows they all died that night...

Teufel: ...all except one...

Anna: ...and their bodies were cremated and their ashes scattered to the winds.

Teufel: Even the Reds whisper that Anastasia escaped...

CLOSE UP ANNA

Anna: They were shot and nothing was left.

CLOSE UP TEUFEL

Teufel: The American journalist says a Red guard named Eugenev noticed that the Grand Duchess Anastasia was not dead. He stole her away unconscious.

CLOSE UP ANNA

Anna: Romantic gossip.

MEDIUM ANNA AND TEUFEL

Teufel: Hear me, Duchess...

TEUFEL pulls at ANNA's shielding pillow.

Teufel: Anastasia's jaw was broken by a rifle butt.
Anna: No!
Teufel: Your jaw has been broken.
Anna: In a train accident in Poland.
Teufel: When?
Anna: Ten years ago.
Teufel: The year the Imperial Family was shot.
Anna: You're a crazy old woman. You scrub toilets in an asylum.
Teufel: I am Head Nurse of this section.
Anna: No one will believe anything you say.

CLOSE UP TEUFEL

Teufel: I say exactly what the American newspaperman says. The
Grand Duchess Anastasia is alive and she is in hiding. She
fears the Red Communists still wish her dead. The American
thinks Anastasia hides in a German convent.

CLOSE UP ANNA

Anna: The Grand Duchess is not in a convent.

CLOSE UP TEUFEL

Teufel: No. She is like you in an asylum.

TIGHT CLOSE UP ANNA

Anna: Anastasia is dead.

TIGHT CLOSE UP TEUFEL

Teufel: You are Anastasia.

CLOSE UP ANNA

Anna: You are Napoleon Bonaparte. Let me alone.

MEDIUM ANNA AND TEUFEL

Teufel: Anastasia's foot was stabbed by a bayonet.

TEUFEL pulls at the bed covers.

Teufel: Let me see your foot.
Anna: No!
Teufel: On rainy days, you limp. Why?
Anna: The train accident!
Teufel: No!
Anna: Don't touch me.

ANOTHER ANGLE

Teufel: Hear me, Duchess. Miss High and Mighty Grand Duchess. I'll do what I like. This is not old Russia. This is the new Germany. *Verstehst du?* This is a new day. Now you take this news clipping and read it. See, my Romanov sweet, how close the American journalist is on your trail.
Anna: Leave me.
Teufel: Leave you? Ah no. You need me. Now. And I need you.
Anna: You need me?
Teufel: You are my ticket away from this madhouse.
Anna: I am not the Grand Duchess Anastasia.
Teufel: Not now. But once you were. And you will be again. There is much money...I have written to your relatives.
Anna: What relatives?
Teufel: Your uncle, the Grand Duke Ernst Ludwig. His sister, your aunt, the Grand Duchess Olga.
Anna: Those people are nothing to me!

CLOSE INSERT

NEWSPAPER ARTICLE displaying *New York Blade*

Teufel: (Voice Over) But you are everything to them. You are the sole living heir to all of Russia.

MEDIUM ANNA AND TEUFEL

Anna: No.

ANNA cries, buries her face in the pillow. TEUFEL turns smugly into camera and exits. SHOT HOLDS on the sobbing ANNA for three beats.

DISSOLVE

INT. SANITARIUM. ANNA'S ROOM—MORNING

FULL ANNA

ANNA sits in a rocker covered with a lap robe. She has been reading, and she sits in a glow of sunshine. Flowers are at the window. It is springtime in Berlin. FRAU TEUFEL enters. ANNA is startled from her pleasant reverie.

Teufel: A special morning, Duchess.
Anna: I told you. Do not call me that.
Teufel: There are some who remember you were once upon a time somebody very special.
Anna: Never. I am not special. From before my train accident there is little "special" I remember.

MEDIUM ANNA AND TEUFEL

TEUFEL begins to brush ANNA's hair. The girl does not resist.

Teufel: Your mother, the Czarina, was German. You have fled to the proper country.
Anna: Germany?
Teufel: Like you, we understand the political convenience of "amnesia."
Anna: Sometimes it is better not to remember.

TEUFEL touches some rouge to ANNA's cheeks. ANNA flinches slightly.

Teufel: Your face is her face—grown up.

Anna: You paint on a mask.

Teufel: If you will not tell me, the hungry Romanovs will tell me who you are.

Anna: I am nobody.

Teufel: Nobody is nobody. Nobody disappears. Always someone knows. Someone passes in the street and says, "I remember her."

Anna: I come from nowhere.

Teufel: The left-over Romanov relatives will remember who you are.

Anna: Be suspicious, Frau Teufel, very suspicious of anyone who "remembers" me.

INT. 1928 ROLLS ROYCE. BERLIN—DAY

MEDIUM TWO-SHOT OLGA AND LUDWIG

Driving to the Berlin sanitarium, the Grand Duchess OLGA, the Grand Duke ERNST LUDWIG, and the former Romanov governess KATHARINE are in close conversation as they are chauffeured.

Olga: Spare me more impostors pretending to be my dead nieces.

Ludwig: We must check every possibility.

Olga: They are dead, Ludwig. All dead and lucky.

Ludwig: But if only one of them, only one, is alive. Russia lives.

ANOTHER ANGLE INCLUDING KATHARINE

Olga: Speak to me no more of our Holy Russia. Now it is their Union of Soviet Socialist Republics. Katharine, what does that mean?

KATHARINE smiles and shrugs.

Ludwig: If Frau Teufel's girl is our niece, then Russians everywhere have hope. Anastasia can be crowned empress.

Olga: She can sit on an empty throne.

Ludwig: A restoration of the Romanov dynasty is our only hope.

CLOSE UP OLGA

Olga: Dynasties! I hope only for caviar that is black instead of red.

ANGLE SAME AS ABOVE

Ludwig: My dear sister, Olga, you have changed more than Russia.

Olga: I have met three false Tatianas, one ridiculous imitation of Maria, and two pathetic actresses playing my godchild, my dear dead Anastasia.

MEDIUM KATHARINE

Katharine: But, Excellency, what if the rumor is true?

ANGLE SAME AS ABOVE

Olga: The way the world is now, my dear, better we had all died in 1918. I spit on politics.

CLOSE UP KATHARINE

Katharine: I was her nurse, her governess. At night I lie awake, fearing Anya is alive. Alone. Helpless...

ANGLE SAME AS ABOVE. OLGA AND LUDWIG

Katharine: (Voice Over) ...Afraid for her very life.

LUDWIG turns to OLGA who stares stoically ahead. They ride in silence three beats.

DISSOLVE

EXT. SANITARIUM DRIVE AND PORTICO—DAY

HIGH-ANGLE SHOT PANS entering Rolls Royce

OLGA, LUDWIG, and KATHARINE exit the car and enter the sanitarium doors.

INT. SANITARIUM ENTRY—DAY

Teufel: Your Excellency! Madame! Miss! Welcome to our little hospital. You will not regret my letter. I am Frau Teufel.
Olga: (To KATHARINE) Ask the woman to show us the girl.
Teufel: Anna awaits you.
Olga: No doubt with bated breath.
Teufel: Not very anxiously, I'm afraid.
Olga: Every cheap little actress so far has champed at the bit to prove to me she is my niece the Grand Duchess.
Teufel: Your niece's health is not the best.
Olga: Do not presume she is my niece.
Teufel: You will recognize her as I did.
Katharine: Ten years is a long time.

ANOTHER ANGLE FEATURING OLGA

Olga: Wait.
Katharine: Madame?
Ludwig: Olga, not another game?
Olga: You, Katharine, must wear my coat and muff and hat.
Katharine: Yes, Madame.
Olga: And I shall wear yours. We shall fool this cheap little tart in her own charade. She will confuse the Governess Katharine for her aunt the Imperial Grand Duchess Olga.
Katharine: (Embarrassed) Yes, Madame.
Olga: We shall expose her in record time.

ANOTHER ANGLE

Teufel: I think Madame will be pleasantly surprised. This way, please.

INT. SANITARIUM HALLWAY—DAY

A TRUCKING SHOT of OLGA, LUDWIG and

KATHARINE led by TEUFEL
moves down the shadowed hall

Half-mad PATIENTS stand in the corners, sit on chairs, stare vacantly. OLGA pulls KATHARINE's coat tightly about herself. TEUFEL knocks on Anna's door, but does not wait for an answer. They enter.

INT. SANITARIUM. ANNA'S ROOM—DAY

MEDIUM ANNA
FEATURING TEUFEL, OLGA, LUDWIG

ANNA faces indifferently out the window, backed by LUDWIG.

Teufel: Anna, your visitors are here.
Anna: They are your visitors, Frau Teufel. They are your clients.
Teufel: Say "hello," Anna.

CLOSE UP ANNA

Anna: (Turning, her delivery is flat, by rote) My name is Anna Eisenstein.

MEDIUM OLGA AND LUDWIG
FEATURING ANNA

Ludwig: How do you do? I am the Grand Duke Ernst Ludwig. And this...
Anna: ...is the Grand Duchess Olga.
Olga: I am the Imperial Governess Katharine.
Anna: Madame is mistaken.
Ludwig: The girl is no fool.
Anna: I remember Madame's face.
Olga: You remember.
Anna: From news photos.
Olga: The Imperial Family interests you?
Anna: History is my hobby. Certain history.

Olga: Who are you?

CLOSE UP ANNA

Anna: (Extremely by rote) My father's name was Josef Chernov. He starved to death in the Ukraine in 1917. I married Alex Eisenstein at Sverdlosk in 1920. My husband was killed in the train accident that broke my jaw. I have no family...

TIGHT CLOSE UP TEUFEL

Teufel: Anna!

TIGHT CLOSE UP ANNA

Anna: ...I have no family. My mother died when I was born.

MEDIUM OLGA, LUDWIG, AND TEUFEL

Olga: Your "Grand Duchess," Frau Teufel, is not so very grand. She needs more rehearsal.
Teufel: Please, Anna.
Olga: She has, it seems, learned the wrong part.
Ludwig: The girl is obviously frightened.
Olga: Old men are sentimental old fools around young girls.

MEDIUM KATHARINE

Katharine: Madame, she needs a chance.

MEDIUM TWO-SHOT OLGA AND ANNA

Olga: I'll give her a chance.

OLGA cups ANNA's chin in her hand.

Olga: Look at me, girl. Where was the Imperial Winter Palace?
Anna: I don't know.
Olga: Everyone knows.
Anna: At Tsarskoe Selo.
Olga: And the Imperial Summer Retreat?

Anna: You're hurting me.... They summered at Lavadia on the Black Sea.
Olga: Certainly.
Anna: Everyone knows that.
Olga: Now tell me you are not the Grand Duchess Anastasia.

CLOSE UP TEUFEL

Teufel: (Threatening) Anna!

MEDIUM TWO-SHOT OLGA AND ANNA AS ABOVE

Anna: I am not, I am certainly not, the Grand Duchess Anastasia.

OLGA releases ANNA's chin. OLGA wipes her hands.

Olga: Of course not. Teufel gives you too much powder. Too much rouge.

MEDIUM OLGA AND ANNA FEATURING LUDWIG

Olga: (To LUDWIG) I'll not call anyone here an old fool. Are you satisfied? My instincts were right. A woman can always read...another woman.
Anna: Please, go.
Olga: Come, Ernst Ludwig. Katharine. Let us leave this madhouse. Let us leave Frau Teufel and her rouged little puppet.

OLGA turns on her heel and sweeps grandly out.

MEDIUM TWO-SHOT LUDWIG AND ANNA

Ludwig: ...And when was the last time that Anastasia saw me, her uncle, Ernst Ludwig?
Anna: Some say, Excellency, in 1916 when you entered the back door of the palace in St. Petersburg to effect a separate peace between Germany and Russia.
Ludwig: Only a fool would accuse me of such treason.
Anna: I'm a fool. A fool for everyone.

Ludwig: In Russia! During the war! No, no, no! I was never
   there. Do you understand? Never there.

Anna: So...you want me to remember...what you want me to
   remember.

LUDWIG bows curtly and exits.

CLOSE UP KATHARINE AND ANNA

KATHARINE tentatively reaches out toward ANNA,
but instead pulls her gesture back to touch her own face.
ANNA turns away. Rain has begun to streak the window.
KATHARINE exits.

TIGHT CLOSE UP TEUFEL

Teufel: I should turn you out to the streets.

MEDIUM ANNA AND TEUFEL

ANNA leans into her own rainy reflections at the window.

Anna: Leave me. Leave me.

Teufel: My ugly duckling. My ugly, ugly ducking. I'll turn you
   yet into a swan.

FADE OUT

ACT III

FADE IN
INT. RUSSIAN GYPSY CAFE. BERLIN—NIGHT

SOUND

Gypsy music, up, then under

CLOSE SHOT TEUFEL's

face pulls back
MEDIUM SHOT

TEUFEL sits at linened table elegantly smoking a cigarette, European-style, and sipping a small coffee. Activity and atmosphere people fill the set. American reporter JOHN WILSON enters.

Wilson: Frau Teufel?

Teufel: (Ever the coquette) *Mein Herr.*

Wilson: John Wilson of the *New York Blade.*

Teufel: Such an eager Mr. Wilson. Americans are always eager where money is concerned.

Wilson: You write a persuasive letter.

Teufel: My letter was accurate.

Wilson: The Grand Duchess may be the Woman of the Century.

Teufel: Her whereabouts is very valuable to your newspaper?

Wilson: The Duchess is a good human-interest story. A young girl. Exile. Assassination. Lost identity.

Teufel: A melodrama.

Wilson: A fairytale.

Teufel: The Duchess sells newspapers.

Wilson: Frau Teufel, you deliver her to me. You deliver half what your letter promised, and I guarantee your picture on the cover of our Sunday supplement.

Teufel: You perhaps flatter all women, Mr. Wilson. Spare me. I am a faceless nobody.

WILSON makes no comment. A WAITER saves the dead moment between them by serving him a coffee and TEUFEL a pastry.

Teufel: All that concerns me is my dear Anna. I must protect her. She is very valuable to me.

Wilson: Returning her true identity will be her best protection.

Teufel: The Red Communists wish her dead.

Wilson: She will be safe in Paris or London. She may be in exile. But she can enjoy even exile in New York.

Teufel: The Communists have a price on her head.

ANOTHER ANGLE

Wilson: I suspect you shopped around.
Teufel: Her relatives quarrel over her. One says "She is" in private, then in public says "She isn't." There is pressure.
Wilson: There is money.
Teufel: A fortune.
Wilson: Rumors of a million dollars in the Bank of England.
Teufel: A million! Ha! Several million, Mr. Wilson. Her father, Czar Nicholas, deposited several million in various banks under code names only his children knew.
Wilson: And this girl knows the names.
Teufel: Anna knows.
Wilson: Anna?
Teufel: She calls herself Anna.

CLOSE WILSON

Wilson: And what, Frau Teufel, do you call yourself?

CLOSE TEUFEL

Teufel: I am the protector of the Grand Duchess Anastasia.

MEDIUM TEUFEL WITH WILSON FEATURED

Wilson: How valuable is your protection?
Teufel: Your *New York Blade* is very wealthy.
Wilson: How much?
Teufel: Understand, Mr. Wilson, I am a business-woman.
Wilson: You are in the "Duchess Business."
Teufel: Precisely. I have only one piece of merchandise.
Wilson: What's she worth on the open market?
Teufel: Ten thousand American dollars.
Wilson: Eight.
Teufel: Nine.
Wilson: Sold. Two thousand on delivery. Seven thousand on verification.

MEDIUM TEUFEL

TEUFEL knifes through a rich pastry.

Teufel: Slice it as you wish, Mr. Wilson of the *New York Blade*. But you will slice it with my name on it. Nine thousand American dollars from you or forty thousand Russian rubles from the Reds...

TEUFEL bites into the pastry.

Teufel: ...Anna is merchandise to me.

MEDIUM WILSON

Wilson: There is a name for women like you, Teufel.

MEDIUM TEUFEL

Teufel: And for men like you, Wilson...

TEUFEL wipes her lips.

Teufel: ...You know my business. We needn't name it.

MEDIUM TWO-SHOT TEUFEL AND WILSON

Wilson: When will I see this Anna?
Teufel: Tomorrow afternoon at 2, I will escort the Duchess to the Kino Cinema. You may observe her there.
Wilson: No good, Teufel. More than see her. For nine thousand, I talk to her.
Teufel: She is afraid of strangers. She knows people wish to kill her.
Wilson: After the movie, bring her here. You and I shall pretend, Teufel, that we are old friends.
Teufel: (Amused) Revolutions and money make strange bed-fellows, Wilson.
Wilson: In America, we say, when you lie down with dogs, you...
Teufel: (Nonplused) We also have that saying in Germany.
Wilson: Yeah. *Ja. Ja Wohl! Touche!*

Teufel: Because of Anna, Wilson, we shall both be able to afford
fumigation.
Wilson: You're a tough old doll.

CLOSE UP TEUFEL

Teufel: Armies have marched over me.

CLOSE UP WILSON

Wilson: I couldn't have stated the obvious better.

CLOSE UP TEUFEL

Teufel: I intend to survive, Wilson. This is Berlin, 1928, and I
am a common woman. I am not like the frightened, coddled
woman you seek. A woman left over from a world of royalty
dead and gone. I take my life into my hands. Red blood, not
blue, runs in my veins. Long after the world has forgotten
there ever were Grand Duchesses, women like me will survive.

MEDIUM WILSON AND TEUFEL

TEUFEL rises, smiling, self-satisfied.

Teufel: Good-night, Wilson.

TEUFEL exits.

SHOT SLOWLY TRUCKS INTO
TIGHT CLOSE UP of a reflecting WILSON

DISSOLVE

INT. KINO MOVIE THEATER—DAY

MEDIUM ANNA AND TEUFEL

ANNA and TEUFEL are discovered watching a film.
Light from the projector triangles down through the
darkness over their heads. Behind them an anonymous

MOVIE-GOER sits intent on the newsreel. The NEWS-REEL FOOTAGE screened is of Soviet tanks; Lenin speaking; labor collectives; glorified Revolutionaries.

MEDIUM
holds on ANNA and TEUFEL

Footage Voice Over: "The new Soviet regime, productive, political, on the march..."

NEWSREEL FOOTAGE

Marching Soviet troops, tanks.

NEWSREEL FOOTAGE

A quick cut to St. Petersberg. The Russian Royal family, featuring the children, climb into an Imperial Coach, proceeding through crowds. A longshot of the Czar and Czarina waving from a distant white balcony.

Footage Voice Over: "...a far-cry from the long-exiled Romanov dynasty ended ten years ago with the death of Czar Nicholas II..."

MEDIUM ANNA, TEUFEL, MOVIE-GOER

Anna: Am I supposed to enjoy this?
Teufel: Sit quietly.
Anna: Is this another of your tests to see how I react?
Teufel: Quiet.
Anna: I wish to leave.
Teufel: People are watching.
Footage Voice Over: "...The Soviet military might is matched by its political force...At home in Moscow or exiled to Europe, millions of Russians publicly cheer the Soviets and secretly fear the power of the NKVD, the dreaded Russian Secret Police..."

ANNA turns her profile. The SHOT PANS slightly with

her turn losing TEUFEL completely. The MEDIUM SHOT then loses focus on ANNA and deep-focuses, as if from ANNA's P.O.V. over her shoulder to rest momentarily on JOHN WILSON smoking nonchalantly in his seat.

The SHOT focuses deeper, past WILSON, catches briefly the face of MALENKOV of the NKVD, dismisses him as negligible, and PULLS focus BACK past WILSON, stopping again only briefly, PULLING BACK to OPENING FOCUS on ANNA. She turns full face back into SHOT that simultaneously PANS BACK to original MEDIUM SHOT of ANNA, TEUFEL, and MOVIE-GOER.

Teufel: You disturb the audience.
Anna: Then I shall leave.
Teufel: You will sit. The cinema relaxes your nerves.
Anna: You are a cruel woman.
Teufel: You are a foolish girl.
Movie-Goer: Shhh!
Anna: I want to go.
Teufel: You are impossible...you are ever the Duchess.

ANNA and TEUFEL rise and exit up aisle.

ANOTHER ANGLE

ANNA and TEUFEL exit past WILSON.

SHOT HOLDS on WILSON

ANOTHER ANGLE PARALLEL TO ABOVE

ANNA and TEUFEL exit past MALENKOV. SHOT HOLDS on the NKVD face of MALENKOV with the light from the screen reflecting on his fat features.

DISSOLVE

INT. RUSSIAN GYPSY CAFE. BERLIN—DAY

FULL ANNA AND TEUFEL

ANNA and TEUFEL order under the noise.

SOUND

Cafe music and hubbub drown all voices

WILSON enters, sits, and orders.

MEDIUM ANNA AND TEUFEL

Anna: Who is that man?
Teufel: All men are the same.
Anna: The American who is following us.
Teufel: I can't see him without my glasses.
Anna: Perhaps you know him. He is smiling.
Teufel: Then smile back.
Anna: He is coming to our table. I want to go.
Teufel: "I want! I want!" You are as spoiled as any Romanov.

MEDIUM WILSON—ANNA'S P.O.V.

Wilson: Excuse me. Frau Teufel. Can it be, dear Frau Ilsa Teufel!

MEDIUM ANNA FEATURED
BETWEEN TEUFEL AND WILSON

Teufel: *Gott in Himmel!* Wilson! What a pleasure... It is John
   Wilson! Such a long time.
Wilson: Since the year after the Great War.
Teufel: Oh...how looong!
Anna: Oh, how touching.
Teufel: Frau Anna Eisenstein, Mr. John Wilson.
Anna: Frau Teufel corresponds these days with so many "old"
   friends.
Wilson: A few French postcards back and forth...Yes.
Anna: Frau Teufel writes most revealing letters.
Wilson: Revealing?

CLOSE ANNA

Anna: You know the word, Mr. Wilson. I am not stupid. You know words very well, I think, Mr. John Wilson of the *New York Blade*...
Teufel: (Voice Over) Anna!
Anna: ...Mr. John Wilson, reporter, who hounds innocent people. I may be silent, Frau Teufel, but I am not slow. That American newsclipping you showed me weeks ago. The correspondent's name was—no surprise—John Wilson.

MEDIUM TWO-SHOT ANNA AND WILSON

Wilson: You disliked my article?
Anna: A reporter who pays for fact, Mr. Wilson, buys fiction.
Wilson: Your girl is sharp, Frau Teufel.
Teufel: Sharp-tongued!
Anna: I must protect my...
Wilson: ...self...
Anna: ...privacy. I am a very private person.
Wilson: You were once a very public person.

ANOTHER ANGLE INCLUDING TEUFEL

Anna: Pfff! Teufel here has sold you her obsession. She is mad, you know. She should not be the keeper of a madhouse. She should be kept. She fancies I am the Grand Duchess Anastasia.
Teufel: You are Anastasia.
Wilson: Aren't you?

CLOSE ANNA

Anna: I am no more than myself. Poor Anastasia died with her family. I have great sympathy for that poor girl. They were all shot...Everyone knows that.

CLOSE WILSON

Wilson: I don't know that.

CLOSE ANNA

Anna: Mr. Wilson, people never want the rulers they admire, the heroes they adore, ever to die. I have read that in America rumors abound of soldiers and presidents, who have not really been killed, but who have gone into hiding. Even actors. Your Valentino.

MEDIUM ANNA, WILSON, FEATURING TEUFEL

Teufel: Nonsense!

CLOSE UP ANNA

Anna: Even Jesus, as long ago as Jesus. He was not left for dead. Mary Magdalene saw Him alive. The Apostles saw Him alive. Today most of Europe, most of America, believes Jesus is not dead. They believe in Easter. They believe He rose again.

MEDIUM ANNA, WILSON, AND TEUFEL

Teufel: And her very name...
Anna: ...not my name...
Teufel: ... Anastasia's name. Anastasia's name means in English: The Woman Who Stands Again.
Wilson: Anastasia: The Woman Who Rose Again.

INSERT SHOT FROM RUSSIAN CELLAR
CLOSE ANASTASIA SLOW MOTION

In the cellar, bloodied, ANASTASIA rises.
Insert duration: fast enough to be the observable side of subliminal.

CLOSE TEUFEL

Teufel: The woman who rose again. Indeed!

CLOSE ANNA

Anna: Blasphemy! She was not Jesus. (ANNA crosses herself)

MEDIUM ANNA, WILSON, AND TEUFEL

Teufel: The Resurrection of the Duchess. That is your angle, Wilson. A Princess who would not die.
Anna: An angle on a lie. I am an expert on lies.
Wilson: I'm an expert on deceitful women.
Anna: Men never believe women anyway.
Wilson: Not since Eve taught Adam better. Nice try, Teufel. Find yourself a new Cinderella. (To ANNA) You're a pretty girl...
Anna: ...for me "pretty" is nothing.

CLOSE TEUFEL

Teufel: Anna lies. Of course, she lies. She lies about lies. WILSON!

TIGHT TWO-SHOT ANNA AND WILSON

Wilson: Then I'll ask her once and for all. Are you Anastasia?
Anna: (By rote) I am Anna Eisenstein. My father's name was Josef Chernov. He starved to death in 1917. I married Alex Eisenstein at Sverdlosk. I have no family.

MEDIUM ANNA, WILSON, FEATURING TEUFEL

Teufel: Lies! Liar! Lies!

TEUFEL strikes ANNA with a finger slap.

Wilson: Hold it!
Anna: (Crying) I am Anna Eisenstein.
Wilson: Maybe, sweetheart. It makes no difference who you are. Maybe the better story is about Anna Eisenstein.
Teufel: You make a fool of me.
Anna: You were a fool long before I was born.

ANNA exits.

MEDIUM TWO-SHOT WILSON AND TEUFEL

Wilson: Sorry, Old Girl. I think the bottom just fell out of the

Duchess business.

EXT. BERLIN GARDEN CAFE—DAY

MEDIUM LUDWIG AND ANNA.

ANNA unwraps a small package at the table.

Ludwig: My thanks for your coming.
Anna: A cross, Your Excellency. It is so very lovely.
Ludwig: Olga thinks me foolish.
Anna: Not foolish. Your note spoke with the kindness I needed.
Ludwig: You are easy to be kind to.
Anna: The cross was Anastasia's?
Ludwig: Once Anya lived in Peterhof Castle.

CLOSE ANNA

Anna: I have read Lenin. To the Revolutionaries she was a prop
in a royal play.

MEDIUM ANNA AND LUDWIG

Ludwig: The girl was real. She was warm.
Anna: So much...you miss her?
Ludwig: I miss them all.
Anna: The world has changed.
Ludwig: So Olga says.
Anna: She might at least rent a castle in Spain.

ANOTHER ANGLE

Ludwig: Anna?
Anna: Excellency?
Ludwig: Secretly. Trust in an old uncle who longs for his niece,
for his past. Say you are Anastasia.
Anna: Please, Your Excellency.
Ludwig: Anya!
Anna: The person I am is Anna Eisenstein.
Ludwig: Anya, my heart—for all of Russia—hears otherwise.

Anna: I am not...

CLOSE LUDWIG

Ludwig: No. Please. If for you, you must now be Anna Eisenstein, then be Anna Eisenstein.

CLOSE ANNA

Anna: I am not...

CLOSE LUDWIG

Ludwig: But for me, at least do not say you were never Anastasia.

MEDIUM ANNA AND LUDWIG

ANNA tries kindly to leaven the situation.

Anna: Excellency, who I am is easy to say. Who I have never
been, ah, that is a list longer than the Berlin telephone direc-
tory.
Ludwig: (Smiles) You have reason to trust no one.
Anna: Thank you.
Ludwig: One day yet, Anna Eisenstein, I shall raise you from
the underground and prove you and the Grand Duchess Olga
royally wrong. She has bet me 10,000 Deutsche marks.
Anna: (Smiles) I am sorry you will lose.

INT. LUDWIG'S GRAND HOTEL SUITE—NIGHT

CLOSE BORODIN REVEALING OLGA

CLOSE SHOT of the jewel-encrusted hand of a male
Russian aristocrat, BORODIN, who feeds caviar on a
cracker to a hyper-groomed poodle. The dog eats a lick.
BORODIN raises the cracker to his own face as the
SHOT PULLS BACK. He nibbles and returns the rest to
the dog. OLGA, ever the Dowager Grand Duchess, sits

opposite him. They are in the midst of a SMALL PRESS RECEPTION.

Olga: Caviar for the dog?
Borodin: The animal, Olga, has no way of knowing the Great Days are gone.
Olga: But not forgotten.
Borodin: (Baiting OLGA) And perhaps soon revived. A restoration. A return of the Romanovs.
Olga: Nonsense, Borodin.
Borodin: Ernst Ludwig believes he has found her.
Olga: Ernst Ludwig grasps at straws. The way he caters to these foreign reporters...

ANOTHER ANGLE REVEALING
THE THREE REPORTERS
WILSON, ROBERTS, AND LORRE

Roberts: My London editor thinks this new girl an equal fraud.
Lorre: Frankly, so do I.
Roberts: In the last six months, I've interviewed three Tatiana's, one Maria, and a dwarf Czarevitch Alexis.
Lorre: *Ja.* Imagine a dwarf Czarevitch!
Roberts: Sounds economical. He could be his own court jester...

SHOT catches WAITER with tray and PANS with him from REPORTERS as he offers tray to BORODIN and OLGA.

Borodin: ...But what of the Russian throne? What if poor little Anastasia survives alone. Penniless. Terrified.
Olga: I have no more politics. And no more pity.
Borodin: Think of the money Anastasia may claim in the Bank of England.
Olga: Mere rumor! Nicholas had no secret accounts. I would have known.
Borodin: Ah, yes.
Olga: Believe me, if Anastasia had the good fortune to survive,

she'd have the good sense to keep her fortune to herself.

Borodin: Certainly the Grand Duchess Anastasia, when restored, will set up a court in exile.

Olga: So the likes of you can stuff your dogs with caviar? Never!

Borodin: I was an Imperial Officer.

Olga: You were ever impotent, Borodin…Where were you "officers" when the Imperial Family needed rescue? I would not give you a ruble.

BORODIN rises in a huff, tucks his poodle under his arm, and pushes off. The SHOT FOLLOWS him and HOLDS, as he exits out of shot, on the three REPORTERS.

Roberts: (About BORODIN) That is certainly the "end of the line."

Lorre: That man hopes against hope. He has called my newspaper already with two false Anastasias.

Wilson: Even if she survived the shooting, no self-respecting Anastasia could survive this circus.

Roberts: Of those two Anastasias, one was a venereal chambermaid from the Berlin Hotel…

Lorre: …and the other a lunatic woman from a Bavarian mental ward. Cuckoo.

Roberts: …"Survive the shooting," Old Man? No one survived the shooting.

Wilson: You miss the point.

Roberts: The point?

Wilson: All accounts agree. All the witnesses agree: Anastasia was not killed in the first volley of shots. She stood up. She rose up among all the bodies of her dying family.

Roberts: But the Chekas clubbed her down again.

Lorre: They bayoneted her right foot.

Wilson: Provable points on any claimant. The chin. The foot. Evidence.

Lorre: Europe is full of wounded people.

Roberts: The entire family of Czar Nicholas Romanov is dead.

Wilson: Then why are you here?

ANOTHER ANGLE ROBERTS AND LORRE
FEATURING WILSON

Roberts: To sell newspapers, Old Boy.

Wilson: So you resurrect Anastasia. Why not the little boy, the little Czarevitch? Why not the direct male heir?

Roberts: My dear Wilson, the Czarevitch Alexis was already at the age of 12 an incurable hemophiliac.

Lorre: He was a bleeder.

Wilson: ...The slightest cut...

Lorre: Hemophiliacs do not survive beatings, shootings, stabbings.

Wilson: (Dripping irony) You're a delightful little man... But why, Roberts, resurrect Anastasia?

Roberts: Because she was young and pretty. She was only 17 the night of the murders.

Lorre: Death at such an early age is romantic.

Wilson: Romantic?

Roberts: Quite romantic...Quite.

Lorre: ...and her story sells newspapers.

Wilson: Quite.

MEDIUM LUDWIG, OLGA, KATHARINE

LUDWIG makes an entrance escorting OLGA. KATHA-RINE is two steps behind.

Ludwig: My dear friends. Gentlemen of the Press. My only announcement at this, our monthly official reception in exile, is that we are near, very near, to finding and presenting my niece, the Grand Duchess Anastasia, heiress to all of Russia.

Wilson: Quite.

MEDIUM WILSON FEATURING MALENKOV

Over WILSON'S shoulder, NKVD AGENT, MALEN-KOV, discovered standing in the doorway, toasts LUD-WIG'S announcement with a glass of blood-red wine.

MALENKOV smiles.

FADE TO BLACK

ACT IV

FADE IN

INT. HOTEL ODEON LOBBY—NIGHT

FULL ESTABLISHING
FEATURING WILSON, CLERK, AND MALENKOV

Outside, through the lobby windows, it is raining. WILSON is seen through the window approaching the modest hotel. He enters through door shaking rain from himself in front of a brass plate reading HOTEL ODEON. WILSON crosses the small lobby. A large man, MALENKOV, has his back to WILSON and to the CAMERA as he stands at the registration desk. MALENKOV is completing his transaction.

Clerk: Thank you, Mr. Malenkov. *Danke schön.*

MALENKOV turns into CAMERA and WILSON who pays him no heed. MALENKOV steps into foreground. WILSON glances at MALENKOV who stares back.

MEDIUM WILSON FEATURING MALENKOV

Wilson: The room number of Frau Anna Eisenstein, *bitte.*
(MALENKOV smiles and exits)
Clerk: 203, sir.

INT. HOTEL ODEON LOBBY
FEATURING STAIRS—NIGHT

MEDIUM STAIRWELL WILSON

WILSON climbs to room 203. Knocks. ANNA answers through the door.

Anna: Who is it?
Wilson: John Wilson.
Anna: Go away, Mr. Wilson.
Wilson: I want to talk with you.
Anna: We have nothing to say to each other.
Wilson: Listen, sister, I want to make a deal. (Silence: two beats) You know what a deal is. (The door opens part way)

CLOSE UP ANNA

Anna: How did you find me?

CLOSE WILSON

Wilson: I read Frau Teufel's palm. It said "money."

CLOSE ANNA AND WILSON

Anna: For money she told you where I am?
Wilson: For money she'd give you a permanent vacation in Moscow.
Anna: (Opening door) Come in, Mr. Wilson...

INT. HOTEL ODEON. ANNA'S ROOM—NIGHT

MEDIUM ANNA AND WILSON

Wilson: I believe you're telling the truth.
Anna: What is the truth?
Wilson: You're just a nice kid. You're not Anastasia.
Anna: Thank you, Mr. Wilson.
Wilson: But all the right and all the wrong people insist you are. Why?
Anna: They wish to use the Grand Duchess Anastasia.
Wilson: Use?

Anna: Come, Mr. Wilson. You understand *use*. American reporters use everyone, everything.

Wilson: Hold it, Duchess.

Anna: Why do you still call me "Duchess"?

Wilson: Maybe it's habit.

Anna: Habits can be changed.

CLOSE WILSON

Wilson: Maybe if I closed my eyes and believed very hard, I could take you for Anastasia. I've studied the royal pictures. Your nose. Your ears. They resemble her nose. Her ears.

CLOSE ANNA

Anna: But my chin is different.

CLOSE WILSON

Wilson: (Almost tenderly with a touch of romance) Broken, you say. Like hers. And your eyes....

CLOSE ANNA

Anna: Yes? My eyes?

MEDIUM ANNA AND WILSON

Wilson: Your eyes say more than your lips. They hide secrets.

Anna: You become too personal, Mr. Wilson. I have led a sad life. Like many Europeans since the Great War. No better, no worse than most. (She lights a cigarette nervously) I smoke too much. Do you smoke too much, Mr. Wilson?

Wilson: Everyone in Europe smokes too much.

Anna: We are a very nervous continent...What is it you want, Mr. Wilson? What is your deal for me? To be Anastasia or not to be Anastasia? That is the question. Will you offer me more than Ernst Ludwig to play the Duchess? Or will you offer me more than his sister Olga to not play the Duchess? They play against each other. Life is a stupid chess game.

Wilson: Either way you can be a rich woman.

CLOSE ANNA

Anna: I am a dead woman.
Wilson: Dead?
Anna: I am followed everywhere by the Soviet Secret Police.

MEDIUM ANNA AND WILSON

Wilson: The NKVD?
Anna: At first I thought my imagination tricked me. The Soviets are everywhere. They want no Anastasia rising from the grave. They want no Duchess around whom the Russian royalists can rally. The Soviets especially fear an imposter Anastasia. She would be a Romanov puppet! Impossible to control.
Wilson: So your game turns dangerous.
Anna: Not my game. I am in danger no matter what I do because of what others wish to believe about me. Belief is always stronger than fact.
Wilson: What are the facts?
Anna: People, certain people, make me very nervous, Mr. Wilson.
Wilson: You have been ill.
Anna: ...and I have been reading. A novel from America...
Wilson: In America we read Russian novels.
Anna: ...a novel by Nathaniel Hawthorne. *The Scarlet Letter*. A story of a marked woman. She suffers because others make her into something she's not.
Wilson: It's about the sin of adultery.

CLOSE ANNA

Anna: No. It's about a sin called the violation of the human heart.

MEDIUM ANNA AND WILSON

Wilson: The violation of the human heart?
Anna: *Use*, Mr. Wilson. Using another person to get what you

want. That's the greatest sin of all.
Wilson: I'm not much on God.

CLOSE ANNA

Anna: I am glad Anastasia is dead. I have read and studied about her. I think I would have liked her. I would not like to think that so simple a young girl should have to suffer so much, be shot, and rescued by a soldier named Eugenev, and then used by her own relatives and hated ten years after by her father's enemies. Because of adventurous reporters like you, Mr. Wilson, her ghost cannot rest.

MEDIUM ANNA AND WILSON

Wilson: Anastasia possesses you?
Anna: (Laughs) No, Mr. Wilson. I need no exorcism. The world, perhaps, needs an exorcism. I need only sleep and safety.
Wilson: Then leave Berlin.
Anna: I have no money.
Wilson: I will pay you for your story.

CLOSE UP ANNA

Anna: Which story?

CLOSE UP WILSON

Wilson: That you are truly Anna Eisenstein whom the Russian exiles wish to turn into the Grand Duchess Anastasia. (ANNA laughs) Why do you laugh?

MEDIUM ANNA AND WILSON

Anna: Because, Mr. Wilson, you reduce my life to an operetta. You make my life into a silly American musical comedy.
Wilson: Either way, I will give you money. I will see you safely out of Germany. Tonight.
Anna: Not tonight.
Wilson: Then tomorrow.

Anna: Not tomorrow.

Wilson: You are afraid for your life, but you will not leave Berlin.

Anna: The Soviets are in no rush to kill me. They are not fools, even though they are Communists. They toy with me. They play cat-and-mouse with Ernst Ludwig. All these people—these Europeans, these Russians—they love to play politics with people's lives, Mr. Wilson. They love the chase.

Wilson: Will you sell me your story?

Anna: You are charitable, Mr. Wilson. But my story will not make interesting reading.

Wilson: Why not?

CLOSE ANNA

Anna: Because it has no ending.

CLOSE WILSON

Wilson: No ending?

CLOSE UP ANNA

Anna: Not yet.

MEDIUM ANNA AND WILSON

Wilson: But with your own lips you have said you are not Anastasia.

Anna: And my lips repeat that. My body gives contrary evidence.

Wilson: Your body?

FULL ANNA AND WILSON

Anna: My chin has been broken like hers. (ANNA sits) And look, Mr. Wilson, if you will, as I remove my slipper. She would not remove her slipper for anyone. Look! My right foot has been pierced.

Wilson: Anastasia's foot was pierced by a bayonet.

Anna: My lips say my foot was pierced by a metal slat in the same train accident that broke my jaw. You see, my story is too contradictory for your paper to buy. My body testifies against my lips.

CLOSE UP WILSON

Wilson: Who are you?

CLOSE UP ANNA

Anna: I am a chess piece.

CLOSE WILSON

Wilson: You are a woman.

MEDIUM ANNA AND WILSON

Anna: Don't be tiresome, Mr. Wilson. You will please leave now. I am not feeling myself.
Wilson: Think about my offer.
Anna: I will consider your...deal.
Wilson: Tomorrow I'll call.
Anna: Goodnight, Mr. Wilson.
Wilson: Promise me one thing.
Anna: Yes?
Wilson: Promise me you will not leave this room.
Anna: Single rooms make me nervous. This room makes me claustrophobic.
Wilson: For your own safety, promise me.

CLOSE UP ANNA

Anna: Perhaps I promise. Good-night, Mr. Wilson.

FULL ANNA AND WILSON

WILSON leaves ANNA alone in the room. ANNA crosses to window, pulls curtain to watch WILSON depart through separate pools of streetlight. ANNA drops curtain back. She crosses herself in front of an icon. A tremor runs through her body.

SOUND

Faraway the MAIN THEME music
FLOATS FROM A CAFE

MEDIUM ANNA

The curtain at the window rises and falls. The candle before the icon flickers and gutters out. ANNA walks to the table and spills a large quantity of pills across the wood. She pours a glass of water and takes two pills, contemplates and takes two more. She pulls on her coat and slips a careless handful of remaining pills into her pocket and exits.

INT. HOTEL ODEON LOBBY
FEATURING STAIRS—NIGHT

MEDIUM ANNA

ANNA descends the worn but clean stairs of the HOTEL ODEON and exits the lobby into the night.

EXT. BERLIN STREET
LANDWEHR CANAL—NIGHT

LONG SHOT

The night is foggy. ANNA bears a trace of her limp. She walks along the LANDWEHR CANAL. The fog is melancholic. At the water's edge, ANNA stands meditatively. She stares into the water as lights from across the canal reflect.

DISSOLVE INSERT

Over the water shot, MONTAGE appears of happier royal moments which build to a nightmare pitch.

1. CLOSE ANASTASIA's joyous young face; she runs, unlimping, down a flight of stairs.

2. CLOSE UP NICHOLAS' face turning into camera and smiling.

3. DISSOLVE to NICHOLAS' face in the Royal Photograph.

4. SOUND of young Grand Duchesses laughing in echo mixed with the sound of a long-forgotten Imperial Orchestra playing discordantly a familiar and sentimental Russian melody in a minor key.

5. SOUND: a harsh chord.

6. NEWSREEL FOOTAGE from the cinema as seen before.

7. CLOSE UP KARKOV'S face.

8. CLOSE UP ALEXANDRA standing up.

Alexandra: My sweet Jesus!

9. SOUND of gunshots

10. CLOSE UP ANASTASIA

Anastasia: Eugenev!

11. FULL of lonely peasant wagon cutting across the horizon.

12. CLOSE UP ANASTASIA lying unmoving under rags in wagon.

13. MEDIUM EUGENEV turns from driver's seat to look down at her. (Is the handsome young guard hauling her dead body to the secret burial site or is he making good

her escape?)

14. MEDIUM NICHOLAS sitting in cellar chair holding ALEXIS.

Anastasia: (Voice Over) Father!

DISSOLVE

EXT. BERLIN STREET
LANDWEHR CANAL—NIGHT

CLOSE UP ANNA

Anna: LEAVE ME ALONE!

(Here the tension must build with some ambiguity toward
a possible plunge into the canal)

Anna: I...am...not...you. Leave me alone! You will not...possess...
me. Leave me. I am not you. Not you!

LONG ANNA

ANNA collapses toward the water, and falls to the edge
of the canal.

MEDIUM ANNA REVEALING MALENKOV

Next to ANNA's face, her hand hangs in the murky canal.
A pair of Soviet shoes steps in next to her face. A cigarette
hits the cobbles and is ground out. Camera pans slowly
up the heavy suited body of MALENKOV. He smiles
enigmatically.

CUT TO

ACT V

EXT. BERLIN STREET
LANDWEHR CANAL—NIGHT

MEDIUM TWO-SHOT ANNA AND MALENKOV

MALENKOV stoops, kneels next to ANNA's body, and rummages through ANNA's pockets. The pills spill out. He pulls her papers and flips through the booklet.

CLOSE UP INSERT ANNA'S PAPERS

ANNA's papers reveal an official photo and her name: ANNA EISENSTEIN.

MEDIUM TWO-SHOT ANNA AND MALENKOV

MALENKOV shrugs. ANNA moans. He begins to roll the unconscious girl over the lip of the canal. A voice calls out.

FULL ANNA, MALENKOV, GUNTHER, MONIKA

A young man, GUNTHER, and a young woman, MONIKA, bicycle up. MALENKOV drops ANNA's papers. GUNTHER and MONIKA dismount. MONIKA kneels next to ANNA. GUNTHER faces the rising MALENKOV.

CLOSE UP GUNTHER

Gunther: Hey!

CLOSE UP MONIKA

Monika: Is she your friend?

MEDIUM SHOT MALENKOV, GUNTHER, MONIKA
FEATURING ANNA

MALENKOV shakes his head *no*. MONIKA picks up a few pills. GUNTHER peddles off toward a police kiosk for an ambulance.

Monika: Help me roll her over.

MONIKA looks around but MALENKOV has disappeared.

DISSOLVE

FULL

ANNA is being loaded in ambulance which pulls out during the following dialog.

Gunther: Who is she?
Monika: Here are her papers. (Policeman takes them) Who is she?
Policeman: Another nobody.
Monika: Where will you take her?
Policeman: To the public hospital.
Gunther: Will she be alright?
Policeman: Who knows. The streets these days are filled with such people. Wanderers.
Monika: A man was with her.
Gunther: He was only passing by.
Monika: Was he?
Policeman: These days everyone is anonymous. (He inspects a key which MONIKA hands him) Hotel Odeon.

INT. HOSPITAL ROOM—MORNING

MEDIUM ANNA AND NURSE

ANNA asleep. A NURSE attends her, takes her pulse, touches her fevered forehead.

CLOSE UP WILSON

WILSON, unshaven, sits next to ANNA's bed. His vigil is

obvious. The ashtray is full. ANNA stirs in bed.

Wilson: Anna?

MEDIUM ANNA AND WILSON

Anna: You are here.

WILSON rises. ANNA puts out her arms. They embrace.

Anna: Oh, Wilson, I am so afraid. I have never let myself be afraid before. (WILSON kisses her lightly, then fully) Never let me go.
Wilson: I called back to your hotel.
Anna: I was suffocating. I had been reading about...her.
Wilson: I told you to stay put.
Anna: (Pulling out of clinch) Women these days are other than obedient.
Wilson: OK, Duchess. *Touché*.
Anna: Last night you offered me a deal. Perhaps...
Wilson: Anastasia may be the biggest hoax of the century.

TIGHT CLOSE UP ANNA

Anna: You asked *me* for *my* story. Not hers.

CLOSE UP WILSON

Wilson: Your story too.

MEDIUM ANNA AND WILSON

Anna: Help me and you may have my story.
Wilson: How can I help you?

CLOSE UP ANNA

Anna: Save my life. Prove to them all...prove that I AM NOT THE GRAND DUCHESS ANASTASIA!

INT. RUSSIAN GYPSY CAFE

BERLIN—AFTERNOON

MEDIUM SHOT WILSON

Behind WILSON in a phone booth, the Russian Cafe bustles with sound. WILSON, who cannot be heard over the music and chatter, is talking on the phone and is montaged with each of the following talking isolated on the phone. Lips move in heated unheard conversation.

CLOSE UP KATHARINE

KATHARINE nods *yes, yes.*

CLOSE UP LUDWIG

LUDWIG shakes head *no, yes, yes.*

CLOSE UP OLGA

OLGA wags her finger, *no, no, no.*

CLOSE UP TEUFEL

TEUFEL is very animated, furious. She hangs up.

CLOSE UP WILSON

WILSON looks into receiver.

CLOSE UP TEUFEL

TEUFEL places phone call.

CLOSE UP MALENKOV

MALENKOV's Russian-pudgy hand picking up phone. He is slurping borscht. Intercut between TEUFEL and MALENKOV. TEUFEL says silent good-bye and hangs up. MALENKOV replaces receiver on hook, wipes lips, and eats impassively.

INT. HOTEL ODEON. ANNA'S ROOM—NIGHT

MEDIUM ANNA AND WILSON

Wilson: Everything is set.
Anna: Olga will silence Ernst Ludwig?
Wilson: Katharine will see to it.
Anna: And Frau Teufel?
Wilson: Loyal to the highest bidder. I hope I bid high enough.
Anna: Oh Wilson. (ANNA hugs him) I'm not in love with you.
    But I love you.
Wilson: You're some kid, Duchess.
Anna: No matter who I am? For now? For this moment?

CLOSE ANNA AND WILSON

ANNA and WILSON kiss. Play this as a "classic" love
scene: music full. They embrace. A bare shoulder. They
sink to the couch. Pan to the icon and the burning candle.
PAN to the rain streaking down the windows. PAN back
to the candle burnt much lower, then to the couple lying
lovingly together.

ANOTHER ANGLE CLOSE ANNA AND WILSON

Anna: The spring rain changes everything. I think with you I am
    safe...

EXT. HOTEL ODEON—NIGHT

MEDIUM MALENKOV
EXTREME ANGLE FEATURING HOTEL

MALENKOV, in deep shadows, is loading his pistol.

INT. HOTEL ODEON. ANNA'S ROOM—NIGHT

MEDIUM ANNA AND WILSON

Anna: ...so long as Frau Teufel is silent.
Wilson: As long as Olga keeps Ludwig quiet. He spooks me.
Anna: Why?
Wilson: Ernst Ludwig is a much too ambitious man.

INT. LUDWIG'S GRAND HOTEL SUITE—DAY

CLOSE OLGA

The table is laden with Russian Easter eggs and paraphernalia. OLGA's hands are painting an egg.

FULL OLGA, KATHARINE, LUDWIG

KATHARINE sits across the small table helping.

Olga: No!

Ludwig: Russian Easter is the right time for Anya's resurrection.

Olga: No, Ernst Ludwig. You are my brother, but you are impossible.

Ludwig: A man should never deal with a woman.

Olga: A woman can never deal with a short man.

Ludwig: I am not short.

Olga: I am short...and you are shorter than I. (OLGA fires up a stylish cigar for herself)

ANOTHER ANGLE

Ludwig: It is time to restore a Romanov to the Russian throne.

Olga: Romanov...Romanov.

Ludwig: Not any Romanov will do...

Olga: The girl herself denies she is Anastasia.

Ludwig: She is close enough for me.

Olga: You are mad for power.

Ludwig: I am the head of this family.

Olga: And I am the backbone.

Ludwig: Then I shall break your back.

Olga: It is not because you are short, Luddie, that I look down on you.

Ludwig: Russian Easter is tomorrow. The Sunday papers must carry our official announcement: The Grand Duchess Has Been Found.

CLOSE OLGA

Olga: She is the wrong person.

MEDIUM OLGA AND LUGWIG

Ludwig: You are the wrong person, sister.
Olga: One can't choose one's relatives.

CLOSE UP LUDWIG

Ludwig: In Anastasia's case—I can.

ANOTHER ANGLE MEDIUM OLGA AND LUDWIG

Olga: The poor girl. You will use anyone—anything—to restore your power.
Ludwig: I have expensive tastes.
Olga: In horses and whores!
Ludwig: My niece, the restored Grand Duchess Anastasia, will be most generous.
Olga: Except she denies she is Anastasia.
Ludwig: She lies...I truly believe, sister, that she is our niece. She looks as the child Anastasia might look as a woman. But more, in her gestures, in her face, ah, in her face is the face of her father, Nicholas.
Olga: Is it now?

ANOTHER ANGLE OLGA AND LUDWIG
FEATURING KATHARINE

Katharine: I too see her resemblance to the Czar, Madame.
Olga: (Grinding out her cigar) If the truth be known...
Katharine: Yes, Madame?
Ludwig: ...nothing. Truth can never be known.
Ludwig: What truth?
Olga: I was closer to Nicholas than to Alexandra. Nikki confided in me. Things...
Ludwig: What things?...Katharine, leave us.
Olga: Katharine, stay.
Ludwig: Olga, you are an insinuating woman.

ANOTHER ANGLE MEDIUM OLGA AND LUDWIG

Olga: ...things Nikki took to his grave.
Ludwig: Women other than Alexandra!
Olga: ...things I will take to mine.
Ludwig: You lie. You will imply anything to stop me.
Olga: True.
Ludwig: Katharine, you heard nothing.
Olga: These days servants hear everything...
Katharine: I will never speak, Sir.
Olga: ...then they write books to tell everything.
Katharine: Madame, I will never speak.
Olga: Then you shall disappoint me, Katharine...I want the world to know the Grand Duke Ernst Ludwig is short—on sense.

ANOTHER ANGLE

Ludwig: I am ringing up that English reporter, Roberts.
Olga: If you recognize that girl officially, Luddie...
Ludwig: Yes?

CLOSE UP OLGA

Olga: I shall break with you forever. To me she is dead.

CLOSE UP LUDWIG

Ludwig: To me she is risen.

CLOSE UP OLGA

Olga: I want her to remain dead.

MEDIUM OLGA, LUDWIG, KATHARINE

Ludwig: Then, Madame, good-bye. Good luck. And good riddance.
Olga: You short old fool. Come, Katharine.
Katharine: Yes, Madame.

Olga: (Tossing LUDWIG an egg) And to you, brother, a very happy Resurrection!

Ludwig: (Misses the decorated egg which breaks in a splat)

MEDIUM OLGA AND KATHARINE

OLGA and KATHARINE exit.

ANOTHER ANGLE FULL LUDWIG

Ludwig: Operator, ring the Berlin office of *The London Chronicle*...Nigel Roberts, please...Yes, Mr. Roberts. This is Grand Duke Ernst Ludwig. We are about to have a most splendid Easter. I have found my niece, the Grand Duchess Anastasia. (LUDWIG's finger moves about in the broken mess of egg)

FADE TO BLACK

ACT VI

INT. RUSSIAN CHURCH. BERLIN—NIGHT

ESTABLISHING FULL
LOW ANGLE

Pre-dawn of Easter Vigil. ESTABLISHING FULL of church interior heavy with candles and incense. MUSIC is liturgical. FULL SHOT faces of Russian-émigré church-goers. MEDIUM SHOTS of the Russian choir, the pageantry of the priests in their robes swinging censers over the people.

CLOSE UP ANNA

Blue incense smoke billows around Anna's face.

EXT. STREET. RUSSIAN CHURCH. BERLIN—NIGHT

WILSON double-times running up steps. A newspaper is folded under his arm.

INT. RUSSIAN CHURCH. BERLIN—NIGHT

In the vestibule light, WILSON opens a newspaper. A box on the front page contains LUDWIG's announcement. WILSON folds paper, slaps his thigh, strides into the church.

MEDIUM ANNA TO INCLUDE WILSON

ANNA is standing. WILSON sidles into frame and stands next to ANNA. Both face into CAMERA. This church exchange is a *sotto voce* whisper. Neither ANNA nor WILSON moves.

Wilson: Happy Easter, Duchess.
Anna: I love you, Wilson.
Wilson: You're a sweetheart of an actress.
Anna: Actress?
Wilson: You've got a show to do. (Flashes newspaper) Ernst Ludwig wants to make you a star.
Anna: Oh dear God! I swear, Wilson, I know nothing about this.
Wilson: "Gold Diggers of 1928."
Anna: Believe me.
Wilson: (Mocking) "Hold me, Wilson." "Never let me go, Wilson." "I love you, Wilson."
Churchgoer: Shhh!
Anna: I swear I'm telling the truth.
Wilson: You are a creation of lies.
Anna: There is truth in me.
Wilson: Who are you?
Anna: I...don't...know...anymore.
Wilson: So long, sweetheart.

WILSON exits up aisle.

ANOTHER ANGLE MEDIUM ANNA
FEATURING CROWD

ANNA, bewildered and crying, leaves her place and like a boat against the current pushes her way back up the aisle suddenly crowded by a procession of priests and deacons and acolytes, singing, with candles and incense. CAMERA back-trucks partway to show her subjective P.O.V.

CLOSE UP WILSON

WILSON reacts to something fearful he sees outside the door of the church.

EXT. STREET. RUSSIAN CHURCH. BERLIN—NIGHT

FULL
EXTREME ANGLE FEATURING BLACK CAR

A severe black car pulls to the deserted curbing.

MEDIUM TEUFEL AND MALENKOV

TEUFEL sits framed against the backseat window. Her face is lit by a low-angle light. MALENKOV jumps from the car, gun prominently in hand.

EXT. STREET. RUSSIAN CHURCH. BERLIN—NIGHT

MEDIUM WILSON FEATURING ANNA

ANNA catches up to WILSON.

Anna: Wilson!

CLOSE UP TEUFEL

Teufel: (A breathily exhaled whisper) An-na!

EXT. STREETS. BERLIN—NIGHT
MONTAGE OF THE CHASE

MALENKOV running. WILSON grabbing ANNA. Main Theme MUSIC up-tempo and rampant. ANNA and WILSON run down the dark street, through narrower and narrower alleys. Along the Landwehr Canal. MALENKOV chases. The chauffeured car carrying TEUFEL tries to follow. Once the car cuts ANNA and WILSON off. They turn and retrace their steps. MALENKOV fires a shot. They dodge. They catch a moment of safety in the shadows behind some trash bins.

SOUND

WHISTLES, WHEELS, STEAM ESCAPING,
TRAINS CHUGGING

EXT. RAILROAD YARD TRACKS.
BERLIN—NIGHT

ESTABLISHING FULL TILTED ANGLE
RAILROAD YARD

TIGHT TWO-SHOT ANNA AND WILSON

Anna: Leave me here.
Wilson: I love you, Anna.
Anna: More than me, you love the idea of me.
Wilson: You are an obstinate woman.
Anna: Let them kill me if it is so important to them.
Wilson: I love you.
Anna: Let them do me a favor.

Wilson draws ANNA near and kisses her.

SOUND

Faraway train whistle

Wilson: Who are you?
Anna: You hold me. You tell me.

MEDIUM TRUCKING MALENKOV

MALENKOV running.

CLOSE UP MALENKOV

MALENKOV's shadowed face looks right and left.

SOUND

Train whistle

INSERT CLOSE UP TEUFEL

TEUFEL points in the direction she thinks
ANNA and WILSON are hiding.

SOUND

Screeching train whistle

INSERT ALLEY TRASH CANS

EXT. RAILROAD YARD TRACKS.
BERLIN—NIGHT

MEDIUM SHOT ANNA AND WILSON

Anna: Other women claim to be Anastasia. Why does no one
   believe them?
Wilson: They are too hungry.
Anna: I have never claimed to be the Grand Duchess. Why does
   no one believe me?
Wilson: You are not hungry enough.

CLOSE UP ANNA

ANNA screams, hands covering face, seeing MALENKOV.

SOUND

Screeching train whistle

CLOSE UP MALENKOV

FULL RAILROAD TRACKS

A TRAIN in the far distance is rushing toward CAMERA. MALENKOV jumps down into frame and rolls into ANNA and WILSON.

FULL WILSON, ANNA, AND MALENKOV

WILSON and MALENKOV wrestle for MALENKOV's gun. They fall on the tracks.

SOUND

Screeching train whistle

Wilson: Anna! Run!

FULL TEUFEL

TEUFEL exits her car even as it is pulling up to a halt.

MEDIUM WILSON AND MALENKOV

WILSON and MALENKOV struggle to a standing position.

MEDIUM ANNA

ANNA escapes across tracks.

ANOTHER ANGLE
FULL WILSON AND MALENKOV

The train roars down upon WILSON and MALENKOV. The gun is in the air.

TIGHT TWO-SHOT WILSON AND MALENKOV

A struggle to the death.

MEDIUM MALENKOV TO INCLUDE WILSON

The train roars past and, with a mighty surge, WILSON pushes MALENKOV into the side of the passing train. MALENKOV's throat is caught on a hook and he is carried off by the train into the darkness like a dead and broken doll.

CLOSE UP MALENKOV

MALENKOV's face, bulging in the surprise of death as he vibrates hanging on the side of the speeding train.

CLOSE UP TEUFEL

TEUFEL, assessing the situation, is furious, and rushes to the car.

FULL WILSON

WILSON runs toward the car. The DRIVER peels out into the distance making good TEUFEL's escape, as well as her continuing threat. WILSON looks around.

SOUND

The train rattles off into the dark,
then SILENCE

CLOSE WILSON

Wilson: Anna!

FULL WILSON

WILSON cuts across the shadows of the empty train tracks.

Wilson: Anna!

WILSON searches. ANNA is not in sight.

Wilson: Anna!

CLOSE UP ANNA

ANNA is hiding, her face lit by a pinpoint of street-light.

Wilson: (Voice Over) Anna!

ANNA looks in his direction. Ambiguity. Is she about to answer? Then WILSON calls not her name but her controversial title.

Wilson: (Voice Over) Duchess!

ANNA closes her eyes. Nothing will ever change.

Wilson: Duchess!

ANNA opens her eyes crying; then she turns off into the dawn shadows.

LONG WILSON

Wilson: Duchess!

SOUND

Music up. Main love theme swells.

HIGH ANGLE

CAMERA shoots down on WILSON. The BOOMSHOT grows higher and higher as WILSON shrinks on screen into a puzzle of wet cobblestones gray with the coming Easter dawn.

EXT. DOCK AND BOAT RAILING—DAWN

MEDIUM ANNA

ANNA is one of a huddled group of women boarding a

crowded boat.

SOUND

LONELY BOAT HORNS

CLOSE UP ANNA

ANNA's face is partially covered. She turns into CAMERA. She is crying.

Wilson: (Voice Over: Echo) Anna!

FREEZE FRAME

TIGHT CLOSE UP ANNA

EXT. HARBOR—DAWN

ESTABLISHING HIGH ANGLE
FEATURING BOAT AND HORIZON AT DAWN

Under the FREEZE FRAME of ANNA's face, the boat pulls away into the harbor to grow smaller and smaller. The push-pull energy of this last MONTAGE image should continue as the credits roll over the MAIN LOVE THEME MUSIC.

THE END